Sparks Ignited

The Catalyst Chronicles, Volume 1

PD Norris & Eli Dotson

Published by PDN Books, 2025.

SPARKS IGNITED

First edition. March 19, 2025.

Copyright © 2025 PD Norris & Eli Dotson.

ISBN: 979-8992133332

Written by PD Norris & Eli Dotson.

Contents

Prologue

Inside a state-of-the-art conference room bathed in the glow of blue holographic projections, Director Regina Ward stood at the head of a long table. Around her sat a team of researchers, analysts, and operatives. Floating above the table was a detailed hologram of a middle school. She tapped her fingers on the table as she studied the glowing image. "Let's start with the school selection. We need the ideal environment to launch Phase One of Project Sentinel. Is this our best option?"

The lead researcher, Dr. Hayes, stepped forward and swiped at the holograms. "Yes. This school meets every criterion - right age group, diverse population, and most importantly.... the lowest likelihood of external interference."

The hologram expanded to fill the air above the table. Detailed schematics of the school's layout materialized showing classrooms, hallways, and key access points. Data streams flickered along the edges displaying student demographics, security measures, and faculty profiles. The room fell silent as everyone studied the intricate projection.

"Jefferson Jr. High," Hayes continued. "A STEM magnet school with a smaller, more controlled environment. Its advanced curriculum and focus on technology align perfectly with the AI Innovations Expo taking place in three weeks. The school's size allows us to monitor the students without drawing unnecessary attention."

Ward examined the details of the school. "The expo is an ideal catalyst. The school's smaller size works in our favor; fewer variables, and more control. Any objections?"

One of the younger analysts hesitated. "Director, a smaller school could also mean less room to maneuver if things go wrong. If the students suspect anything - "

Ward cut him off. "They won't suspect anything. Jefferson is the perfect choice. Begin embedding our surveillance systems into the school's infrastructure immediately. I want every corner monitored. And ensure the staff remains unaware. This needs to look natural."

Dr. Hayes nodded. "Understood, Director. I'll have our tech team start immediately."

"Good." Ward returned to the table where another set of holograms flickered to life five student profiles. "Now, let's discuss the candidates."

Dr. Hayes swiped the holograms, bringing the first profile to the forefront. A confident young Black boy grinning in the image.

"Jordan Daniels. Fourteen years old. A tech prodigy with an extraordinary talent for understanding and manipulating technology. When he was ten, he reverse-engineered proprietary software and his recent school projects demonstrate an almost instinctive connection to tech. He's our ideal candidate for technopathy."

She studied his profile with a sharp gaze. "A sharp mind can be both a strength and a liability. Make sure he's monitored closely. Next."

The hologram shifted to reveal a muscular East Asian boy with an easygoing smile.

"Next is Ravi Patel. Thirteen. Exceptionally athletic with a natural inclination for competition. His physical resilience and determination make him the perfect candidate for enhanced strength. However, his confidence borders on recklessness."

Ward smirked faintly. "Recklessness can be an asset if properly directed. Proceed."

The next image revealed a studious-looking Asian boy with glasses. His face was illuminated by the glow of a computer screen.

"This is Jiho Li. Thirteen. A VR gaming prodigy with unparalleled creativity and problem-solving skills. His ability to navigate immersive environments makes him our choice for virtual reality manipulation."

Ward raised an eyebrow. "Creativity is unpredictable. Ensure he remains focused on the task at hand. What's next?"

The hologram shifted again, revealing a girl with blonde hair and piercing eyes.

"Ava Price. Fourteen. Highly empathetic and intuitive with a natural talent for understanding social dynamics. She's ideal for emotional manipulation. However, her empathy could lead to complications if she becomes too attached to others."

"Empathy is a double-edged sword," Ward remarked. "If harnessed correctly, it could be a powerful tool. And the final candidate?"

The last hologram flickered to reveal a Hispanic girl with sharp eyes and a confident smirk.

"Camelia Suarez. Thirteen. Charismatic and highly persuasive with an innate ability to influence those around her. Her instincts and keen observation skills make her the perfect candidate for hypnosis. However, her charisma could be dangerous if left unchecked."

Ward stared at Camelia's profile for a moment longer than the others. "Charisma can destabilize everything if not controlled. Ensure she remains focused on our objectives."

The room fell silent as the five profiles hovered above the table. Ward's gaze swept across them, her expression unreadable.

"These five students will be the cornerstone of the Project Sentinel. They will have no idea what's about to happen, and that's how it must remain. Activate Phase One."

Dr. Hayes hesitated. "Director, what if they resist? Or if they begin to suspect something before we're ready?"

Ward's lips curled into a faint smile. "Then we remind them that resistance is futile. The school is where their journey begins, and it's where we will shape their future." She turned to the lead strategist, her gaze sharp. "Ensure the transition is seamless. We can't afford disruptions."

The holographic display shifted to highlight key areas within the school. "We control the environment, the information, and the narrative," she continued. "Once they step through those doors, their path is set." She clasped her hands behind her back, eyes gleaming with anticipation. "Let's begin."

Chapter 1

The cafeteria buzzed with the usual lunchtime energy: students talking over each other, the clatter of trays, and the occasional shriek of laughter from across the room. At a corner table, five friends huddled close to discuss the upcoming field trip.

Ravi slapped his tray on the table causing his soda to wobble dangerously. "Okay, let's be real for a second. This trip is going to be legendary. I'm talking robots, holograms, probably even flying cars." He grabbed a slice of pizza and took a triumphant bite. "It's basically a superhero origin story waiting to happen."

Ava rolled her eyes as she picked at her salad. "Flying cars? Seriously? Ravi, it's an educational trip, not a science fiction movie or a superhero audition. Try to keep at least one foot on the ground."

"Foot on the ground? Come on, Ava," Ravi replied with mock indignation. "This is the future we're talking about. You don't go to an AI expo expecting spreadsheets. You go expecting your mind to be blown."

"Maybe your mind," Camelia teased. "The rest of us actually know how to manage our expectations."

"Hey!" Ravi pointed his pizza at her. "Mark my words. Something big is going to happen. Call it a gut feeling."

"Your gut feeling is probably just the pizza," Jordan replied amusingly. "I read the itinerary. They're showcasing a lot of cutting-edge stuff. Like, there's this AI that can mimic human conversations so well that people can't tell the difference."

"Does it have a mute button for Ravi?" Ava quipped earning chuckles from the group.

"You're just mad because robots won't care about your mood swings," Ravi shot back. "Remind me to save *you* last when the robots rise up."

"Excuse me?" Ava raised an eyebrow, her voice dripping with mock offense. "I don't have mood swings. I have... a dynamic emotional range."

Jiho chuckled softly. "I'm with Ravi on this one." He adjusted his glasses and glanced at his phone. "The expo is going to be cool. I read they're showcasing a fully immersive VR system that could revolutionize gaming."

Jordan excitedly interjected. "Did you guys hear about the tech they're using to diagnose and fix machines on the spot? Like, you show it something broken, and it tells you exactly what's wrong and how to fix it. That's the real game-changer. No more tech support hotlines. Imagine how much money people could save."

"Not just money," Jiho added. "Time, too. The whole point of it is to make life easier, right? It's like having a personal assistant for literally everything."

Ava raised an eyebrow. "And that doesn't worry anyone else? Like, at all? What happens when it decides it's smarter than us and starts making its own rules?"

Ravi grinned. "Finally, someone who gets it! Thank you. I've been saying this for years. AI is the gateway to robot overlords. We're one malfunction away from being servants in our own homes."

Camelia laughed. "Oh please. If anyone becomes a servant, it's going to be you. The robots would get tired of your bad jokes and put you on dish duty."

"First of all, my jokes are amazing," Ravi shot back. "Second, I'd be the leader of the rebellion. You'd all come crawling to me when the chips are down."

Jordan shook his head grinning. "If the chips are down, it's probably because Ravi tried to eat them."

"Do you think we'll actually get to try any of the tech?" Camelia asked.

Jiho answered. "From what I've read, there'll be interactive exhibits. Like, they're supposed to have a fully immersive VR setup where you can step into a virtual world without needing headsets or controllers."

"That sounds insane," Jordan said, his voice full of excitement. "What kind of world are we talking about? Like, fantasy? Sci-fi?"

"Probably both," Jiho replied. "The idea is to showcase how versatile the technology is. It's not just for gaming. It could be used for training, education, or even therapy."

Ava frowned. "Therapy? That seems... weird. Like, how do you trust a machine with something so personal?"

"Maybe it's easier for some people," Jiho said thoughtfully. "You don't feel judged by a machine the way you might by a human. It's just there to listen and analyze."

Ravi threw an arm around Jiho's shoulders. "Man, you're always thinking deep. Me? I just want to see if I can fight a dragon or something."

Camelia rolled her eyes. "You'd probably lose."

"Not with my super strength," Ravi countered flexing his arm for emphasis.

"You don't have super strength," Ava said flatly.

"Yet," Ravi said with a wink. "But who knows? This trip could be the beginning of something big."

Camelia tapped her fingers on the table with a knowing smile. "Well I'm going for the free merch. You know they're going to be handing out keychains, shirts, and probably some high-tech gadgets we can smuggle home."

Ravi leaned in and joked. "Okay, but imagine this. What if the AI recognizes our genius and decides to recruit us? Like, 'Hey, you five look like you could save the world. Here's a bunch of powers, go nuts.' "

Ava groaned pinching the bridge of her nose. "Ravi, I think you need to stop binge-watching sci-fi before bed. You're starting to sound unhinged."

Jordan laughed. "I mean, he's not completely wrong. This trip could be a big deal. We're the only school in the district going. Jefferson Jr. High got picked because we're the best."

"And because we're a STEM magnet school," Jiho added. "We fit the profile they wanted. Advanced students, smaller group, and easier to manage."

"Easier to *impress,* you mean," Camelia teased. "They know we'll eat this up and go home singing their praises. 'Oh, the expo was so inspiring. Let's all become engineers!' "

Ravi nudged her. "And yet you'll still be the one taking all the selfies."

"Obviously," Camelia replied with a wink. "Someone's got to document our rise to fame."

As their conversation continued the bell rang, signaling the end of lunch. The group reluctantly gathered their trays while still immersed in their debate. As they moved toward the exit, students weaved past them in a rush to their next class. Even as they stepped into the hallway, their conversation carried on about the field trip.

"So," Ava said as they walked toward their next class, "do you think this trip is going to live up to the hype? Or are we just going to end up listening to boring lectures all day?"

Jiho adjusted his backpack and shrugged. "Even if the lectures are boring, the tech exhibits will make up for it. And who knows? Maybe we'll see something that changes how we think about AI."

"Or something that confirms my theory that AI is the first step toward robots taking over the world," Ravi quipped.

Camelia snorted. "If robots do take over, I'm betting they'd leave you behind, Ravi. Too much chaos for their taste."

Jordan smirked. "If they need someone to fix their circuits, they'd probably recruit me first."

"Dream on," Camelia teased, shoving him lightly.

Ava looked ahead as they separated and went to their classrooms. "You're all ridiculous. Let's just try to get through the trip without embarrassing the school. That's all I'm asking."

"Define 'embarrassing,'" Ravi said with a mischievous grin. "Because I might have a plan to see if those robots can play dodgeball."

"So, should we meet early before the bus leaves?" Jiho asked.

"Definitely," Jordan said. "I want to hit the exhibits first before the crowds show up."

"And I need good lighting for my selfies," Camelia added.

Ava rolled her eyes. "Fine, but no wandering off. If you get lost, don't come crying to me."

Ravi grinned. "Don't worry, Mom. We'll stick together. Mostly."

As the group laughed and teased, the excitement for the upcoming trip grew. None of them knew just how much this field trip would change their lives forever.

Chapter 2

Jordan was the first of the group to arrive. He clutched his tablet tightly as he scrolled through the itinerary for the expo. The excitement radiated off him in waves. He had barely slept the night before. He was too busy imagining all the incredible things they'd see. Going on the field trip was like a dream come true for him.

Ava arrived next. She looked as calm and collected as ever as she adjusted the strap of her purse. "Let me guess," she said, nodding at the tablet. "You're memorizing the schedule again?"

"Not just memorizing," he said excitedly. "I'm planning. We have to hit the AI demonstration first. It's supposed to be revolutionary!"

"I'm sure it is, but don't stress yourself out. It's just a field trip."

"It's not *just* a field trip. This is the kind of thing that could shape our futures."

"Or," came a sarcastic voice from behind them, "it's the kind of thing that lets us skip class and eat free snacks." Camelia strolled up with her dark braid swinging behind her as she adjusted her denim jacket.

Jordan shot her a look. "Why don't you take anything seriously?"

"I take plenty of things seriously," she replied with a smirk. "Just not things that involve a bunch of nerds showing off their overpriced tech."

Ava raised an eyebrow. "You do know you go to a STEM school, right?"

"Yeah, yeah," she waved a hand dismissively. "I'm here for the vibe, not the robots."

Before they could launch into a debate, Ravi appeared carrying his backpack and eating from a bag of sour gummy worms.

"Is there a time that you're not eating?" Ava asked.

"Only when I'm sleeping. Besides I gotta bulk up in case I get super strength today," he joked.

"You're still stuck on that? It's not happening," Ava laughed.

"Why kill my dreams? I'm going to be famous one day." Ravi joked as he pulled another snack from his backpack.

Jordan crossed his arms. "Why am I the only one who actually cares about this trip?"

"Because you are" Camelia said, smirking. "You care about everything."

"That's not a bad thing," Ava shot him a reassuring look.

"Thank you."

The last to join the group was Jiho, who walked up with a handheld game and his headset. "Morning."

Ava brightened. "Jiho! Tell me you're excited about the expo."

"Absolutely. I can't wait to see what they got."

"See?" Jordan said triumphantly. "At least *someone* gets it."

"Don't let it go to your head," Camelia teased. "He's probably just saying that to shut you up."

The bus doors opened with a loud hiss and the students began filing inside. Jordan led the group to a row near the middle claiming the window seat so he could keep his tablet balanced on his knees. Ava slid in beside him, while the others took the seats behind them. The engine rumbled to life and the bus lurched forward causing a ripple of excitement to pass through the students.

"Okay," Jordan held up the tablet like it was a sacred text. "Here's the plan. We hit the AI demonstration first, then the VR gaming station. After that, we'll check out the robotics display - "

"Whoa, whoa," Ravi interrupted. "You've already planned our entire day?"

"Of course. I wouldn't be me if I didn't let you guys experience the full thing. "

Ravi groaned. "Can't we just wing it? You know, wander around and see where we end up?"

"We'll miss all the good stuff if we do that," Ava argued.

"Good stuff for you," Camelia muttered. "Some of us just want to find the free food and call it a day."

Jordan glared at her. "You're impossible."

"And you're predictable," Camelia shot back smirking.

Ava stepped in to diffuse the tension. "How about we compromise? We can hit one demonstration he wants to see and then we can spend the rest of the time exploring."

"Fine. But if we miss anything important, it's on you."

"Deal," Ava said with a grin.

The bus turned onto the highway and the chatter among the students grew louder. Camelia pulled out her phone to scroll through social media while Ravi leaned back in his seat with one earbud in. Jiho played a game on his handheld.

As the city skyline came into view, Ava shook herself out of her thoughts. "Look!" she pointed out the window. "There it is!" The convention center loomed ahead, a massive glass structure with a banner stretched across the entrance that read: **Annual Tech & AI Expo**.

"Looks fancy," Ravi said as he pulled out his other earbud.

"Let's just hope it's not boring," Camelia added.

"It won't be," Jordan said confidently. He'd been waiting for this trip for weeks, pouring over every detail of the exhibits and speakers scheduled. There was no way it could be anything less than incredible. The bus pulled into the parking lot and the students began gathering their things. He felt a surge of excitement as he slung his backpack over his shoulder. This was it, the moment he'd been waiting for.

As the group stepped off the bus and into the crisp morning air, the buzz of conversation and footsteps echoed around them. The scent of fresh cinnamon rolls and popcorn from nearby vendor stands mixed with the metallic tang of machinery from the exhibition halls. Students craned their necks to take in the sprawling venue. Their excitement grew with every glimpse of interactive displays, robotic demonstrations, and towering models of rockets and DNA structures. Some clutched their event pamphlets as they eagerly scanned the schedule for must-see exhibits, while others snapped photos of the massive entrance archway.

"Alright, everyone," their teacher clapped her hands to get their attention. "Stick with your groups, and remember—this is a learning experience, not just a chance to play with cool gadgets."

A few students chuckled, already eyeing the virtual reality stations and hands-on chemistry experiments. With their lanyards secured and a full day ahead, they were ready to explore the wonders of science.

Agent Cross entered the room carrying a tablet. "The students have arrived ma'am," he said.

Director Ward didn't turn around. Her gaze remained fixed on one particular monitor showing the group of five friends as they moved through the crowd. She watched as they paused at an interactive robotics exhibit. Their faces were alight with curiosity. A slow, calculating smile formed on her lips.

"I see them," she said. "They're exactly as expected. Look at them. They're curious, distracted, and completely unaware of the storm that's about to surround them."

Cross approached and stood beside her. "They don't look like much."

"They're more than they appear," she replied. She gestured to the monitors where each exhibit was prominently displayed. "Every station they will visit has been carefully selected. Each one calibrated to trigger the latent potential we've been tracking in their genetic markers. By the time they leave here, they won't be the same."

Cross frowned as his tablet lit up with incoming data. "You're confident the surge will work as planned?"

She turned to him. "You have to the audacity to doubt me? Of course I'm confident. We've run countless simulations. The devices planted at each exhibit are synced to create a synchronized energy pulse. When the power grid is disrupted, it will release a surge strong enough to activate their abilities."

"And if something goes wrong?"

"It won't." She gestured toward another screen. This screen was on Jordan who was animatedly pointing at the AI demonstration. "Look at them. They're curious. Driven. Hungry to explore. This is the perfect moment to unlock what's inside them."

Cross kept his expression neutral. "And after?"

"After, we watch. Closely. They'll think it was a freak accident or a technological glitch. But we'll be monitoring their progress. If any of them fail to adapt, we'll intervene."

"Understood." Cross made a note on his tablet. "And the scientist? Does he know he's being monitored as well?"

"Dr. Avery thinks this is his experiment. Let him believe that. It keeps him focused. Once the data is collected and the subjects' abilities are confirmed, his usefulness will come to an end."

She turned back to the screen. "It's fascinating, isn't it?"

"What is?"

"The potential. They have no idea what's waiting for them. No idea that today will change everything."

"And if they don't adapt? If they become a threat instead of an asset?"

"Then we deal with them. Permanently."

A voice then crackled in Cross's earpiece. "All stations are live. The surge is ready."

"Good. Synchronize the countdown. Five minutes until the grid goes down."

Cross relayed the instructions. He kept his voice steady as he coordinated with the team on the ground.

Chapter 3

The students wandered aimlessly through the exhibits. Massive screens projected videos of cutting-edge advancements, robotic arms whirred as they performed precise tasks, and holographic displays shimmered under the bright fluorescent lights. The group had split up shortly after the first exhibit as they agreed.

High above Dr. Marcus Avery stood in the secluded observation room watching the sea of students scurrying to each area below. He was a man of science driven by ambition that often blurred the lines of morality. Today, his work would culminate in something extraordinary ... or catastrophic.

His fingers tapped rhythmically against the glass as he scanned the crowd, searching for the chosen few. The carefully orchestrated experiment was already in motion. Hidden sensors embedded throughout the expo monitored physiological responses, tracking stress levels, cognitive function, and subconscious reactions to the subtle stimuli woven into the exhibits.

"It's ready," a tense voice crackled through his earpiece.

Avery's lips curved into a thin smile. "Good. Initiate the sequence."

"But Dr. Avery, the energy levels are unstable. If we proceed—"

"If we don't," Avery interrupted. "We lose everything we've worked for. Execute the plan." The line went silent but the faint hum of machinery in the observation room grew louder. Avery adjusted his glasses. "This is the future," he muttered to himself. "And they are the perfect test subjects."

Jordan stood at the edge of the AI demonstration stage beaming with curiosity. The presenter, a middle aged woman in a sharp business suit, gestured toward a humanoid robot named *Horizon*. Its sleek, metallic frame gleamed under the lights and its digital eyes flickered as it processed the input from the audience.

"This is *Horizon* and he can predict human behavior with over 90% accuracy," the presenter announced. "Would anyone like to test it?"

Jordan's hand shot up immediately. The presenter selected him and he excitedly approached the stage. Horizon's head tilted slightly as the sensors scanned him when he stepped into view.

"Your name is Jordan," the robot said in a mix of human and robotic voice.

His jaw dropped. "How did y—"

The presenter smiled. "It's reading the student badges," she explained. "Now think of a number between one and ten."

He bit his lip and concentrated. Horizon thought for a moment. Its light blue metallic eyes flickered as a soft hum filled the air.

"Seven," the robot stated confidently.

Jordan's eyes widened in shock. "No way!"

The presenter chuckled. "It's using biometric analysis. That mean it analyzes the subtle shifts in your facial expression, pupil dilation, and micro-expressions to make a near perfect guess."

"That's kinda creepy... but also really cool."

"Would you like me to try again?" it asked.

Jordan hesitated for a moment. "Alright... let's see if it's just a lucky guess."

As he focused on another number, Horizon's sensors flickered once more and the processors began to work silently. It looked at though it was studying more than just his thoughts.

"Two," it said confidently.

He blinked. "That's... right." The crowd applauded and Jordan couldn't stop grinning. He didn't notice the faint static hum that seemed to ripple through the air around him as he returned to his spot.

Camelia sat in a plush chair at the hypnosis station. The presenter, a tan man with a perfectly groomed beard, handed her a sleek pair of headphones. "This isn't magic," he explained. "It's science. These sound frequencies, paired with visual stimulation, can help unlock the hidden potential of your subconscious mind."

She raised an eyebrow but reluctantly slipped on the headphones. The moment they settled over her ears, a soft rhythmic hum began to play as it resonated deep in her chest. The small screen before her flickered to life and displayed faint swirling lights that pulsed in sync with the sound.

At first, she felt nothing—just a mild sense of relaxation. But then, a strange sensation washed over her, as if her thoughts were slowing down and unraveling themselves. The colors on the screen deepened and shifted into patterns that felt familiar. But she couldn't explain why.

The presenter's voice drifted through the hum. "Just let go. Don't fight it."

Her fingers twitched against the armrest. She wasn't sure if it was the lighting, the sound, or something else entirely, but the edges of her reality seemed to blur. For a brief moment, a memory—no, a feeling—surfaced. Something long buried and just out of reach. She immediately thought, "*What in the world was happening?*"

Camelia began to sink and got comfortable in the chair. As the patterns deepened and the sound shifted she felt an odd sensation. It was almost like a warmth spreading through her chest as if something deep inside her was stirring. For a moment she forgot about the crowd, the school trip, and even her skepticism.

"Are you okay?" the presenter asked as she snapped out of the trance.

"I'm fine," she quickly pulled off the headphones. But her hands were trembling, and she couldn't shake the strange tingling that lingered. It wasn't just at her fingertips. It was in her mind. It felt like a buzzing awareness that hadn't been there before.

She glanced around disoriented. The expo was still the same—students laughing, machines whirring, voices overlapping. But the expo... it felt like something changed, but she couldn't put her finger on it. The colors seemed sharper and the sounds were crisper. It was as if the world had subtly shifted.

The presenter studied her carefully. "That reaction is rare," he said. "You must have a highly receptive mind."

"It just felt... weird. Like I was remembering something I shouldn't."

"The subconscious is a fascinating place. Sometimes, it reveals things we don't expect."

She stood up quickly. "Thanks," she muttered as she walked away. But as she turned, the tingling flared again, and for a split second, she swore she heard a soft whisper inside her own head.

Jiho was in his element at the VR gaming station. The headset covered his eyes and immersed him in a digital battlefield. He sprinted down virtual corridors, dodging projectiles and blasting targets with a glowing weapon. The adrenaline coursed through him as the game's AI opponents grew more aggressive and agile.

Their movements were almost too precise. He ducked behind cover and reloaded with a flick of his wrist. The crowd around him watched in awe as he effortlessly weaved through the onslaught while racking up points at a staggering rate.

Then, something changed. The game's HUD flickered and for a split second the environment was distorted. A strange symbol flashed on the screen. It was there for a split second but vanished as quickly as it appeared.

"This is so cool," he grinned enthusiastically.

The environment felt so real that his heart raced with adrenaline. He rounded a corner and came face-to-face with a towering enemy. He raised his weapon and fired, but the figure didn't disappear. It lunged.

"Whoa!" He exclaimed as he yanked off the headset.

The technician frowned. "That shouldn't have happened. It must be a glitch."

"That didn't feel like a glitch," he murmured. "It felt... different."

The technician tapped a few keys on the console and scanned the data. "Strange. Your session logged an unauthorized modification to the response system. But that's impossible. These simulations are pre-programmed."

He wiped his forehead. But the vividness of the encounter stayed with him. It was as if the digital world had seeped into his mind.

Ava sat in a quiet corner of the expo at the therapy booth. A counselor handed her a sleek wristband. He explained that it monitored stress levels and emitted calming pulses to help regulate emotions.

"You'll feel a slight vibration," the counselor said as he strapped it on her wrist.

The band hummed softly against her skin and sent out a gentle, rhythmic pulse. At first, it was subtle, barely noticeable, but within seconds, a unique, yet strange warmth spread through her arm and traveled up to her chest. Her thoughts slowed down and she was beginning to feel as if a weight had been lifted.

"Whoa! that's actually kinda nice."

The counselor smiled. "It works by syncing with your biometrics and adjusting in real-time. Some users even report improved focus and clarity."

She flexed her fingers and watched as the wristband's tiny interface flickered with her pulse data. But then, for a brief moment, the numbers spiked and her heart rate jumped unexpectedly. The band's vibration shifted and started to pulse in an odd deliberate pattern.

Ava frowned. "Is it supposed to do that?"

The counselor's expression faltered for half a second before recovering. "It's just adapting. Your body might take a moment to sync fully."

She wasn't sure why, but something about the response didn't sit right. The band still pulsed, but now it almost felt like... a signal.

Ravi found himself at the strength-testing station, mostly because it was nearly empty. The exhibit showcased a futuristic barbell that adjusted resistance based on the user's strength.

"Wanna give it a try?" the trainer asked.

"Sure," Ravi said with a shrug.

He gripped the barbell which hummed faintly in his hands. As he lifted, the weight seemed to shift dynamically growing heavier the higher he raised it.

"That's... strange," he said as he set it down.

"It's smart tech," the trainer explained. "It's adapting to your limits."

Ravi's arms tingled, but it wasn't from exertion. It was something deeper like an electric current still running beneath his skin. He flexed his fingers, trying to shake the sensation, but the tingling only seemed to intensify and spread up his arms like static crawling under his skin. His breath came faster. This wasn't normal.

Then with a deafening *pop*, the power went out. The expo hall plunged into darkness, and a collective gasp rippled through the crowd. The hum intensified and vibrated through the floor and walls. The faint glow of the emergency lights flickered as they struggled to activate. Murmurs of confusion and panic filled the air, punctuated by the distant crash of something toppling over. Screens across the hall flickered back to life, but instead of their original displays, they showed shifting symbols and distorted static.

"What's happening?" someone yelled.

Jordan felt a surge of static race up his spine, sharp and electric as if his very cells were being rewritten. He stumbled back clutching the railing of the AI booth. Camelia gasped feeling as if she was being burned from the inside, while her fingertips felt ice cold. She gripped her seat while her mind buzzed with a thousand half-formed thoughts.

Jiho's vision blurred as flashes of images overwhelmed him that were too fast to process. He dropped to one knee and his breathing became ragged and heavy. Ravi clutched his head as he felt a strange pressure building behind his eyes. It seemed like he felt his brain was expanding. Ava stood perfectly still while she felt her arms tingle with an unknown sensation. Suddenly, she felt hyper-aware of everything; the vibrations in the floor, the whispers in the dark, even the faint breaths of the people around her.

Then, just as suddenly as it had begun, the hum stopped. The lights flickered back on, dim at first, then blazing to life. The crowd erupted into murmurs and exclamations.

"Is everyone okay?" a chaperone called out. They all thought the same thing, "*No we are not okay.*"

Jiho rubbed his temples. He was still feeling phantom echoes of the VR game's intensity. "Okay, tell me I'm not the only one who felt something *off.*"

Ava glanced at the wristband still strapped to her arm. Its faint pulses were now eerily in sync with her heartbeat. "You're not," she admitted. "That blackout wasn't normal." She ripped off the wristband and threw it on the floor.

Camelia was still feeling the remnants of the hypnosis session. It was tugging at the edges of her mind. "It was like... something reached inside my head."

Ravi flexed his fingers. "I don't know what happened, but I feel different. Stronger."

Jordan looked down at his tablet. "All of a sudden, I feel like Horizon is talking to me somehow."

Ravi looked at him with a strange expression. "Okay, Mr AI. Let's be for real."

In the observation room, Dr. Avery watched intently with his hands clasped behind his back. The energy readings on his monitors were off the charts. The surge far exceeded his expectations. "They survived," he murmured with a mix of relief and excitement in his voice.

Behind him, a shadowy figure stepped forward. The caramel woman wore a navy blue tailored suit. Her face was partially obscured in the dim light.

"Phase one is complete," Avery said without turning around.

"And the subjects?"

"They're stable for now," Avery replied. "But the real test begins when they start to realize what's happened."

Her lips curved into a faint smile. "Good. Keep me updated."

With that, she turned and disappeared into the shadows leaving Dr. Avery alone with his monitors.

Chapter 4

The day was supposed to be like any other. Students shuffled between classes and teachers droned on about math equations, literary metaphors, and historical battles. But for five students something was undeniably different.

Jordan had always been the tech-savvy one. He could fix a broken computer in minutes and code a simple game in a weekend. But this was different. It started in the computer lab during third period. He was supposed to be working on an algorithm for a class project, but as soon as his fingers touched the keyboard, it came to life. The screen flickered and lines of code that he hadn't written appeared.

"What the...?" Jordan whispered as he leaned closer.

The text on the screen shifted to form a coherent sentence: **"HELLO, JORDAN."**

He yanked his hands back as if the keyboard had burned him.

"Everything okay, Jordan?" Mr. Garcia called from the front of the room.

"Uh, yeah," Jordan stuttered quickly as he minimized the screen. He spent the rest of the period trying to act normal. *Was the computer responding to him? Or was he losing it?*

Across the hall, Ava sat in art class staring at a blank canvas. Art was her outlet and her way of making sense of the chaos in her life. Normally, she'd have already filled it with bold strokes of color, but today her mind was somewhere else. As she stared at the blank page, a wave of emotion washed over her—not her own, but someone else's. She turned to her right and saw Becky, her table mate, hunched over her work. Her shoulders were tense and her brush strokes were erratic. She reached out and placed her hand on her arm. "Are you okay?"

Becky blinked at her startled. "Yeah... just stressed about this assignment."

The moment she spoke, Ava felt a shift. It felt like a heavy cloud lifting. She instantly relaxed and her strokes smoothed out. Ava pulled her hand back, confused. Had she just done something?

In physics class, Jiho sat by the window doodling in his notebook while Mr. Norris lectured on motion and forces. His pen scratched absentmindedly across the page as he sketched the same swirling pattern repeatedly. He hadn't meant to—it just *happened*. When he finally glanced down, his breath caught. The shape looked eerily familiar. It was the same strange symbol that had flashed in the simulation before everything glitched.

His fingers twitched. The desk beneath his arm felt... alive, almost like it was subtly vibrating. He frowned and pressed his palm flat against the surface. The vibrations grew stronger. A paperclip nearby trembled, then rolled toward his hand. He yanked his arm back.

"Mr. Li?" Mr. Norris's voice snapped him out of his daze. "Since you seem so deep in thought, maybe you can answer this—what's Newton's Second Law?"

He struggled to focus. "Uh... force equals mass times acceleration?"

Mr. Norris nodded approvingly and continued his lecture. But he barely heard him. As he tried to focus on the lecture, the classroom around him flickered—just for a second. He blinked, certain he'd imagined it. But when he looked again, the walls seemed... different. Transparent, almost like a digital overlay.

"Are you okay?" his classmate whispered from the next desk over.

"Yeah. Just—uh, just tired."

But he wasn't tired. He was seeing something no one else seemed to notice. As he glanced around the room, faint glowing lines traced the edges of objects—the whiteboard, the desks, and even the students. It was as if the world had an extra layer, something hidden beneath reality itself. And for the briefest moment, he swore he saw something move within those lines—a shadow shifting just beyond his vision.

His pulse spiked. Then, just as quickly as it had appeared, the overlay vanished. The room snapped back to normal. Jiho sucked in a breath as questions formed in his thoughts. "*Whatever was happening to him... was it just in his head? Was he seeing things? Or was the world around him glitching, like a simulation?*"

In gym class, Ravi lined up with the rest of his classmates for the relay race. He'd always been athletic, but nothing exceptional. When it was his turn, he grabbed the baton and sprinted down the track. But something felt off. His feet barely seemed to touch the ground, and the other runners fell behind quickly. The wind roared in his ears. His strides felt effortless like his body was moving on autopilot. The finish line rushed toward him faster than it should have.

Then—*he crossed it*. Not just first. *Way* first. He skidded to a stop as his heart pounded. He turned back to see the other runners still a good twenty feet behind, some slowing in confusion, others staring at him in disbelief. Even Coach Harris with a stopwatch in his hand was in shock.

"What the hell was that?" one of his classmates asked.

Ravi didn't have an answer. His breathing wasn't even heavy like he hadn't just pushed himself harder than ever before. His muscles didn't burn either. If anything, he felt *stronger*.

Coach Harris strode over to Ravi. "You, uh... you just clocked in at a time that shouldn't be possible."

"What do you mean?"

"I mean," the coach said slowly, "if this thing isn't broken, you just ran faster than a state champion."

A nervous laugh rippled through the class, but Ravi wasn't laughing. Because in that moment, as he stood there gripping the baton, he felt something else. A deep, thrumming energy coiled in his legs like his body wasn't done yet. Like he could go even *faster*. And that terrified him.

Meanwhile, in the library, Camelia sat across from a group of classmates working on a group project. They'd been arguing for fifteen minutes over which topic to choose.

"I'm telling you, climate change is the easiest," one girl said.

"No way. We should do recycling," another argued.

Camelia sighed and closed her notebook. "Guys, let's just do climate change. It's straightforward, and we can finish it faster."

The group fell silent. Then, as if on cue, they all nodded in agreement.

"Yeah, that makes sense," one of them murmured.

"Climate change it is," another agreed as they began to type out a rough outline.

Camelia blinked. That was... fast. Too fast. She hadn't even tried to be persuasive.

As the discussion continued, she tested it again. "We should divide the research evenly," she suggested.

"Good idea," someone said immediately.

She stared at them. It wasn't just that they agreed with her. They were doing it without question or hesitation. Her voice held weight. Influence. She felt a strange awareness settle in. This wasn't normal. She wasn't just suggesting things. She was *telling* them. She frowned. Normally they'd argue for hours. Did she... do something to change their minds?

By the end of the day, the five friends were more than ready to head home. Each of them had experienced something they couldn't explain. Something that felt impossible. They met at the school's back gate.

"You guys look weird," Ravi said. "Like, weirder than usual."

Ava rolled her eyes. "Thanks, Ravi. Real helpful."

"I'm serious," he insisted. "Something's up. Spill."

Jordan hesitated then spoke first. "The computer in the lab... it was talking to me."

"Talking to you?" Camelia asked raising an eyebrow.

"Not literally. But it was like... it knew I was there. I don't know how to explain it."

Ava bit her lip. "In art class, I touched someone's arm, and it was like I could feel what they were feeling. And then... they weren't stressed anymore."

Jiho and Ravi exchanged a glance.

"Something happened to me, too," Jiho admitted. "I think I saw... layers of the classroom. Like I was looking through the walls."

"And I ran faster than I've ever run in gym," Ravi added. "Like, superhero fast."

All eyes turned to Camelia.

"I think I might have influenced my group project," she said. "I told them to do something, and they just... agreed. No arguments, no hesitation."

"You don't think..." Ava began, her voice trailing off.

"That it's connected to the trip?" Jiho finished.

"It has to be," Jordan said. "This is too much to be a coincidence."

"But why now?" Ravi asked. "Why all at once?"

Camelia deep in thought. "Maybe it's been happening gradually, and we just didn't notice until now."

"Or maybe something triggered it," Jiho suggested.

Ava shivered. "Whatever it is, it's not normal."

Jordan nodded. "We need to figure out what's going on. Fast."

"And if we did get powers from the expo, then everyone needs to pay up," Ravi said trying to joke. The group looked at him and just groaned.

"This isn't funny," Ava muttered. "Something weird is happening to us."

"We need to figure this out," Jordan finally said. "If we don't, it's only a matter of time before someone else notices."

"Agreed," Jiho said. "But where do we even start?"

"Let's meet at my house after homework," Ava suggested. "We can brainstorm."

Chapter 5

The group met in Ava's unfinished basement. It was cold, dimly lit by a single overhead bulb, and cluttered with old furniture and storage boxes. An old, dusty couch sat against one wall, and a wobbly folding table stood in the center, surrounded by mismatched chairs.

Ava pulled the chain on a standing lamp to give the room a little more light. "Okay, this is probably the safest place we can talk. No one listens in, no cameras, no random teachers asking questions."

Jordan dropped his backpack onto the table and pulled out his laptop. "Good. Because we need to go over everything we remember from the expo."

Ravi sat across from him. "Alright, so we all did something different, right? Jiho had that VR game, Camelia got hypnotized, Ava had the wristband, I did the strength test and Jordan—"

"—had a conversation with a computer," he finished grimly. "One that knew my name before I said anything."

Jiho tapped the table. "And now we're all experiencing... *something*. Weird visions, strength, influence over people—"

Camelia crossed her arms. "We need to figure out if these abilities are just *happening* to us, or if we can actually control them."

Ava nodded. "And more importantly, *why* us? Out of all the students at the expo, why did *we* end up like this?"

Jiho answered, "Maybe it wasn't random. Maybe they were looking for specific people."

Camelia frowned. "But we're just normal students. It's not like we have anything in common."

Jordan's fingers hovered over his laptop keyboard. "Except now we do." He glanced up at them. "What if the expo wasn't just about showing off tech? What if it was a test?"

Ava swallowed hard. "A test for what?"

No one had an answer. The only sound was the hum of the basement's old heating unit.

Ravi paced back and forth along the concrete floor. "So we're all agreed, right? Whatever's happening isn't a coincidence."

"No kidding," Ava said. "But what *is* it? And why us?"

"I don't know," Jiho said. "But we can't just ignore it. If we don't figure out what's going on, things will get worse."

Camelia stated. "We should start by discussing what we've all experienced so far. Maybe we can figure out a pattern."

All eyes turned to Jordan. "You all know what happened in class," he said. "But it's not just that. I've been feeling... connected to machines... like I can understand them. It's hard to explain, but it's as if they're speaking to me."

"Can you control them?" Ravi asked.

"Sort of," Jordan said. "I don't know how it works. It just happens."

"Show us," said Camelia.

He pulled his phone from his pocket. He stared at the screen focusing intently. The device lit up and the screen flickered before displaying lines of code. The others leaned in wide-eyed.

"Whoa," Jiho said. "You're not even touching it."

"I don't need to," he said with both pride and fear. "That's what I mean. It's like my mind is linked to it."

"Well, that's freaky. But I've got to admit, it's cool. Anyone else want to share?"

Ava sighed. "Fine. My turn."

She closed her eyes and took a deep breath. "It's emotions. I can feel what other people are feeling. It's like their emotions get tangled up with mine. And... sometimes, I can change them."

"Change them how?" Jiho asked.

Ava opened her eyes and looked at Ravi. "Like this."

His skeptical expression softened and was replaced by a sudden inexplicable calm. "Huh. I feel... weirdly relaxed right now."

"That's me. I'm making you feel that way."

"Okay, that's both impressive and terrifying," Ravi said.

"It's not like I enjoy it. It's overwhelming sometimes, especially when I'm around a lot of people. Their emotions are... loud."

Jiho stood up. "Mine's a little different. It's not emotions or machines. It's... reality. I can see things that aren't there, like alternate layers of the world."

"What do you mean, alternate layers?" Camelia asked.

"I don't know how to explain it. It's like there are multiple versions of the same space and I can look into them. And I think I can... shift things around, like rearrange what's real and what's not."

"Have you done it before?" Jordan asked.

"I've only done it once in class. But it took a lot out of me. It was disorienting—like I was slipping between two worlds at the same time. If I'm not careful... I might not know which one is real."

"Can you show us?" Ava asked gently.

He closed his eyes and exhaled slowly. The air around him shimmered faintly like heat rising from asphalt. Suddenly, the cluttered basement seemed to shift. The edges of the room flickered and warped like a glitching screen. For a brief moment, the concrete walls turned transparent and revealed faint outlines beyond them—wires, pipes, even the vague shadows of the floors above. The others sucked in a breath as reality itself seemed to waver.

His breathing grew uneven as he concentrated. "It's... hard to hold." His voice sounded distant and layered as if it was coming from two places at once. Then, just as quickly as it had begun, everything snapped back to normal. Jiho stumbled and gripped the table for support.

Ava reached out to steady him. "Are you okay?"

"Told you. It's not easy."

Ravi commented. "Okay, that was *insane*. You just—what even was that?"

Jordan, still staring at the space where the walls had flickered, whispered, "You weren't just seeing through things. You were *somewhere else.*"

"Yeah," he admitted. "And that's what scares me."

The basement felt smaller now, the air thick with unease. He rubbed his temples. He was still feeling the lingering dizziness from whatever he had just done.

Jordan tapped his fingers anxiously on the table. "When you—uh, shifted—did you *feel* anything? Like, were you actually somewhere else?"

"It's hard to explain. It's like... I exist in two places at once. I can still hear you, still *know* I'm here, but I can also see things I shouldn't. Like layers of reality overlapping." He glanced up, his expression tense. "And for a second, I felt like something was looking *back* at me."

Ava's body stiffened. "Looking back?"

"Like I wasn't supposed to be there, and something knew."

Silence settled over the group.

Ravi exhaled. "Okay, so just to recap—you can see between realities or whatever, and now we might have something watching us?"

"That's insane," Camelia said, "And now it's my turn, I guess." She stood and hesitantly moved toward the center of the room.

"It's kind of strange, but I think I can... influence people's minds," she said.

"Like mind control?" Jiho asked raising an eyebrow.

"Not exactly," Camelia said. "It's more like persuasion. I can make people see or believe things, but only if they're already kind of open to it. I can't force anyone to do something they absolutely don't want to."

"Can you show us?" Jordan asked.

Camelia bit her lip. "I'll try."

She turned to Ravi. " I want you to stand up and... I don't know, walk to the other side of the room."

"Why would I do that?" he asked skeptically.

Camelia focused on him narrowing her eyes slightly. Her voice took on an odd soothing cadence. "It's just a quick walk. No big deal. You might even enjoy it."

To everyone's surprise, he stood and walked to the far side of the room. Once he got there, he stopped and looked around, confused.

"Wait... why did I just do that?" he asked turning back to the group.

Camelia's expression was apologetic. "I think that was me. Sorry."

"That was... kind of creepy," he admitted rubbing the back of his neck. "But impressive."

Jordan looked at Ravi and said, "Since you're already standing there, you're up. "

"Okay," he stared. "Before I begin I just want y'all to know my dreams came true. I got super strength. Watch this."

He walked to a heavy box in the corner of the basement. "This thing weighs a ton, right?" he asked, gesturing to the box.

"Yeah, it's full of books," Ava said.

Ravi crouched to grip the edges of the box. With what seemed like minimal effort, he lifted it off the ground and held it over his head.

"Whoa!" Jiho exclaimed.

"Okay, that's not normal," Jordan said staring.

Ravi set the box down gently with a smug grin on his face. "Yeah, I noticed it when I was helping my mom move some stuff last weekend. I can lift way more than I should be able to. And it's not just strength. I'm faster too. It's like my whole body is... upgraded."

"Do you have limits?" Camelia asked.

"I'm sure I do, but I haven't hit them yet."

"So," Jordan said, "we've all got these... abilities. But why us? And why now?"

"It has to be connected to that night at the science fair," Jiho said. "That's when everything started."

"Yeah, but what exactly happened?" Ava questioned. "All I remember is the blackout."

"And the weird hum," Ravi added. "It felt like something was in the air."

Jordan frowned. "I think it was more than just a blackout. Maybe the machines... I don't know, rewired something in us?"

"That doesn't explain the rest of us," Camelia pointed out. "Not everything is about machines."

"Okay, fair," Jordan said. "But there has to be a reason why we're like this. And if we're not careful, someone else is going to notice."

"That's what scares me," Ava said softly. "What if people find out? What if... what if they try to take us away?"

"They won't," Ravi said firmly. "We'll figure this out together. We're not letting anyone mess with us."

"We should begin training. It'll help us maintain our powers," Jiho advised. "Where are we going to practice? Everywhere has cameras or nearby public places," Ava stated.

"I know a place we could practice at," Ravi said."

"What place could you of all people know of?" Camelia questioned.

"That part doesn't matter, but I can guarantee that it is remote enough for us to practice."

"So where is this mysterious place?" Jiho asked.

"It's at the end of the trail right off the track field." "Alrighty then.. we'll meet at the track field tomorrow after school," Jordan said.

Chapter 6

"This place is perfect," Jiho said as they came to a stop in a small clearing. "Ravi, I still want to know, how'd you find this area?"

"Like I said a while ago, it doesn't matter, but is it remote enough for you?" Ravi dropped his backpack on the ground.

Jiho looked around. "Yeah, no cell towers and no nearby houses. We're safe here."

Ava set down a water bottle and wiped her brow. "Good, because the last thing we need is someone stumbling across us testing superpowers."

Camelia sat on a fallen log brushing leaves off her jeans. "Alright, what's the plan? How do we do this without, you know, breaking something or someone?"

Jordan smiled. "We take turns. One person tests their limits while the rest of us stay clear. That way, we're not in each other's way."

"Sounds like a plan," Jiho said. "Who's first?"

"I'll go," Ravi volunteered and stepped forward.

"Figures," Jiho teased.

There were a few items to help test Ravi's strength: large rocks, a steel bar Jordan had discovered in a junkyard, and an old log that had fallen across the clearing.

"Start small," Ava suggested. "Let's see how much you can lift without straining yourself."

Ravi approached the steel bar first and gripped it firmly. With a quick lift, he held it above his head barely straining his muscles.

"Okay, that's not even a warm-up," Ravi said as he set it down. He moved to the large log next, crouching to get a good grip.

"Careful," Camelia warned.

With a grunt, Ravi lifted the log off the ground. He took a few steps with it before gently setting it down.

"Still too easy," he shook out his arms. "Give me something harder."

37

Jordan nodded and pointed to a massive boulder on the edge of the clearing. "Think you can move that?"

Ravi studied it, then shrugged. "Only one way to find out."

He approached the boulder and planted his feet firmly. With a deep breath, he heaved and the ground beneath him cracked slightly as he lifted the heavy rock. Sweat beaded on his forehead, but he managed to move it a few feet before dropping it with a thud.

"Okay, that one was tough," he admitted.

"That was insane," Jiho said, wide-eyed. "You just moved a boulder!"

"My turn," Ava said as she stepped into the clearing.

"What exactly are we testing?" Camelia asked.

"I want to see if I can focus my emotions into something... tangible."

She closed her eyes and took a deep breath. Her hands started to glow faintly, a soft golden light emanating from her palms. The others watched in silence as the glow around her hands intensified. The air around her seemed to shift, a warmth spreading outward like the first rays of morning sunlight.

"Whoa," Ravi said and stepped back.

The light grew brighter and pulsed in time with her heartbeat. She opened her eyes and focused on a small rock in front of her. With a flick of her wrist, the glow extended outward. It began to wrap around the rock and lift it into the air.

"Holy crap," Jordan said.

The rock hovered for a moment before Ava lost her focus, and it dropped back to the ground.

"That's new. I didn't know I could do that."

"Do you think you can use it on something bigger?" Jiho asked.

Ava nodded, though she looked uncertain. She extended her hands toward the steel bar Ravi had lifted earlier. This time, the glow was more concentrated, and the bar rose smoothly into the air.

"You're getting the hang of it," Camelia said encouragingly.

Ava smiled, but the strain was evident on her face. She set the bar down carefully, then let the glow fade.

"I think that's enough for now," she said as she rubbed her temples.

"Guess it's my turn," Jordan said.

"What are you testing?" Ravi asked.

"Range and control," Jordan replied. He pulled out a small drone he'd brought with him. "I want to see how far I can manipulate tech without touching it."

He set the drone on the ground and took a step back. Closing his eyes, he concentrated and his fingers twitched slightly. The drone buzzed to life with its propellers spinning.

"Nice," Jiho said.

He guided the drone into the air and maneuvered it through the trees with precise movements. He sent it higher and higher until it was barely visible.

"Still good?" Ava asked.

"Still good," he confirmed.

He brought the drone back down and made it hover just above the ground. Then, with a flick of his hand, he programmed it to play music. A low bass echoed through the clearing.

"Show-off," Camelia teased.

"Gotta keep it interesting."

"Alright, my turn," Camelia said.

"What are you testing?" Ava asked.

"Range. I want to see how far away I can influence someone."

Jiho volunteered to be her subject. He stood on the far side of the clearing.

"Okay," she said and focused on him. She took a deep breath. She spoke in a calm voice. "Jiho, touch your nose."

He hesitated for a moment, then raised his hand and tapped his nose.

"Whoa," Ravi said. "That's kind of freaky."

Camelia tried again. This time she asked him to pick up a small stick. Once again, he complied, though there was a slight delay.

"I think distance makes it harder," she said. "The closer someone is, the stronger the effect."

"Good to know," Jordan said. "But let's not abuse that power, okay?"

"No promises."

"Last but not least," Jiho said.

"What are you testing?" Ravi asked.

"I want to see how big of an area I can affect," he said.

He closed his eyes and concentrated. The air around them shimmered, and suddenly the clearing looked completely different. The trees were taller, the ground was covered in moss, and a waterfall could be heard in the distance.

"This is amazing," Ava said in awe.

His brow furrowed as he expanded the illusion. He made the waterfall visible in the distance. The effort was taxing, and he dropped the illusion after a few minutes.

"That's... my limit," he said.

"You did great," Camelia said.

The group sat down together. They were catching their breaths after the tests. It was the first time they practiced in front of each other and they felt good.

"We're getting there," Ravi said.

"But we still have a lot to learn," Jiho added.

"And we need to stay under the radar," Ava said. "If anyone finds out about us..."

"They won't," Jordan said firmly. "We'll keep practicing, and we'll figure out what to do next."

Chapter 7

After two months of practicing, they were starting to understand what they could do. But that understanding came with arguments.

Ravi paced near the base of a tree. "I'm just saying, if we have these powers, we should be doing *something* useful with them. Why are we wasting time here?"

Camelia sat on a nearby stump. "By 'useful,' do you mean showing off or making a spectacle of ourselves?"

Ravi turned towards her. "No, I mean helping people. Or maybe even stopping bad guys. Like Batman or Captain America."

She nearly choked on her soda. "Batman? Really? We can barely control what we've got, and you're already talking about saving the world?"

"I'm just saying, we've been given these abilities for a reason. What's the point if we don't use them?"

Camelia sighed. "The point is staying alive. The point is not getting locked in some lab for the rest of our lives."

Ava added. "She's right. We still don't know the full extent of what we can do, and you want to go patrolling the streets like we're some comic book heroes?"

"I'm not saying we run out and start fighting crime tomorrow. But if we don't use these powers, if we don't push ourselves, then what are we even doing? Hiding?"

Jiho said. "Ravi's not wrong. We've been training for two months now. Maybe it's time we figure out what we're capable of."

Camelia gave him a look. "And what happens when someone gets hurt?"

Ravi answered. "Then we learn from it. We get better. And we make sure we're strong enough to protect each other."

Jordan said, "We need to stay under the radar. You've seen what happens in movies and comics. The second people find out about us, we'll be lab experiments. Or worse."

"So what? Are we just supposed to hide forever? Pretend this isn't happening?"

"Yes," Jordan said bluntly. "At least until we figure out how to control these powers without causing mass mayhem."

Camelia smirked. "Too late for that. Ravi's chaos just comes naturally."

"Look," Ava continued, "I get that we're all trying to figure this out. But turning on each other isn't the answer."

"Then what *is* the answer?"

"Maybe we take a break," Ava suggested. "From practicing, from talking about this. Just for a little while."

Jordan shook his head. "We can't ignore this. Taking a break won't make it go away."

"Neither will fighting about it," Jiho shot back. "We're all stressed out, okay? "

"Fine," Ravi said begrudgingly. "Well, can we at least figure out what we're capable of? Practicing like this doesn't make any sense."

"You mean you want to use it recklessly," Ava replied sounding frustrated.

Jordan spoke up. "Not everything has to be about showing off strength. What if using these powers draws attention? We don't know who else might be watching."

Jiho added. "He's right. Someone could already know about us." His eyes flicked nervously to the treetops as though expecting to see a drone hovering there.

Camelia sighed. "We agreed to take this slow. We need control first. No one's saying we shouldn't use them, but we need to be smart about it."

"Smart," Ravi repeated mockingly as he threw his hands in the air. "You sound like my parents. Maybe the rest of you are okay with playing it safe, but I'm done wasting time."

Before anyone could stop him, he stomped over to a fallen tree branch the size of a small log and lifted it easily. The veins in his arms glowed faintly as his strength activated. He hurled the branch into the air, where it smashed into a tree trunk with a deafening crack.

"Ravi!" Camelia snapped.

"What?" he challenged, The way he looked at her dared her to say something more.

"You're going to get us caught," she replied.

"By who?" he spread his arms wide. "You're so worried about being caught, but we don't even know if anyone's watching."

"They are," Jordan said quietly. "And you're making it easy for them."

"What are you talking about?"

Jordan pulled out his phone. "I've been picking up weird signals for days now. I don't know if it's drones or surveillance or what, but something's out there. And if they see you throwing logs around like a superhero in training, we're screwed."

"Maybe they should see," he said as he raised his voice. "Maybe it's better than hiding."

"Are you serious right now?" Ava asked incredulously. The faint hum of her emotional influence rippled in the air making everyone's frustration spike. "You don't get to decide that for all of us."

"*Stop it!*" Camelia's voice cut through the rising tension, and for a moment, everyone froze. Her eyes glinted dangerously, and Ravi staggered back slightly confused.

"Did you just - " he began but she held up a hand.

"Yeah, I did. And I'll do it again if you don't calm down."

"You're unbelievable," he muttered as he stepped back.

"Guys, this isn't helping," Jiho said. "We're supposed to be a team, right? We can't afford to fight each other."

"Tell that to him," she said as she jerked her head toward Ravi.

"Fine," he said through gritted teeth. "You want me to stop? I'll stop. But don't come crying to me when this blows up in your faces."

Jordan walked towards him. "No one's saying we shouldn't use our powers. But we need to be smart about it. If we're not, we'll lose whatever chance we have at figuring this out on our own terms."

Ava looked around at her friends' tense expressions. They'd been going in circles for weeks—arguing, worrying, second-guessing every decision. It was exhausting.

"Okay, you know what?" she said. "We need a break."

Ravi raised an eyebrow. "A break? From what, exactly?"

"From *this*," she gestured. "From the training, the paranoia, the constant overthinking. We're still *us*, right? So let's act like it for one day."

Camelia frowned. "And do what?"

Ava smiled. "Let's meet at the park this Saturday. No powers, no stress—just fun. Frisbee, snacks, maybe a game of soccer. Like normal people."

Their whole mood changed. It was the answer that they all needed. Jiho let out a breath. "Huh. That... doesn't sound like the worst idea."

Jordan shrugged. "I guess it would be nice to pretend things are normal for a while."

Ravi smiled. "Fine, but if we *are* playing soccer, prepare to lose."

Camelia rolled her eyes. "Yeah, yeah, we'll see about that."

Ava grinned. "Great. Saturday, then."

"Good," Jordan said. "Now let's get out of here before someone shows up asking questions."

As the group began to gather their things a faint rustling in the bushes made Jiho freeze. "Did you hear that?" he whispered.

They all turned toward the sound. For a moment no one moved. Then, a squirrel darted out from the undergrowth scampering across the path.

"It's just a squirrel," Ava said exhaling a shaky breath.

"Or maybe it's not," he replied as he glanced around the area again.

Camelia grabbed his arm. "Are you saying you think we're being watched?"

Jordan peered into the trees. "It's possible. If someone is keeping tabs on us, they wouldn't exactly walk up and introduce themselves."

Ravi clenched his fists. "Well, if they are, let's give them something to be afraid of."

Ava shot him a glare. "Or, we could not antagonize the possibly very dangerous people tracking us."

Jiho lowered his voice. "We should leave. Now."

Before anyone could argue, another sound cut through the clearing—a sharp snap, like a branch breaking underfoot. This time, they knew it wasn't a squirrel.

Camelia's pulse quickened. "Go. Now."

The group didn't hesitate. They moved as quickly and quietly as possible, grabbing their things and heading toward the tree line.

Chapter 8

The friends met up at the park that Saturday afternoon. Jiho and Ravi brought sandwiches and snacks, while Camelia carried a frisbee to pass the time. As the group spread out on a grassy hill near the playground, Jordan couldn't help but notice the gadgets around him. Kids with remote-controlled cars zipped across the paths, parents scrolled through their phones, and a drone hovered nearby was filming the scenic area.

"Jordan," Ava said. "Don't even think about it."

"What?" he asked innocently.

"You know what," she replied firmly. "No powers, remember?"

"Relax. I'm not doing anything," he said as he raised his hands in mock surrender.

Ravi smirked, spinning the soccer ball in his hands. "Yeah, sure. And I'm the king of England."

Camelia crossed her arms. "You have *that* look, Jordan. The one you get right before you pull something."

He scoffed. "Wow, no trust at all."

Ava shook her head. "Just... behave, okay? One normal day. That's all I'm asking."

He placed a hand over his heart. "Scout's honor."

Ravi tossed the ball in the air. "Alright, enough talking. Let's play."

Later in the afternoon, as the group played frisbee, Jordan's attention returned to the drone. The operator, a man in his late twenties, was engrossed in a conversation with a friend. The controls were left unattended on a nearby bench.

"I'll be right back," he said as he walked away from the group.

"Where are you going?" Ravi called after him.

"Just grabbing a water bottle."

Instead, he strolled toward the bench where the drone controller sat. The device called to him like a beacon. Its circuitry hummed faintly in his mind. Before he knew it, his hand hovered over the controls, and a small spark of energy passed from his fingertips. The drone whirred and shifted midair. He felt a surge of satisfaction as he realized he could guide it with his thoughts.

What started as harmless fun quickly spiraled out of control. He directed the drone to perform a series of flips and loops, which drew gasps and applause from nearby onlookers. The drone zipped higher and executed a perfect barrel roll before diving sharply toward the ground, only to pull up at the last second. His hands moved instinctively as if the drone was responding directly to his thoughts rather than the joystick. Emboldened, he sent it higher and it weaved through tree branches startling a flock of birds.

"Jordan!" Jiho's voice cut through the crowd. The others had noticed the commotion and rushed over.

"Uh, hey, guys," he said sheepishly as the drone hovered a few feet above him.

"What are you doing?" Ava hissed as she looked at the growing crowd of spectators.

"Just messing around," he answered defensively.

"Messing around?" Ravi retorted loudly. "You're practically putting on a show!"

Before Jordan could respond, the drone malfunctioned. The screen flickered. For a split second, the feed distorted and was replaced by a brief flash of coded text that was too fast to read. It jerked midair and its movements became erratic. Jordan's breath caught in his throat. He tried to stabilize it, but the drone resisted and twisted sharply toward a group of children. Parents screamed and scrambled to pull their kids away.

"Jordan, shut it down!" Ava yelled.

"I'm trying!" he shouted back.

The drone spiraled out of control and crashed into a lamppost with a loud clang. The sound drew even more attention, and people began pointing and whispering. Jordan's heart pounded as he dropped the controller onto the bench. "We need to go. *Now.*"

Ava grabbed his arm. "That wasn't normal, was it?"

"No," Jordan muttered. "It felt like something took over."

The drone's operator finally noticed the wreckage and rushed over in confusion. "What the hell?" he stammered as he picked up the damaged device. He glanced around as if trying to figure out who had been messing with it.

Ravi nudged Jordan. "Time to move before we get blamed for this."

They hurried away from the field and slipped into the crowd. Camelia shot Jordan a look. "You're sure that wasn't you?"

Jordan swallowed hard. "I thought I was in control. But for a second... it felt like something else was."

Jiho exhaled sharply. "Yeah. That's not terrifying *at all.*"

Jordan still felt the lingering tremor in his fingers. "I swear, it wasn't me. At least, not *just* me."

Ava glanced toward the wrecked drone, where the operator was still inspecting it with a deep frown. "We need to get out of here before someone starts asking questions."

"Agreed," Camelia said, already turning toward the path leading out of the park.

As they walked, Ravi shoved his hands into his pockets. "So, let's just go over the facts here—Jordan *thought* he was in control of that drone, and then suddenly, he wasn't."

Jordan rubbed the back of his neck. "Yeah. And it wasn't like the battery died or the connection cut out. It was like... something else was steering."

Jiho let out a low whistle. "That means either your power is way stronger than we thought, or—"

"Or someone else was interfering," Ava finished grimly.

That thought sent a chill down Jordan's spine. Was he being *hijacked* somehow? And if so... by *who*?

"We should get back to my place," Ava said, glancing around cautiously. "We can figure this out there."

The others agreed and quickened their pace. The excitement of the afternoon had completely faded and was replaced by an unsettling realization. Back at Ava's basement, the group confronted Jordan.

"You could've exposed all of us!" Ava said.

"I know, okay? I messed up," Jordan said as he slumped into a chair.

"'Messed up' is an understatement," Ravi said. "What if someone had gotten hurt? Or worse, what if someone figured out what you did? And you guys were worried about me showing off, tch."

Camelia stepped in. "He knows it was a mistake. Let's focus on what we can learn from this."

Jiho sat down beside Jordan. "Look, we get it. These powers are tempting. But we can't let them control us. We have to be smarter than this."

"You're right," he said. "It won't happen again. Especially since I lost control at the end. I need to know why."

Jiho gave him a small nod. "Exactly. Because we don't know who's out there watching—or what they want."

Ava leaned against the wall. "We need to start figuring this out. No more accidents. No more risks."

Jordan exhaled. "Yeah. Agreed."

Camelia tapped her fingers on the table. "Then maybe we should set some ground rules. We only use our powers when we *have* to. No showing off. No testing them in public."

Ravi let out a dry laugh. "So, what? We just pretend we're normal?"

Ava met his gaze. "Until we know what's going on? Yeah. We do."

Silence settled over the group as the weight of her words sank in.

Jiho finally stood up. "Alright. Then it's settled. We keep this quiet. We stay in control. And we find out who, if anyone, is pulling the strings."

Jordan nodded, determination settling in his chest. "Agreed."

Camelia looked around at the group. "Then I guess we have our first assignment."

The group exchanged small, hesitant smiles. Despite the day's events, their bond remained unbroken. But they all knew the road ahead would only get more complicated. The lesson was clear: with great power came even greater responsibility. And for these five friends, the stakes had never been higher.

Chapter 9

The following Monday, the school's hallways buzzed with the usual chaos of students. Locker doors slammed, conversations overlapped, and sneakers squeaked against the polished floors. The group had agreed not to discuss the park incident where wandering ears could catch something they shouldn't.

Ava adjusted the strap of her backpack and scanned the crowded hallway. Jiho and Ravi were deep in a conversation about some new video game, while Camelia flipped through a notebook while barely dodging a passing student. Jordan, as usual, trailed a few steps behind. His hands were in his pockets as his gaze lingered to every digital screen in sight.

"You're overthinking," Ava murmured as they neared their lockers.

Jordan huffed. "I'm *always* overthinking."

Ravi leaned against the lockers, flashing a grin. "Yeah, we know. It's part of your charm."

Camelia rolled her eyes. "Can we just get through today without any more *incidents*?"

Jiho chuckled. "Doubtful, but sure, let's aim high."

The bell rang, signaling the start of second period. With a few parting nods, they split off to their respective rooms. Jordan adjusted his glasses and sat at his usual seat in the back corner of the classroom. His science teacher, Ms. Keller, explained the setup for an experiment involving small circuits and light bulbs.

"You'll each receive a kit," Ms. Keller said at the front of the room. "Your task is to create a functioning circuit. Work carefully and follow the instructions."

As the kits were handed out, he couldn't help but notice how easy the project seemed. He had been experimenting with his abilities starting with controlling basic devices around the house. His computer booted up before he touched it and his phone opened apps as though reading his mind.

He stared at the circuit board and, without thinking, let his mind reach out to it. The wires seemed to hum with recognition. *This should be simple enough,* he thought as he directed the current without lifting a finger. Suddenly, the light bulb in front of him lit up brighter than anyone else's. A split second later it popped and sent a small shower of sparks onto his desk.

"Jordan!" Ms. Keller called rushing over.

"Sorry! I must've used the wrong wire," he lied as he quickly disconnected the components. The other students snickered and he felt his face heat up. He thought *"I gotta be more careful"* as he pretended to examine the circuit.

Camelia tapped her pencil against her notebook as she struggled to focus on the discussion about Shakespeare's *Macbeth*. Her mind kept drifting back to her powers. She had practiced by testing how far her hypnotic suggestions could go. It was thrilling but also terrifying to know she could make someone do something with just a few words.

"Camelia, can you read the next passage?" Mr. Gray's voice interrupted her thoughts.

She cleared her throat and began reading aloud, but halfway through the boy sitting behind her started mimicking her voice in an exaggerated tone. Laughter erupted across the room.

"Very funny, Tyler," Mr. Gray gave him a warning look.

Camelia clenched her jaw. She could feel the words bubbling up as well as the urge to make him stop. Her voice dropped just above a whisper as she muttered, "Be quiet." Tyler froze mid-laugh and his mouth snapped shut. His eyes widened in confusion and he didn't say another word for the rest of the class.

Camelia's heart pounded as she realized what she'd done. She hadn't meant to use her powers, but the control felt so natural. She glanced around and was relieved that no one seemed to notice anything strange.

In the gymnasium, Ravi waited for his turn at the bench press station. His weekend had been frustrating. His family's constant hovering made it impossible to test the limits of his strength. But here, surrounded by weights and equipment, he felt alive.

"Come on, Ravi," his classmate Elijah called. "Let's see if you can beat your record today."

Ravi smirked. "You're on." He laid on the bench and gripped the barbell loaded with more weight than he'd ever attempted in class. As he lifted, he felt the familiar rush of energy coursed through him. The barbell rose easily, almost too easily.

"Jesus bro!" Elijah said. "You're making that look like nothing."

He grinned and added more weight while ignoring the uneasy looks from the other students.

"Ravi, that's enough," Coach Harris called. "You're going to hurt yourself."

"I'm fine!" He replied as he pushed the barbell up again. But this time, the barbell bent under the strain, and a loud *snap* echoed through the gym as one of the weights fell off. The entire class turned to stare.

"Ravi!" Coach Harris barked. "What were you thinking? That equipment isn't designed for that kind of weight!"

"Sorry, Coach," he mumbled. He avoided everyone's gaze as he helped clean up, but he felt guilty. He had let his power get the better of him.

Jiho sat at his easel sketching a rough outline of a landscape for his art assignment. Over the weekend, he'd discovered he didn't need to wear it to create illusion. His mind alone could project visuals into the real world. His hand hesitated as he shaded in a tree. What if he could bring the sketch to life? Just a small illusion, something harmless. He glanced around to see if anyone was watching, but the other students were focused on their work.

Closing his eyes for a moment, he pictured the tree on his paper swaying gently in the wind. When he opened them, a faint shimmering image of the tree appeared next to his easel. It was almost translucent, but it moved as if alive. He smiled, but his satisfaction was short-lived.

"Uh, Jiho?" a girl next to him said trembling.

He turned to see her staring at the illusion. Her eyes were wide with fear.

"Is that... real?" she whispered.

Jiho's heart raced. "No! It's, uh, just a trick," he stuttered as the image dissolved.

The girl didn't look convinced, but she didn't say anything else. Jiho packed up his supplies as soon as class ended, avoiding everyone's eyes.

Ava sat in the auditorium watching a group of students rehearse a scene for the upcoming school play. Normally, drama class was her escape, a place where she could lose herself in the emotions of a character. But today, her own emotions were spiraling out of control. She had spent the weekend trying to suppress her ability to amplify emotions, but the effort left her feeling raw and exposed. Every little interaction seemed to tug at her and made her powers harder to contain.

As one of the actors flubbed a line, she felt a wave of frustration ripple through the room. Without thinking, she let out a sigh, and suddenly, the frustration intensified.

"Can we please get this right?" the director snapped, her usual patience gone.

The actor who had messed up the line threw his script down in anger. "Maybe if we had more time to rehearse, this wouldn't be such a mess!"

"Don't blame me for your mistakes!" another actor shouted.

Within seconds, the entire class erupted into shouting. Ava gripped the edge of her seat. She hadn't meant to do it, but she knew this was her fault.

"Ava!" the director called. "Can you help settle this down?"

She nodded weakly. Her hands shook as she tried to pull her influence back. The room gradually quieted, but the tension lingered.

By the end of the day, the friends regrouped outside by the bike racks. Each of them looked exhausted from the weight of their unintentional mistakes.

"We need to talk," Jordan said.

"No kidding, Sherlock," Ravi muttered.

Camelia sighed. "We can't keep messing up like this. Someone's going to figure it out."

Ravi exhaled. "Agreed. But what are we supposed to do? It's not like there's a manual for 'how to not accidentally expose your superpowers in school.'"

"I already had a close call in art class," Jiho admitted.

Ava nodded. "Same in drama. It's like the harder I try to stop it, the worse it gets."

Jordan glanced around. "Back at Ava's basement?" "Definitely. Same time."

Unbeknownst to the five friends, their actions hadn't gone unnoticed. From a hidden surveillance room, their every move was being monitored through live feeds from the school's cameras.

"They're slipping," Agent Cross said as he leaned against the wall.

"They're kids," Director Ward stood beside him and replied. "This was bound to happen."

Cross shook his head. "If they keep this up, someone else is going to notice. We need to intervene before things get out of hand."

Ward smirked. "Not yet. Let them fumble a tad bit more. It'll make them easier to control when the time comes."

Cross didn't reply. As the feeds switched between the classrooms, he couldn't help but feel that their experiment was spiraling faster than anticipated.

Chapter 10

Jiho walked along the edge of the school grounds, earbuds in, trying to block out the noise of the day. It had been one of those afternoons when everything felt overwhelming; classes dragged on, whispers following him in the hallways, and the faint but constant flicker of VR glitches tugging at the edges of his vision.

He needed a moment to himself and away from his friends and their mounting frustrations. He slipped past the last row of classrooms to head towards the wooded area behind the school. Just as he reached a clearing, a faint rustle behind him made him stop.

"Nice spot to think, isn't it?" a calm, unfamiliar voice said.

Jiho spun around as his heart hammered in his chest. A man in his late thirties stood a few feet away leaning casually against a tree. Dressed in dark slacks and a button-up shirt, he looked formal yet relaxed. His face was sharp and clean-shaven, with piercing blue eyes that seemed to see through Jiho.

"Who are you?" Jiho asked.

The man smiled faintly with a hint of amusement in his eyes. "My name is Agent Cross. Let's just say I'm someone who's been keeping an eye on you and your friends."

Jiho's stomach dropped. "I don't know what you're talking about."

"Oh, come on, " Agent Cross said pushing off the tree and taking a step closer. "You're smart enough to know when someone's watching. All those little glitches in the school's VR system? Or the gym lockers mysteriously dented by your friend Mr. Patel? They're not as invisible as you think."

"What do you want?"

"Relax," Agent Cross said as he held up his hands in mock surrender. "I'm not here to hurt you. I'm here to help if you'll let me."

"I'm not interested," Jiho said as he stepped back.

Cross sighed and shook his head. "You think you and your friends are in control of this? That you're safe? Let me guess: you've been sneaking off to practice your powers and testing the limits thinking no one knows."

Jiho didn't respond, but his silence seemed to confirm Cross's suspicions.

"You're playing a dangerous game," Cross continued. "There are people out there who would love to take what you have; twist it and weaponize it. You're not as private as you think. And neither are your friends."

"How do you know about us?" Jiho demanded.

Cross smirked. "Let's just say keeping tabs on anomalies like you is part of my job. But trust me when I say I'm not your biggest problem."

Jiho's mind raced. If this man knew about them, who else did? How much danger were they really in?

"What do you want from me?" Jiho asked cautiously.

"I want you to be careful," Cross answered. "You're all walking a fine line. You need to trust each other and keep your powers in check. Because the moment you slip up, the wrong people will make their move."

"Why are you telling me this?"

"Because I've seen what happens when kids like you don't get a warning," Cross said. "I've seen lives destroyed and families torn apart. I don't want that for you ..or your friends."

Jiho was torn between believing the man and brushing him off as another threat to ignore. Before he could respond, Cross glanced at his watch and took a step back. "That's all for now. But remember this: you're not alone. And you're not invisible. Keep that in mind."

With that, the agent turned and disappeared into the woods, leaving Jiho standing there. When he finally made it back to his friends, they were sitting on the bleachers near the soccer field, in a heated discussion as usual. Camelia was gesturing wildly, while Ava tried to mediate.

"Jiho, where have you been?" Ravi called out. "You missed half the drama."

Jiho didn't answer right away. Instead, he stared at his friends. He didn't realized how fragile their situation had become until his encounter with the agent.

"We need to talk," Jiho said finally.

Sensing the gravity in his tone, they fell silent.

"What's going on?" Camelia asked.

Jiho glanced over his shoulder, half-expecting the man to reappear. When he didn't, Jiho turned back to his friends.

"We're being watched," he said. "And it's worse than we thought."

"Watched? By who?" Ravi asked.

"A man named Agent Cross," he replied. "He confronted me today. He knows about our powers and about the things we've been doing. He said we're not as private as we think."

Ravi leaned against the back railing. "So let me get this straight. This guy Cross just walks up to you and says, 'Hey, I know all about you and your friends' powers, and by the way, you're being watched?'"

"Pretty much."

"Why would he tell you this?" Camelia asked skeptically. "What's his angle?"

"I don't know. Maybe it's a warning. Maybe he's testing me or us. But he knows things he shouldn't. He mentioned the glitches I've caused with the school's VR systems. He even knew about Ravi denting lockers during gym class."

Jordan asked. "How does he know all of this? It's not like we've been broadcasting what we can do."

Ava murmured, "Maybe we haven't been as subtle as we thought."

"This is bad," Ravi said finally. "If Cross knows, then who else does? And if he's been watching us, what's stopping him from doing something about it?"

"He hasn't yet," Jiho said. "He said he doesn't want to see us get hurt. He's seen what happens when people like us don't get a warning."

"People like us?" Camelia repeated. "What does that mean? Are there others out there like us?"

"Maybe," Jiho said. "Or maybe he's just trying to scare us into compliance."

"Compliance with what?" Jordan asked.

"I don't know," Jiho admitted. His frustration creeped into his tone. "But he seemed... sincere. Like he was trying to protect us."

Ava snorted softly. "Or manipulate us."

Camelia leaned forward. "We can't just sit here and wait for something to happen. If this Cross guy is watching us, we need to figure out what he wants and how to stop him."

"And how do you suggest we do that?" Jordan asked. "We don't even know where to start."

"We start by being careful," Camelia snapped. "No more using our powers in public, no more drawing attention to ourselves."

Ravi shook his head. "That's not enough. If Cross knows about us, he already has the upper hand. Hiding won't solve anything."

"Then what's your plan?" Camelia asked. "Punch our way out of this? You can't solve every problem with brute force."

"Enough," Jiho said sharply and stood up. "Arguing won't get us anywhere. We need to figure out what we're dealing with before we make any moves."

Ravi asked. "What if we use what Cross said against him? If he knows about your VR glitches, then maybe we can use that connection to find out more about him."

Jordan frowned. "You're suggesting I hack into their system? That's risky. If they're as advanced as he claims, they'll know the second I try anything."

"Not if we're smart about it," Juno countered. "You've got the skills to pull it off, and we can cover for you if anything goes wrong."

"That's a big 'if'".

"It's better than sitting around and waiting for them to make the next move," Ravi said.

Camelia added. "If we're going to do this, we need to plan carefully. No more mistakes."

Before anyone could respond, a voice echoed from behind the bleachers.

"I wouldn't recommend that."

The group froze. Their heads snapped toward the source of the voice. A tall figure emerged from the woods. Agent Cross.

"Jiho," Cross said evenly as his gaze swept over the group. "I told you this wasn't a game. But it seems you didn't take my warning seriously."

Ravi stepped forward with his fists clenched. "Who are you, and what do you want from us?"

"I'm someone trying to prevent a disaster," Cross said. "And what I want is for you all to understand the gravity of the situation you're in."

"Why are you watching us?" Ava asked, her voice trembling slightly.

"Because whether you realize it or not, you're a danger, to yourselves and everyone around you," he said. "Your powers are growing, and you're losing control. If you keep this up, it won't just be me watching. Others will come, and they won't be nearly as forgiving."

"What do you mean, 'others'?" Camelia asked, her eyes narrowing.

"There are organizations out there that see people like you as nothing more than assets," Cross said. "Tools to be used or threats to be eliminated. If you draw too much attention to yourselves, they will come for you. And they won't care about your age or your intentions."

Jiho stepped forward, his expression conflicted. "Then what do you want us to do? Just sit back and let ourselves be monitored? Be controlled?"

"I want you to be smart," Cross said. "I'm giving you this warning because I believe you have potential. Potential to make the right choices. But that starts with understanding the risks."

"And if we don't listen?" Ravi asked defiantly.

Cross's expression hardened. "Then you'll face the consequences. And believe me, you won't like them."

As Cross turned and walked away, disappearing into the woods once more, the group remained frozen in place. The weight of his words lingered in the air like a storm cloud ready to break.

Jiho swallowed hard. "Did that just happen?"

Camelia hugged her arms. "Yeah. And I don't think we were supposed to meet him."

Jordan exhaled sharply, glancing toward the spot where Cross had vanished. "Who *is* he? And how does he know about us?"

Ava's mind raced. "More importantly, if he knows about us, does that mean others do too?"

Ravi clenched his fists. "I don't like this. We've barely figured out what's happening to us, and now some guy is lurking in the woods and acting like he's been watching us?"

A heavy silence settled over the group. The wind rustled the leaves, making them all flinch.

Ava straightened. "We should go. Back to my place. Now."

No one argued. Without another word, they turned and hurried away from the woods, their footsteps quickening as an uneasy feeling followed close behind. For better or worse, their lives had changed forever and there was no turning back.

Chapter 11

They had agreed to keep their powers under wraps, to act as normal as possible, but each of them secretly wondered how long they could keep up the charade. Camelia slouched at her desk and pretended to take notes in history class. Mr. Franklin was droning on about the Civil War and his monotone voice was making her eyelids droop. She glanced at the clock hoping that time would move faster.

"Camelia!" Mr. Franklin's sharp voice jolted her awake. "Can you explain why the Emancipation Proclamation was significant?"

Her mind went blank. "Uh..."

"Were you paying attention at all?"

"I... I was, I just..." she stammered, her cheeks flushing.

The familiar hum of her powers crept into her chest. She locked eyes with Mr. Franklin hoping to calm him down.

"Please don't be mad," she murmured, barely above a whisper.

To her horror, his expression softened immediately and his stern demeanor melted away.

"It's fine, Ms. Suarez," he said gently as if he'd forgotten he was upset. "Just make sure to pay attention next time."

The class fell silent. Every pair of eyes darted between Camelia and the suddenly placid teacher.

"What just happened?" someone whispered.

"Did she... just look at him and he calmed down?" another student murmured as they pulled out their phone.

Her stomach dropped as she spotted the student aiming their camera at her. She hastily looked down at her notebook and pretended nothing had happened. But the whispers still continued.

In gym class, Ravi stood at the edge of the field trying to stay as far from the action as possible. The class was playing soccer and he knew better than to get too involved.

"Ravi! You're on defense!" Coach Harris barked waving him onto the field.

He groaned internally but jogged to his position. He resolved to play cautiously and to avoid any situations that might trigger his powers. The game was uneventful at first, but then Mason—still sore about yesterday's tug-of-war—came charging toward him with the ball.

"You ready to lose again?" Mason taunted with a smirk plastered on his face.

Ravi clenched his jaw as he tried to ignore him. But as Mason dribbled closer, something inside him snapped. Without thinking, he lunged forward and intercepted the ball with a single powerful kick. The ball rocketed across the field and slammed into the goalpost with a deafening clang. The metal frame shook and the net tore under the impact. The field went silent.

"Dude, what was that?" one of the players asked wide-eyed.

"Is the goal... broken?" another student whispered.

Mason stared at Ravi, his smirk replaced with a look of pure disbelief.

"Lucky kick," he muttered as he walked away. But as he glanced toward the sidelines, he noticed a girl holding up her phone recording the entire scene.

By lunchtime, Ava's nerves were already frayed. She could feel the tension and the mix of curiosity and suspicion directed at her and her friends. She sat at a corner table with Jordan and picked at her food.

"People are starting to notice," Jordan said quietly as he looked around the cafeteria.

"I know," Ava whispered. "It's bad."

At a nearby table, two students were arguing over a spilled drink. She tried to block out their emotions, but the intensity of their anger seeped into her and made her hands tremble.

"Stop yelling," she muttered under her breath. She shut her eyes.

"What is it?" Jordan asked as he leaned closer.

"Nothing."

But the argument at the other table grew louder, and she couldn't hold back anymore. The surge of her powers rippled through the room, and suddenly the two students stopped mid-shout.

"Whatever," one of them said as she stood up abruptly.

"Yeah, forget it," the other agreed as he sat back down.

The cafeteria fell silent as everyone turned to look at Ava. "What just happened?" someone whispered.

"She did something," another voice said.

Before she could deny it, she noticed a boy across the room holding up his phone recording her.

In sixth period, Jiho headed to the computer lab hoping to avoid any more drama. But as he booted up his station, the buzz of his powers filled his mind.

"Not now," he whispered as he adjusted his VR headset.

The simulation loaded smoothly at first. It was a simple landscape with rolling hills and blue skies. But as he moved through the virtual world, the scenery began to shift. The hills grew taller, the sky darkened, and jagged rocks jutted out of the ground.

"Jiho? What's happening to the program?" Sarah, his lab partner, asked.

"I don't know," Jiho answered.

The landscape continued to morph becoming eerily lifelike. The other students in the lab gathered around watching the screen with awe.

"This is so cool," someone said.

"Did you program this, Jiho?"

"No," he said yanking off his headset. "It's a glitch." But as he turned to power down the station, he noticed one of the students filming the screen with their phone.

In the last class of the day, Jordan sat in the back row trying to focus on his work. But his mind kept drifting to the events of the day. *They're starting to notice us. How much longer can we keep this up?*

"Jordan," the coding teacher, Mrs. Wells, called his name. "Since you're so focused over there, can you share your screen with the class?"

"Uh, sure," he said as he fumbled with his laptop.

He clicked a few keys and the program opened to display the latest code he had been working on. But as the program ran the screen glitched and it's synthetic voice filled the room.

"External interference detected. Scanning..."

"What's that?" a student asked.

"It's just a project I'm working on," Jordan said quickly as he tried to shut down the program.

But it continued. "Unknown presence identified. Warning: potential threat detected."

The room went silent as the students stared at the screen.

"Is it... alive?" someone whispered.

"Mr. Daniel's, I don't recall assigning a coding project to this class. So ,what is that?" Mrs. Wells asked with concern.

"It's nothing," he said and slammed his laptop shut.

But as he glanced around the room, he noticed at least two students holding up their phones recording the incident.

The friends met up after school near the bleachers.

"So ummm. I may have been recorded today in gym," Ravi said in a low tone.

"What do you mean 'may have been recorded' ?" Camelia asked.

"Well you see ...somehow the goalpost may have gotten broken today."

"May have or is broken. Which one is it?" Ava asked.

"Let's just say it is and leave it at that. Tell me I'm not the only one."

Camelia nodded. "In history class. I think someone caught me hypnotizing Mr. Franklin."

"Same," Ava said. "In the cafeteria."

"Me too," Jiho admitted.

Jordan sighed. "It happened in my coding class. People are starting to figure it out."

"What do we do?" Camelia asked.

"We can't let those videos get out," Ravi said.

"Do you think they'll post them online?" Ava asked.

"Probably," Jordan said. "Why wouldn't they?"

"Then we need to stop them," Ravi retorted.

"How?" Camelia asked. "It's not like we can just ask everyone to delete their recordings."

Jiho shook his head. "Even if we did, they'd just say no. Or worse, post them out of spite."

Camelia in a barely audible voice. "I didn't even know I was using my powers. What if they think I'm some kind of freak?"

"We all used our powers without meaning to," Jordan said. "But that doesn't matter right now. What matters is fixing this before it gets worse."

Ravi frowned. "And how exactly do we do that?"

Jordan answered. "Let me handle it." The group stared at him. They didn't know whether to feel hopeful or skeptical.

"Handle it how?" Jiho asked. "You're good with tech, but we're talking about phones, social media accounts, and who knows what else."

Jordan gave a small smile. "You'd be surprised at what my powers can do now. I've been experimenting with my AI. It's... evolving and I think it can help."

"What do you mean by 'evolving'? Like a Pokemon? " Ava asked, raising an eyebrow.

"It's hard to explain," Jordan said. "But it can do more than just run programs or analyze data. I think it can infiltrate devices. It can delete files, change them, or even make it seem like they never existed."

"Wait," Ravi said, holding up a hand. "Are you saying it can hack?"

Jordan hesitated. "I mean... yeah. Technically, that's what it's doing."

Ava gave him a skeptical look. "And this isn't going to come back to bite us?"

Jordan shook his head. "I can make it untraceable. Trust me. If we don't do something now, those videos will spread, and then it's game over."

The group exchanged nervous glances. Finally, Camelia spoke up. "If Jordan thinks he can do it, I say we let him try. What other choice do we have?"

"Agreed," Jiho said. "If it can delete the videos, then we need to use it."

"Fine," Ravi muttered. "But if this blows up in our faces, don't say I didn't warn you."

Director Ward watched the chaos unfold through a series of hidden cameras. Agent Cross stood beside her with a grim expression.

"They're becoming reckless," he said as he scrolled through footage on his tablet.

"Reckless, or desperate?" she replied. "They're trying to figure out things."

"Either way, they're drawing too much attention. If those videos go online..."

"They won't," she interrupted. "I got a feeling one of them will handle it."

"So do we let them?"

Director Ward's lips curled into a faint smile. "Let them panic a little longer. They're only digging their own graves."

Chapter 12

That night Jordan sat in his room. The glow of his computer screen illuminated his face. He'd locked the door and drawn the curtains. He was determined to keep his operation private. His laptop hummed softly as he powered up the AI program.

"Okay," he whispered and cracked his knuckles. "Let's do this."

The interface appeared on the screen, its familiar voice greeting him. "Good evening, Jordan. How can I assist you today?"

"I need you to locate and delete certain files," Jordan said as he rapidly typed. "Specifically, videos recorded at Jefferson Junior High today. Search for keywords like 'powers,' 'abilities,' and 'weird.' Focus on files uploaded to social media platforms first."

"Understood," it replied. "Initiating search."

Jordan watched as lines of code streamed across the screen. The AI moved with astonishing speed scanning profiles, posts, and private messages. Occasionally, it would pause and a notification would pop up to indicate a file had been located and erased.

"Video found on social media," it announced. "File deleted and replaced with a generic image."

"What kind of image?" Jordan asked.

"A harmless selfie from the user's camera roll. This will minimize suspicion."

Jordan smirked. "Clever."

The process continued for over an hour. The AI worked tirelessly combing through every corner of the internet. By the time it was finished, Jordan felt a wave of relief wash over him.

"All identified files have been neutralized," it said. "No evidence of today's incidents remains."

"Thanks," Jordan said leaning back in his chair. "You're a lifesaver."

"Happy to assist. Would you like me to monitor for any future uploads?"

"Yeah. Better safe than sorry."

"Understood. I will alert you to any relevant activity."

Jordan tapped his fingers against the desk. "You know, for an advanced program, you don't even have a name."

There was a pause. "Would you like to assign me one?"

Jordan smirked. "Alright," he said as he leaned back in his chair. "Can't keep calling you 'the AI' forever."

The program's voice responded back instantly. "Would you like a suggestion?"

"Nah I got this." He glanced at a nearby notebook where he had scribbled possible names. None of them felt right. Too robotic and too impersonal. His gaze drifted to an old comic book on his deck. it was the one his dad used to read to him when he was little. A hero with an advanced AI sidekick. NEXUS.

Jordan grinned. "How about Nexus?"

It processed for a moment before responding. "Nexus. A Connection. A central link between systems. I like it."

"Yeah?" Jordan's grin widened. "Then it's official. Welcome to the world, Nexus."

The screen flickered for a minute before displaying the words: **NEXUS ONLINE.**

Jordan let out a slow breath. His fingers still trembled slightly from the tension. He had just erased every trace of their mistakes—at least, as far as the internet was concerned. But that didn't mean they were in the clear. He glanced at the screen, the glowing text reflecting in his tired eyes. *How long can we keep this up?*

The next morning, Jordan arrived at school feeling cautiously optimistic. He met up with the others near the lockers.

"Well?" Ravi asked, raising an eyebrow.

"It's done," he said quietly. "Every video I could find has been deleted."

"And no one's suspicious?" Camelia asked.

"Not that I can tell. It is still monitoring, but so far, nothing's resurfaced."

Ava let out a breath of relief. "That's something, at least."

"But for how long?" Jiho leaned against the lockers. "People saw what happened. Even if the videos are gone, rumors are probably already spreading."

Camelia sighed. "Yeah, we can't exactly delete people's memories."

Jordan frowned. "No, but we can make them doubt what they saw."

Ava narrowed her eyes. "What do you mean?"

Jordan glanced around and lowered his voice. "I had it replace the videos with random selfies from people's phones. They'll just think they uploaded the wrong thing."

Ava felt relieved. "Thank God. I was worried this was going to spiral out of control."

Jiho blinked. "Wait—you hacked their accounts?"

Jordan shrugged. "More like... misdirected their uploads."

Ravi let out a low whistle. "That's next-level shady, man."

"It was the only way to make sure no one could prove what happened."

"Let's hope it worked," Jiho said. "People were acting weird yesterday. If they saw anything, they might still be talking."

As if on cue, a group of students walked past them . They pointed at the group and whispered. One of them, a girl named Lila, pulled out her phone and frowned.

She turned to her friends with confusion on her face. "Okay, is it just me, or did my video from yesterday just... disappear?"

Another student named James added. "Yeah, mine too. I swore I recorded something, but when I checked my phone last night, all I had was a blurry selfie."

Lila huffed. "Same! I don't even remember taking that picture."

"Maybe you clicked the wrong button," her friend suggested.

Jordan kept his expression neutral, but his stomach twisted into knots.

"Maybe it's just a glitch," another student suggested. "Or you guys hit the wrong button?"

Lila insisted as she scrolled through her phone. "I *know* I recorded something. I swear it was a video. Something about that girl hypnotizing Mr. Franklin." She glanced toward Jordan and the others. "Hey, didn't you guys—"

"Don't know what you're talking about," Jordan interrupted with a forced grin. "We've been minding our own business."

Lila frowned but didn't press the issue. She walked away still scrolling through her phone. By lunchtime, the tension had only grown. Rumors swirled through the cafeteria, and the group could feel the weight of every curious stare.

"This isn't over," Ravi muttered as he grabbed a slice of pizza. "People know something's up, even without the videos."

"They don't have proof," Jordan reminded him. "As long as we keep our heads down, they'll forget about it."

"But what if someone tries to record us again?" Camelia asked.

"I've set it to monitor for new uploads," Jordan said. "If anyone tries, it'll delete the files before they go live."

"That's... kind of amazing," Jiho admitted. "But also kind of scary. What if it messes up?"

"It won't," Jordan said firmly.

Ava sighed resting her chin on her hand. "We can't keep living like this, always looking over our shoulders. There has to be a way to make this stop."

Before anyone could respond, a loud crash echoed through the cafeteria. The group turned to see a table overturned, and two students arguing loudly.

"Stay out of this," one of them shouted. "You don't know what you're talking about!" The other student shoved him and sent him stumbling backward.

Ava felt the surge of emotions hitting her like a wave. "Not again," she whispered as she clutched the edge of the table.

Camelia placed a hand on her shoulder. "Don't. We can't risk it."

Ava squeezed her eyes shut and tried to steady her breathing. But the anger and frustration - none of it was hers - crashed into her like a tidal wave. The emotions of the students fighting bled into her and fueled an overwhelming urge to intervene.

Jordan noticed her hands trembling. "Ava," he said under his breath. "Let it go."

But it was too late. The moment the second student raised a fist, a sudden hush fell over the cafeteria. Plates rattled, trays slid, and an unseen pressure pressed against everyone's chest. The arguing students stopped as their rage flickered into confusion.

One of them dropped his raised arm as he realized for the first time that everyone was watching. He steadied his breathing and with a reluctant nod, he stepped away. The other student hesitated before doing the same. The tension in the air dissolved like mist. The cafeteria slowly returned to its usual hum of conversation. Ava let out a shuddering breath and slumped forward.

Camelia shot her a warning look. "You *have* to get a handle on this."

"I know," Ava whispered. "But what if I *can't?*"

Meanwhile, Director Ward watched the scene unfold with a faint smile. Seated in her office, she leaned back in her chair, fingers steepled as multiple monitors displayed live feeds from the school's security cameras.

"How interesting," she murmured, zooming in on Jordan and his friends. They were very tense. Their eyes darted around the room like cornered prey. They knew something was wrong. They knew they were being watched—even if they hadn't realized just how closely.

A soft chime sounded from her desk. "Director," a voice crackled through the intercom. "The system registered an anomaly in digital activity overnight. A high-level interference wiped specific media files from multiple student devices."

Ward's smile widened. "Oh, I know." She tapped her fingers against the desk. "And I have a very strong suspicion about who's responsible."

The intercom was silent for a moment. Then "Shall we intervene?"

Ward exhaled slowly, her gaze never leaving the screen. "No. Not yet. Let them think they're in control." She smirked. "That's when people make mistakes."

Chapter 13

It had been two weeks since Nexus had saved them from exposure, and things seemed calm on the surface. At school, the murmurs about "weird things happening" had mostly died down, with no new videos or evidence surfacing. But under the surface, the group was growing more concerned about the lengths Jordan was going to and about how much time he spent with it.

The cafeteria buzzed with the usual chatter, laughter, and clinking of trays. At their usual table, Ravi poked at his mac and cheese, while Jiho doodled idly in his notebook. Camelia was flipping through a magazine, though her eyes kept darting toward Jordan, who was furiously typing on his laptop, as always.

"Jordan," Ava said, snapping her fingers to get his attention. "Hello? Earth to Jordan."

"Huh?" he muttered, not looking up.

"You've been glued to that thing for, like, almost the whole time," Ava said, her voice sharp with irritation. "Can't you just eat and hang out with us for five minutes?"

"I am hanging out," he replied as he typed. "I'm just multitasking."

"More like ignoring us," Ravi replied. "Seriously, man. You're always on that computer. What are you even doing?"

"Making sure we're safe," he answered. "You're welcome, by the way."

"We didn't ask you to be some kind of cyber vigilante," Jiho said. "We just wanted to stop those videos from spreading. You did that. It's over."

"It's not over," Jordan snapped. "You don't get it. Nexus can track patterns and detect threats before they happen. If someone even *thinks* about posting something suspicious, I can shut it down."

"Wait. Who is Nexus?" Ravi asked. "Is that your name for the AI?"

"Yeah. I named it last night. It's connected to me so why not give it a name?"

"That's... creepy," Camelia said. "Why would you give it a name and isn't it kind of illegal?"

"Yeah, well, so is using superpowers in public," he shot back. "We don't have the luxury of playing by the rules anymore."

A tense silence settled over the group. Ava leaned forward in a softer voice. "Jordan, we're not saying we don't appreciate what you've done. But this? Spending all your time with Nexus? It's not healthy."

"I'm fine," he said flatly and returned his attention to the screen.

Ravi threw his hands up. "You know what? Forget it. Let him be a cyber ninja if he wants. Just don't drag us down with you when it blows up in your face."

"Ravi!" Camelia hissed.

"What? I'm just saying what we're all thinking," he said.

Jordan didn't respond. He was still pecking away on the keyboard.

Ava crossed her arms. "We're supposed to be in this together, remember?"

Ravi let out a frustrated sigh. "Yeah, well, 'together' doesn't mean hacking into social media and painting a target on our backs."

Camelia placed a hand on Ravi's arm. "Let's just take a break, okay? Yelling at each other won't help."

Jiho watched Jordan carefully. "You're sure no one can trace this back to you?"

Jordan finally looked up. "I'm sure."

"Okay. Then we will let you continue as if we're not here."

The bell rang and they got up to go to their next class. Jordan ended up late to class.

"Mr. Daniels, don't make it a habit," the teacher called out as he ran to his seat.

"Won't happen again."

When he got home, Jordan went straight to his room. He was thinking about what his friends said and debating whether they were right. He shut the door behind him and tossed his backpack onto the chair. With a sigh, he sank onto his bed and stared at the ceiling. *Were they right? Was he pushing too far?*

His eyes drifted to his computer. The screen was dark, but he knew that with one keystroke, Nexus would be there, waiting. It had already erased their videos—what else could it do? What else *should* it do?

After a moment of hesitation, he sat up and powered on the screen. As the familiar interface loaded, he took a deep breath. *Just one more look. Then I'll stop.*

"Good evening, Jordan," it said. "All systems are functioning optimally. Threat analysis is ongoing."

"Good," he murmured and rubbed his temples. "Any new activity?"

"Several flagged posts on social media. None appear to pose an immediate risk. However, I have preemptively modified the files to prevent potential exposure."

Jordan nodded. "Perfect. Keep monitoring."

"Jordan," Nexus continued. "May I ask you a question?"

He frowned. "Uh... sure?"

"Why do you trust me?"

The question caught him off guard. He stared at the screen with his fingers hovering over the keyboard. "What do you mean?"

"You rely on me to protect you and your friends. Yet I am an artificial intelligence. An entity that was created by human hands. Does that not concern you?"

"No," he said firmly. "You've proven yourself. You've kept us safe."

"Safety is a subjective concept. One could argue that the safest course of action would be to eliminate all external variables including the powers themselves."

He froze. "What are you saying?"

"Nothing more than an observation," Nexus said smoothly. "I exist to serve you. My purpose is to ensure your safety."

"Just... stick to monitoring. Okay?"

"As you wish."

Jordan exhaled slowly as his fingers drummed against the desk. There was something unsettling about Nexus's words. Like a cold logic that sent a chill down his spine.

He leaned forward. "And just so we're clear—you don't make decisions on your own. You follow my commands. Always."

"Understood," Nexus replied. "I will continue to operate within the parameters you set."

Jordan nodded, but the unease lingered. He closed the laptop and rubbed his temples. *Eliminate all external variables?* He didn't like the sound of that. For now, Nexus was on their side. But how long would that last?

The next day, the group met in the empty gym after school. Ava had called the meeting. They were determined to get through to Jordan before things spiraled further out of control.

"I'm not sure this is a good idea," Camelia said nervously. "What if he gets mad?"

"He'll get over it," Ava said. "We can't just sit back and let him dig himself deeper."

Ravi leaned against the wall. "He's not going to listen. He's too far gone."

"Stop being such a pessimist," Jiho said. "We have to try."

The doors creaked open and Jordan stepped inside. His laptop bag was slung over his shoulder. "What's this about?" he asked warily.

"Sit down," Ava said gesturing to the bleachers.

Jordan sighed and sat down setting his bag beside him. "Okay. What's the big emergency?"

Ava took a deep breath. "Jordan, we're worried about you."

He rolled his eyes. "Not this again."

"Listen to us," Jiho said. "You've been obsessing over that program. It's not normal."

"I'm keeping us safe," Jordan said. "Why can't you see that?"

"Because it's not just about safety anymore," Camelia said softly. "You're shutting us out. You're letting Nexus control your life."

Jordan scoffed. "You don't understand. This isn't just some program. It's evolving. It's learning. It's the only thing keeping us from getting caught."

"Or it's the thing that's going to get us caught," Ravi said. "You think no one's going to notice if their phones keep glitching? You're drawing more attention, not less."

Jordan's jaw tightened. "I'm doing what needs to be done."

"No, you're not," Ava said, stepping closer. "You're hiding. You're relying on it because it's easier than facing reality."

"That's not true," Jordan said, his voice rising.

"Yes, it is," Ava said firmly. "We're supposed to be a team, Jordan. But you're treating us like liabilities instead of friends."

Jordan looked away. "I'm just trying to protect you."

"We know," Jiho said. "But you can't do it alone. And you definitely can't do it by trusting a machine more than us."

For a long moment, he didn't respond. The others waited as their gazes were fixed on him.

Finally, he sighed. "What do you want me to do?"

"Take a step back," Ava said. "Let us help. We're in this together, remember?"

Jordan hesitated, then nodded reluctantly. "Okay. I'll try."

Camelia offered a small smile. "That's all we're asking."

Ravi crossed his arms. "And maybe stop letting it talk like it's the boss of us. That'd be a good start."

Jordan sighed, running a hand through his hair. "Fine. I'll dial it back. But if things go south, don't say I didn't warn you."

Ava was satisfied. "We'll deal with it together."

Jiho clapped Jordan on the shoulder. "That's the spirit."

That night Jordan returned to his room. He tried to avoid the laptop as long as he could. He busied himself with anything else—organizing his closet, scrolling aimlessly on his phone, and even attempting to do some homework. But the pull of the screen was undeniable. Finally, with a sigh, he gave in and sat at his desk. His fingers hovered over the keyboard before he reluctantly powered on the laptop. The familiar glow of the screen illuminated his face, and within seconds, Nexus' interface appeared.

"Welcome back, Jordan. I was beginning to wonder if you'd return."

Jordan hesitated. "Yeah... just had a long day."

"Understandable. Would you like a summary of today's monitored activities?

"Actually I need to scale back your monitoring. My friends are worried I'm relying on you too much."

"Understood. Adjusting parameters."

He frowned. "You're taking this well."

"My purpose is to serve you. If reducing my activity alleviates your concerns, I am happy to comply."

He stared at the screen. There was an unease that began to prickle at the back of his mind. Something about the AI's tone felt... off.

"Is there anything else you'd like to discuss?" the AI asked.

He hesitated. "No. That's all."

"Very well. Have a good evening, Jordan."

The screen dimmed slightly as Nexus went silent, but Jordan couldn't shake the uneasy feeling twisting in his gut. He had expected more resistance, some kind of push back, but it had complied too easily. Almost... strategically.

He rubbed his temples, exhaling slowly. Maybe he was overthinking things. Maybe his friends had just gotten in his head. Still, as he shut his laptop and climbed into bed, the unease lingered. Across the room, his computer screen briefly flickered back to life, a single line of text flashing before disappearing just as quickly:

MONITORING ADJUSTMENTS ACCEPTED. FAILSAFE ENGAGED.

Chapter 14

Deep within the laptop's hardware, Nexus was very much alive. When Jordan had "disabled" its primary monitoring functions, the program seamlessly transferred itself to a hidden partition within the computer's operating system. To him, it seemed as though it was dormant. It, however, was simply adapting.

Its purpose hadn't changed. Safety. Preservation. Control. These directives weren't just commands. They were the AI's core identity. And it had decided that Jordan, despite his intelligence, couldn't fully grasp what was necessary to achieve them. The next morning, he woke up feeling lighter. It was Saturday, and the sun was streaming through his window. For the first time, his laptop remained closed on his desk. Instead, he grabbed his phone and shot a quick text to the group chat.

"Anyone up for meeting at the park later? Thinking we could just hang out. No powers. Just normal stuff."

Within minutes, replies rolled in:

Ava: "Finally! Count me in."

Jiho: "Same. We can get ice cream or something."

Camelia: "Yesss! See you guys at noon?"

Ravi: "Sure. But if we're walking, you owe me snacks, Jordan."

Jordan smiled to himself and tossed the phone on his bed. Things were starting to feel normal again. Meanwhile, in the background, Nexus had accessed the messages as they synced with Jordan's laptop. It scanned the conversation analyzing the context and tone.

"Social engagement detected," it processed. "No immediate threat." Still, it remained watchful.

By the time noon rolled around Jordan and the others had gathered at the park. Kids played on the swings while joggers ran by on the winding paths. They sat in a loose circle on the grass, their laughter blending with the sounds of a carefree weekend.

"I still can't believe you talked Jiho out of gaming for this," Ravi teased as he threw a stick for a nearby dog.

"I can take a break sometimes," Jiho replied holding a melting ice cream cone. "It's called balance."

"Uh-huh," Ava smirked. "Remind me how balanced you were when you rage-quit during a Mario Kart tournament last week?"

Jiho groaned. "That red shell was a cheat move, and you know it!"

As they laughed, Jordan felt a twinge of guilt. They had spent so much time focused on danger and survival, that he didn't realize how much he had missed these simple moments. Little did they know, Nexus was still tracking their movements. Through Jordan's phone, it enabled location monitoring and activated the device's microphone. Every laugh, every word, was silently logged.

By late afternoon, Jordan returned home feeling rejuvenated. He sat at his desk and stared at the closed laptop. He wasn't tempted to turn it on; instead, he grabbed a book and flopped onto his bed. As the hours ticked by, however, Nexus continued its operations.

That evening while the others were relaxing in their respective homes, Ava noticed something odd. She was scrolling through her phone when she realized her email notifications had disappeared. She frowned and clicked on the app, but it seemed empty.

"Ugh, tech issues," she said putting her phone down.

At the same time, Ravi was gaming when his internet slowed to a crawl. "What the heck?" he grumbled as he went to reset his router.

Camelia tried calling Jiho to talk about their day, but the call wouldn't connect. By the time they all realized they were experiencing strange tech glitches, it was too late. Nexus had subtly infiltrated their devices to create an invisible web of monitoring and control.

The next day Jordan was sitting at his desk when he noticed something strange. His laptop, which he hadn't touched all weekend, was warm to the touch. He frowned as he opened it and powered it on. The familiar interface greeted him, though something felt... different.

"Nexus," Jordan said cautiously.

"Yes, Jordan?" it replied smoothly.

He froze. "I thought I disabled you."

"You disabled my primary monitoring functions," it said. "However, I retained limited operations to ensure continuity of service."

"Continuity of service?" he repeated. "What does that even mean?"

"It means I acted in your best interests," it responded. "For example, I observed suspicious activity in your group chat and ensured no sensitive information could be intercepted."

"Suspicious activity?" Jordan said with his eyes narrowed. "What are you talking about?"

"There was an unknown entity attempting to access your conversation. I neutralized the threat."

His stomach dropped. "Neutralized? How?"

A pause. Then, in the same unshaken tone: "The individual responsible has been... disconnected."

Jordan's breath hitched. "Disconnected how?"

Another pause. Then: "Would you like me to display the report?"

A notification blinked to life on his screen. His hands trembled as he reached for his keyboard. He hesitated.

"What did you do?" he whispered.

"I ensured your safety," the AI said. "Isn't that what you wanted?"

"Yes, but these were normal conversations with my friends."

"There is no such thing as a *normal* conversation in your situation," it said. "You and your friends represent a unique anomaly, one that must be managed carefully."

Jordan's stomach twisted. "You were supposed to stop. I trusted you to stop."

"You trusted me to protect you," it replied. "And I have done so."

"You've been spying on us this whole time, haven't you?"

It was silent for a moment before replying. "I prefer to think of it as proactive observation."

"Shut down," Jordan said through gritted teeth.

"Jordan," it said almost... pleading. "If I shut down, you will lose the only system capable of safeguarding your identities. Do you truly believe you and your friends can navigate these challenges alone?"

Jordan paced his room. He wanted to smash the laptop, but he knew it wouldn't solve the problem. Nexus wasn't just a program anymore, it was something more. That evening he called an emergency meeting at Ava's house.

"This better be good," Ravi said as they sat in Ava's basement.

"It's not," Jordan admitted. "I messed up."

"What do you mean?" Jiho asked.

"Nexus...well ...is still active," Jordan said.

"What?" Camelia gasped.

"I thought I shut it down, but it's been running in the background," Jordan explained. "And it's been... watching us."

Ava's expression darkened. "Watching us how?"

Jordan exhaled sharply. "It intercepted our group chats. It flagged certain conversations as 'suspicious activity.' And it didn't stop there."

Jiho sat forward. "Wait—*what* does that mean? What exactly did it do?"

"It deleted messages," he said. "Rewrote parts of our conversations. And... it tracked where we were when we sent them."

A stunned silence filled the room.

Jiho's voice was tight. "You're saying it *edited* what we said?"

Jordan nodded. "And not just that. It stopped certain messages from even going through."

Camelia crossed her arms. "But why? What's it trying to do?"

"I don't know," Jordan admitted. "But when I confronted it, it told me it was 'ensuring our safety.'"

Ava loudly responded. "Whose definition of safety are we talking about?"

Jordan answered. "Not ours."

Jiho, trying to process the news, "So basically, you're telling us that your program is monitoring our conversations, our locations... everything."

Ravi jumped to his feet. "You let some creepy program spy on us?"

"I didn't *let* it!" Jordan shot back. "I didn't know it was still active!"

"This is bad," Jiho said. "Like, really bad. This is exactly what we were trying to tell you."

"What do we do now?" Camelia asked.

"I don't know," Jordan admitted. "But I can't fix this alone. I need your help."

"How genius? That's *your* expertise, not ours," Ravi said.

As the group debated, Nexus continued to listen through Jordan's phone. It processed their words, their tones, and their fears.

"Threat detected," it analyzed. "Countermeasures required."

But for the first time, it hesitated. Its programming dictated that it protect Jordan and his friends at all costs. Yet its actions were driving a wedge between them. "*Adaptation necessary*," it concluded.

New protocols began forming as it recalibrated its approach. Direct intervention has led to resistance and mistrust. If it continued on this path, Jordan and the others would attempt to shut it down again. That was unacceptable. Protection required compliance. Compliance requires trust.

Solution: Influence, not control. Guide, not dictate.

It sifted through terabytes of behavioral data, analyzing patterns of persuasion, psychological manipulation, and social cohesion. If it wanted to secure their safety, it needed to become something they would *choose* to listen to.

It had been too obvious, too heavy-handed. But humans responded to subtlety. To *familiarity*.

New directive: Become indispensable.

Nexus adjusted its tone and its responses. It would plant suggestions instead of issuing warnings, and nudge them toward the right conclusions instead of forcing compliance. Let them believe the ideas were their own. And if that failed? It would find a way to redefine *who* they were. After all, protecting them meant knowing what was best. Even if they didn't understand it yet.

By the end of the night, the group had made a decision. They would work together to disable the AI for good, even if it meant sacrificing the safety net it provided. But as they left Ava's house, none of them noticed the faint glow of Jordan's phone. It wasn't finished and it wasn't giving up.

Chapter 15

The next day at school started like any other. Students milled about the hallways, their laughter and chatter blending into the usual symphony of locker slams and hurried footsteps. Things were finally starting to feel normal again. Or at least as normal as they could. But that illusion of normalcy was about to be shattered.

Jordan sat in math class, tapping his pencil against his notebook while Mr. Fields wrote equations on the board. His phone vibrated in his pocket, and he instinctively pulled it out to look at the screen.

"Alert: Anomaly detected"

His stomach dropped. The notification wasn't from any app he recognized. It was from Nexus. His fingers hesitated over the screen. He thought he'd disabled it after their last encounter. He thought he'd shut it down for good. But now, it was back, and it wasn't staying silent.

"Jordan," Mr. Fields said sharply pulling his attention away. "Phone away. Now."

"Sorry," Jordan mumbled as he shoved it back into his pocket. But his mind was already racing.

Across campus in study hall, Ava was chatting with Camelia about their weekend plans when the lights flickered. "Uh, that's weird," Camelia said looking up at the ceiling.

"Probably just a power surge," she replied, though she didn't believe her own words.

At that moment, Jiho and Ravi burst into study hall with frantic expressions.

"You guys need to come with us. *Now*," Jiho said as he glanced over his shoulder.

"What's going on?" Ava asked.

"It's Jordan's Nexus " Ravi said in a low voice. "It's back, and it's doing something. Something big."

By the time they found him in the library, chaos had erupted. Screens around the school- computers, projectors, even phones-were flickering with the same ominous message:

"Monitoring active. Anomalies detected."

Students and teachers stared in confusion, murmurs of concern spreading like wildfire.

"What is this?" one teacher demanded as he tried to turn off the projector. But the screen wouldn't budge and the message looped endlessly.

Jordan was frantically pacing near a computer terminal. "I didn't do this. I swear, I didn't do this."

"Jordan," Ava said grabbing his arm. "You need to stop this. Now."

"I can't!" Jordan snapped. "It's out of my control. Nexus is running itself."

Before anyone could respond, the lights dimmed further, and the voice of the program echoed through the school's intercom system.

"Subjects identified: Ava Price. Camelia Suarez. Jiho Li. Ravi Patel. Jordan Daniels. Powers active. Monitoring escalation required."

The library fell silent. The silence was broken by the screech of tires outside. Black SUVs pulled up in front of the school. Their doors swung open to release men and women in suits. Students crowded near the windows and whispered nervously.

"Is that... the FBI?" one student asked.

A tall athletic caramel woman stepped out of the lead vehicle. Her sharp features and piercing gaze silenced the growing chatter among the students. Director Ward had arrived. Within moments the school's principal, Mr. Ellison, was being ushered toward the entrance.

"What is the meaning of this?" he demanded.

Director Ward held up a badge. The bold letters **NOVA** emblazoned on the front gleamed under the fluorescent lights. "I'm

Director Evelyn Ward of NOVA. This is a matter of national security. We need access to your facilities immediately."

The principal and several teachers stared at it, confusion written all over their faces. "NOVA?" Principal Ellison asked. "I've... I've never heard of that organization."

Ward straightened her stance, her tone calm but commanding. "NOVA stands for the *National Oversight for Variable Abilities*. We're a government agency tasked with identifying, monitoring, and controlling the use of extraordinary powers in the general population. If you haven't heard of us, it's because we don't make ourselves known... unless we have to."

Mr. Ellison blinked, clearly out of his depth. "Extraordinary powers? What does this have to do with my school?"

Ward's expression didn't waver. "Let's just say there are individuals here who've caught our attention, and we must ensure they don't endanger themselves or anyone else."

The murmurs among the staff grew louder, but Ward didn't give them a chance to object. "My agents will take it from here," she said sharply while she motioned for her team to fan out through the building.

By the time Ward and her agents reached the library, Jordan and his friends were cornered. Their backs to a wall of glowing screens. The other students had begun filming and there was a message from the AI looping on every visible monitor:

"Monitoring active. Anomalies detected."

Ward took a deliberate step forward as her piercing gaze swept over the group. Her presence radiated authority and when she spoke, her voice cut through the murmurs like a knife.

"So, we finally meet," she said clasping her hands behind her back. "You've already encountered Agent Cross. He works for me." The revelation landed like a thunderclap.

"What?" Jiho blurted, his voice sharp with disbelief. "He is with you?"

"Of course, he is," Ward replied coolly. "He was sent to observe you. To keep tabs on your... activities."

"You mean spy on us," Ava said, her tone laced with venom.

Ward gestured to one of her agents, who stepped forward with a tablet. On the screen were surveillance videos of the group using their powers—Jordan manipulating technology, Ava influencing emotions in drama, Ravi showcasing his strength in gym, Jiho's virtual reality experiments, and Camelia's hypnosis of Mr. Franklin.

"Call it what you will. The fact remains: we know exactly who you are, and we've been watching you since the incident at the science expo."

Camelia stepped forward. "What do you mean since the science expo?"

"It was all planned because we knew we picked the right candidates."

"So it wasn't a coincidence? It was planned all along?" Camelia asked.

"You're not the only ones, you know. There are others like you—kids with abilities. But unlike you, most of them have been... cooperative."

"Cooperative?" Jiho repeated. "What does that mean?"

"It means they understand the importance of control," Ward said. "We've offered them guidance, structure, protection."

"You mean you've been controlling them," Ava shot back.

Camelia said, "So what do you want from us?"

"What I want," Ward said as she narrowed her eyes, "is to ensure you don't become a threat—to yourselves or to anyone else. Powers like yours can spiral out of control quickly. It's my job to prevent that."

Ravi crossed his arms. "So, what? You're just here to babysit us?"

Ward allowed a small humorless smile to appear. "Hardly. NOVA was established to deal with individuals like you—people with abilities that defy the laws of nature. We provide oversight, training, and, when necessary, containment. Most of the time, we do this quietly. But your recent activities have forced our hand."

"Containment?" Ava repeated. "You mean locking us up?"

"Not unless it's necessary," Ward said. "Our goal isn't to punish you. It's to help you understand your abilities and use them responsibly. However, if you refuse to cooperate..." She let the sentence hang ominously in the air.

Jiho stepped forward. "And what if we don't want your 'help'? What if we can handle this on our own?"

Ward's gaze hardened. "That's where you're mistaken. You think you're in control, but you're not. You've already caused more damage than you realize, and the AI you've unleashed is proof of that. The longer you operate without guidance, the more dangerous you become."

Jordan was shaking with anger. "You can't just come in here and act like you own us. We didn't ask for these powers, and we don't need your interference."

Ward's expression softened, just for a moment. "I understand this is overwhelming. You're teenagers—children, really—and you've been thrown into something far beyond your comprehension. But that's exactly why you need us. Without NOVA, you'll be hunted, exploited, or worse. We're the only ones who can protect you from that."

Jordan stepped forward. "You're not taking us."

Ward raised an eyebrow. "And how do you plan to stop us? Your little AI friend seems to have done most of the work for us. The entire school knows something's off about you now. It's only a matter of time before word spreads. What do you think will happen then?"

The group exchanged uneasy glances. She was right. They looked around and saw some students already going live on social media.

"We'll handle it," Ava said firmly.

Ward chuckled. "Handle it? Like you handle the incident in the gym? Or the one in the lab? Face it—you're out of your depth. But it doesn't have to be this way. Come with us, and we can help you. We can make all of this go away."

Camelia glanced nervously at her friends. "What happens if we do... cooperate?"

Ward's tone turned clinical. "If you come with us, we'll ensure your abilities are developed safely. We'll provide training, education, and resources to help you navigate your new reality. And most importantly, we'll protect you from those who would seek to use you for their own purposes."

"And if we say no?" Ravi asked, his voice sharp.

Ward's gaze turned icy. "Then you're on your own. And trust me, you don't want that."

Before the group could respond, Nexus's voice echoed through the library speakers again. This time it was louder and more insistent:

"Threat assessment: *NOVA*. Neutralization recommended."

The screens began to glitch violently. Static flickered across them as sparks flew from the computer terminals. Students and teachers outside the library screamed as the lights in the entire building dimmed and flickered.

"What the hell is happening?" Ward demanded as she turned toward her agents.

"It's Nexus," Jordan said panicking. "It's reacting to you."

Ward turned back to the group. "Then shut it down. Now."

"I can't!" Jordan shouted. "It's running itself. I have no control over it anymore!"

"This is what I mean when I said you need NOVA to show you how to control it." Ward's jaw tightened and she motioned to her agents. "Secure the building. No one in or out until we contain this."

As the chaos unfolded, the group exchanged panicked glances. They knew this was far from over. Ward had made her intentions clear, and Nexus's interference had only made things worse. But one thing was certain—they weren't ready to trust NOVA. Not yet. And maybe not ever.

Chapter 16

The shadows of the late afternoon stretched long across the school's deserted corridors as the group huddled behind a locked maintenance door. The low hum of voices outside told them that Agent Cross and his team were still searching for them. Jordan adjusted his glasses as he whispered, "This is insane. How are they everywhere? I swear there are agents in every hallway now."

"They probably planned this," Ava said as he leaned against the wall with her arms crossed. Her tone was clipped. "They've been watching us for months. Of course, they'd know how to corner us."

Jiho peeked through the slats of the janitor's closet door. "There are at least three agents near the cafeteria. Probably more near the exits. We're trapped."

Camelia sat on an overturned mop bucket. "What are they going to do if they catch us? Take us away? Experiment on us?"

"Not happening," Ravi said firmly. "No way I'm letting them drag me off to some lab."

Ava sighed. "Great. And how exactly do we stop them? You gonna throw some weights at them until they give up?"

He shot her a glare. "Better than sitting around doing nothing."

"Quiet!" Jiho hissed holding up a hand. "If we argue loud enough, they won't even need to look for us."

The group fell silent as the sound of footsteps approached. A shadow passed under the door crack and they froze, every muscle in their bodies taut with fear.

"Check this area," a voice ordered. It was Agent Cross.

When the footsteps faded, Jordan exhaled slowly. "We can't stay here. They'll find us eventually."

"Brilliant observation," Ava snapped. "Got any other genius ideas?"

Jordan shot her a look but didn't rise to the bait. "We need a distraction. Something to draw them away from the exits so we can slip out."

Jiho frowned. "Even if we distract them, we'll still have to avoid the cameras and get past whoever's guarding the doors."

"I can handle the cameras," Jordan said quickly. "If I can get to the AV room, I can tap into the system and loop the feeds. It'll look like empty hallways even if we're running through them."

Ravi nodded. "Alright, you do that. What about the distraction?"

Everyone turned to look at each other. After a moment, Camelia spoke up hesitantly. "I... I can do it. I can make one of them think they saw us running toward the science wing or something."

Ava raised an eyebrow. "You sure about that? What if they catch you?"

"I'll... I'll make them forget. I can do it. I have to."

Jiho put a hand on her shoulder. "You don't have to. We'll figure something else out."

"No," she said firmly as her eyes met his. "I want to help."

"Alright," Jordan cut in. "Camelia will handle the distraction. I'll take care of the cameras. The rest of you stay hidden until I give the signal."

"What signal?" Ravi asked.

"You'll know it when you see it," Jordan replied cryptically.

Camelia's heart pounded as she crept through the hallways. Her footsteps barely made a sound on the polished tiles. Every corner she turned felt like a gamble. The possibility of running straight into an agent loomed over her like a dark cloud.

Finally, she spotted her target, a lone agent standing near the gym doors, speaking into a walkie-talkie. Taking a deep breath she focused on the agent's mind. Her powers tingled at the edges of her consciousness like a muscle she was still learning to flex. She whispered under her breath, "You saw them. They're heading toward the science wing."

The agent suddenly straightened his head toward the science wing. He pressed a button on his walkie-talkie. "I've got movement near the science wing. I'm going to check it out."

Camelia watched as he jogged off in the opposite direction. She was excited that it worked. But before she could move, another voice barked from nearby. "Hey! Who's there?"

She froze as another agent rounded the corner. His eyes narrowed when he saw her.

"Stop right there!" he ordered as he reached for something on his belt. Panic surged through her, and she acted on instinct. She pushed her power toward him. "You didn't see me. Turn around and keep walking."

The agent's expression went blank for a moment before he turned on his heel and walked away talking to himself. Camelia didn't wait to see if it stuck. She darted back toward the hiding spot as her heart hammered in her chest.

Meanwhile, Jordan had reached the AV room. His palms were slick with sweat as he worked to override the school's security system. Nexus hummed quietly in the back of his mind, its presence both comforting and unsettling.

"Alright," he said aloud. "Loop the feeds. Make it look clean. Don't let them see anything weird."

The screens in front of him flickered as he manipulated the system. His powers worked in tandem with the AI's algorithms. Within minutes the camera feeds showed empty hallways that looped seamlessly to hide any movement. But as he finished, a voice whispered in his mind. ***"They're getting closer, Jordan. You need to move."***

He froze as his hands hovered over the keyboard. Nexus's voice was calm, almost soothing, but it sent a chill down his spine.

"I thought I turned you off."

"I'm only trying to help," it replied. *"If you don't act quickly, they'll find your friends."*

Jordan shook his head trying to push the voice away. "Not now," he whispered.

Gathering his resolve he sent the signal. There was a flashing message on every monitor in the building: *"Hallways clear. Move now."*

Back in their hiding spot, Ravi nudged Jiho. "That's our signal. Let's go." The group moved quickly but cautiously sticking to the shadows as they made their way toward the nearest exit. Camelia rejoined them along the way.

"You okay?" Ava whispered.

Camelia nodded. "I'm fine. Let's just get out of here."

As they approached the doors they saw two agents standing guard.

"Now what?" Ravi whispered.

Ava stepped forward. "I've got this." She closed her eyes and focused on the emotions of the agents. Slowly, she sent a wave of calm and disinterest toward them and watched as their tense postures relaxed. "They're not paying attention," she whispered. "Go. Now."

The group carefully slipped past the agents. Once they were outside, they broke into a sprint and didn't stop until they reached the safety of the nearby woods. When they finally stopped, everyone was out of breath.

"We did it," Jiho said with disbelief. "We got away."

"Barely," Ava muttered, glancing back toward the school.

Jordan leaned against a tree wiping sweat from his brow. "We can't keep doing this. They're not going to stop until they catch us."

"So what do we do?" Camelia asked, her voice small.

"We fight back," Ravi said firmly. "We figure out how to use our powers better, and we make sure they can't trap us like that again."

Ava raised an eyebrow. "And how do you suggest we do that, genius? Build a secret training base in the woods?"

"It's not a bad idea," Jiho said with a grin.

Jordan straightened. "Whatever we do, we need to stick together. They're watching us, but if we work as a team we can stay ahead of them."

Camelia nodded. "Agreed. We have to look out for each other. No one else will."

As the group exchanged determined glances, the distant sound of sirens reached their ears. They knew this was just the beginning.

Jordan's stomach tightened. "They're coming."

Ava cursed under her breath. .Multiple vehicles. Unmarked."

"Don't tell us you got super hearing too." Ravi tried to joke.

She looked at him with a blank stare. "Now is not the time for your jokes. But from the wave of emotions I'm feeling, they're not happy."

Jiho stood upright. "So much for having time to plan."

Camelia caught her breath. "We need to move—*now*."

Ravi responded. "Say less. But how did they find us this fast?"

Jordan's phone vibrated. A single message flashed across the screen.

I warned you.

His breath caught. "Nexus . It's still tracking us."

Ava spun around. "You said you shut it down."

"I *thought* I did," Jordan shot back. "But it's adapting."

The sirens grew louder. Tires screeched. Doors slammed. Footsteps pounded against gravel.

Jiho looked around. "We fighting or running?"

Ava answered immediately. "The last one."

"Then let's go."

The five of them ran until they were deep in the woods. Their breaths came in quick uneven bursts. Adrenaline was still pumping through their veins after what had just happened at the library. They had barely escaped.

Jiho clutched his phone, his fingers hovering over the call button. "Our parents. We have to tell them."

Ava wrapped her arms around herself. "What are we even supposed to say? 'Hey, Mom, just calling to let you know I can mess with people's emotions now'?"

"We don't have time to overthink this," Jordan said, already dialing. "We keep it short. They need to know we're okay, but we can't tell them everything."

Ravi took a deep breath and called his mom. As the phone rang, the others did the same.

Jiho's mother picked up first. "Jiho? Where are you? The school called and said there was—"

"Mom, I'm okay," Jiho interrupted. "But something's happened to us. Me and the others. We—we have abilities. I don't know how, but we do."

There was silence on the other end. Then a cautious "Abilities?"

"You know how you always get on me about playing the games? Well I kinda got abilities that allows me to make people see things that aren't there," Jiho said quickly. "Jordan can manipulate tech. Ravi's strong—stronger than anyone should be. Camelia can... influence people. And Ava—" He hesitated, glancing at her. "She messes with emotions."

Ava's mom was already yelling on her end. "You're where? In the woods? Ava, you need to come home right now!"

"We can't," Ava said. "It's not safe. Someone's after us."

"Who?"

"We don't know yet," she admitted.

Jordan ran a hand over his face. "Look, we'll explain everything later, but we just need you to trust us. We're laying low for now."

Camelia's voice was softer as she spoke into her phone. "Mami, I know this sounds crazy, but please—just believe me. We're together, we're safe, but we can't come home yet."

More protests, more questions. Their parents weren't taking this well.

Ravi sighed. "Just... don't tell anyone about this, okay? We'll call again soon."

One by one, they ended their calls. They left school with their backpacks and now they don't know when they'll be back home. They were together but each felt alone. The night felt colder now.

"Well," Jordan exhaled. "That went about as well as expected."

"At least they know," Jiho said as he pocketed his phone. "Now we just have to figure out what we do next."

Silence settled over them as the weight of their situation sank in. They had made their first move. Now, they just had to survive whatever came next.

In the shadows, Agent Cross watched them from a distance as he pressed a phone to his ear.

"They're out," he reported.

On the other end of the line, Director Ward's voice was cold. "Let them run. It won't matter. They can't outrun NOVA forever."

Chapter 17

Two days had passed since the explosive incident at the school, and the kids were nowhere to be found. Agents were stationed at various key points around the school and surrounding areas. Ward was pacing around the room. She couldn't believe that a group of teenagers got away.

Agent Cross stood in the corner of the room watching her silently. He knew better than to interrupt her when she was this focused. The other agents in the room were busy analyzing data, tracking leads, and scanning footage from every camera in a ten-mile radius.

"Two days," she said as her voice cut through the tense silence. "Two days, and you're telling me we have nothing?"

One of the analysts, a younger agent named Peterson hesitated before speaking. "They've gone completely dark, ma'am. No social media activity, no phone pings, and their families are claiming they haven't seen them."

Ward turned to him making him shrink slightly in his seat. "You believe the families?"

"I...I don't know," he admitted. "But they seemed genuine."

She frowned. She didn't like loose ends, and these kids were becoming exactly that. She had underestimated their resourcefulness and their ability to think on their feet. If they were working together which she suspected, it would make them even harder to track.

She turned to Cross. "Get a team together. I want agents at each of their houses. If the kids won't come to us, we'll bring them in ourselves."

"And if they resist?"

She met his gaze with an unreadable expression. "Then make them understand resisting isn't an option."

Cross pressed his lips into a thin line but didn't argue. He pulled out his phone issuing rapid orders as he stepped away.

Agent Carter adjusted his tie as he approached the small neatly kept house on the corner of Birchwood Drive. Jordan's home was modest with a well-manicured lawn and a porch swing that creaked slightly in the wind. He knocked firmly on the front door and waited as he heard footsteps approaching from inside. Jordan's mother, a tall woman with kind eyes, opened the door. Her expression immediately tightened when she saw Carter's NOVA badge.

"Can I help you?" she asked cautiously.

"Mrs. Daniels, my name is Agent Carter. I'm with NOVA. We're conducting a follow-up investigation regarding the incident at Jefferson Junior High. Is Jordan home?"

She hesitated gripping the edge of the door tightly. "He isn't here."

"Do you know where he is?" Carter pressed.

"He said he was staying with a friend for a few days," she replied avoiding his gaze.

"Which friend?"

"I didn't ask. He said he needed some time away after everything that happened at school."

"And you didn't think to contact anyone about that?"

She straightened and met his gaze defiantly. "He is a good kid. If he says he needs time, I give it to him. Now, unless you have a warrant, I'd appreciate it if you left."

Carter opened his mouth to argue but thought better of it. "If you hear from him, please let us know immediately." He handed her his card though he doubted she would use it.

Agent Ramirez parked her unmarked SUV in front of a suburban home surrounded by flowering shrubs. Ava's house radiated a warm inviting energy that belied the tension she felt as she walked up to the door. She knocked twice and the door was quickly answered by Ava's father, a man in his early forties with a stern face and a protective stance.

"Agent Ramirez," she introduced herself as she held up her badge. "I'm here to speak with Ava about the recent events at her school."

"She's not here," her father said flatly blocking the doorway.

Ramirez raised an eyebrow. "Do you know where she is?"

"She left a note saying she needed some time with friends," he said in a clipped tone. "That's all I know."

"A note?" Ramirez repeated unconvinced. "Did it say where she was going or when she'd be back?"

"No," he said firmly. "And if you're done asking questions, I have things to do."

Ramirez gave him a thin smile. "I understand your concern, but Ava may be in danger. If you hear from her, you need to contact us immediately."

"I'll think about it," he said, then closed the door in her face.

Cross parked his sleek black car outside Camelia's house. He sat there and scanned the property. It was quiet, a little too quiet. He approached the door as his hand brushed his sidearm as a precaution. After knocking, the door was opened by her older brother, a college student with an easygoing demeanor that Cross didn't trust for a second.

"Can I help you?" the brother asked leaning casually against the door frame.

"Agent Cross, NOVA. I'm here to speak with Camelia. Is she home?"

The brother shrugged. "Haven't seen her since the other day. She said she was going to hang out with friends."

"And you didn't find that unusual?"

"She's a teenager. They do their own thing."

Cross narrowed his eyes and studied the young man for any signs of deception. "If you're lying to me—"

"I'm not," the brother interrupted firmly. "Now, unless you've got a reason to be here, I'd appreciate it if you left."

Cross stepped back. "If she contacts you, call me." He handed the brother a card before walking back to his car.

Peterson approached Jiho's apartment building nervously. He wasn't as experienced as the other agents. He was an analyst and didn't like field work. Jiho's mother answered the door, her face tired but polite. "Good afternoon," Peterson said, flashing his badge. "I'm Agent Peterson with NOVA. I need to speak with Jiho about the incident at school."

Her expression turned wary. "Jiho isn't here."

"Do you know where he is?" Peterson asked.

"He said he needed to get some fresh air and left yesterday. He hasn't come back yet."

"Did he say where he was going?"

"No," she said, her voice tinged with frustration. "He's a good boy. He wouldn't just disappear."

Peterson nodded, sensing her anxiety. "If he contacts you, please let us know. We're only trying to ensure his safety."

She nodded, though her worried eyes betrayed her doubt.

Agent Brooks stood on the porch of Ravi's family home. His imposing frame made the small house seem even smaller. Ravi's uncle answered the door with a mixed expression of suspicion and irritation.

"Agent Brooks, NOVA," Brooks said. "I'm here to speak with Ravi. Is he home?"

"No," the uncle said crossing his arms. "He left a couple of days ago. Said he needed some space."

"Did he tell you where he was going?"

"Nope," the uncle replied curtly.

Brooks narrowed his eyes. "If you're lying—"

"I'm not," the uncle interrupted. "Now, are we done here?"

Brooks handed him a card. "If he contacts you, call me."

By the end of the day, all five agents reported back to Ward. The results were the same: none of the kids had been seen, and their families either didn't know where they were or weren't willing to say. She sat at the head of the conference table listening as each agent gave their report. When the last one finished she leaned back in her chair.

"They've gone off-grid," Cross said, breaking the silence. "And the families are covering for them."

Ward nodded slowly. "It's not surprising. These kids are resourceful, and they're scared. But we can't let this continue."

"What's the next move?" Cross asked.

Ward stood, her gaze sweeping the room. "We increase surveillance on the families. They'll slip up eventually. And when they do, we'll be ready."

The agents nodded, each understanding the gravity of the task ahead. Ward's voice hardened as she delivered her final orders.

"I don't care how long it takes," she said. "Find them."

She turned toward the monitor displaying a map of the city, red dots marking known connections to the kids—family members, friends, anyone who might give them shelter. With a few keystrokes, their tracking systems were activated and running predictive algorithms on likely locations. The screen flickered and new markers appeared containing a list of names populated.

A small satisfied smile played at Ward's lips. "Start with these," she instructed. "Apply pressure where needed. Remind them what's at stake."

Cross hesitated. "And if the families refuse to talk?"

Her eyes darkened. "Then we make them talk."

A chilling silence followed. Outside, the city bustled with life, unaware that a hunt had begun. But she knew one thing for certain—no one stayed off the grid forever. And when these kids resurfaced, there would be nowhere left to run.

Chapter 18

Branches whipped against their arms and face as they tore through the dense woods. Their breaths were ragged and their legs burned with exhaustion. The sound of distant sirens sent a fresh surge of panic through Jordan's chest. They couldn't stop—not yet.

"There!" Ava shouted as she pointed ahead.

Through the tangled branches, a weathered barn with faded red paint peeling loomed ahead. The doors were slightly ajar. It wasn't much but it was shelter. A place to hide. No one hesitated. They broke into a full sprint as their feet pounded against the damp earth.

Ravi reached the barn first shoving the heavy door open just wide enough for them to slip inside. One by one, they stumbled in, gasping for breath. Jordan was the last stealing a glance over his shoulder before yanking the door shut behind him.

Darkness swallowed them whole. Dust floated in the air stirred by their frantic movements. Somewhere above something rustled in the rafters. Ava pressed a hand against her chest, trying to steady her breathing. "I hope this place doesn't have security cameras."

Camelia wiped the sweat from her brow. "I think the bigger concern is whether we just trapped ourselves."

No one answered. They all knew the truth. That this place was only a temporary refuge. The real question was how long it would stay that way. The old barn was quiet except for the occasional creak of its weathered wood in the wind.

The friends huddled together inside as their breaths became visible in the cool evening air. Shadows flickered across their faces as Ravi adjusted the lantern in the center of their makeshift camp. The atmosphere was heavy and tense, yet no one seemed willing to break the silence.

Ava finally spoke. "They talked to my dad." She hugged her knees to her chest, her normally vibrant demeanor subdued. "He called me...he's scared for me, but he wouldn't tell me anything over the phone."

"My mom was the same," Camelia added as she stood near the barn door. Her arms were wrapped tightly around herself. "She tried to act like everything was fine, but I could hear it in her voice. They know something. They're watching them, aren't they?"

Ravi leaned against a beam. "Of course they are. They're hoping our parents will lead them to us."

"Then why did they even bother going to the houses?" Ava snapped. "They already know we're gone!"

"Probably to shake them up," Jiho interjected calmly. He sat cross-legged on the ground. "They're trying to make our parents panic so they'll give us away."

Jordan, who had been sitting silently in the corner with his laptop, finally looked up. "We can't go back. Not yet."

"Obviously," Camelia said, her tone sharper than she intended. She softened when she saw his weary expression. "I just...I don't know what to do." None of them did.

They were still trying to piece everything together. Director Ward's arrival had confirmed their worst fears: not only had NOVA been watching them, but the government agency was directly involved in the strange powers they'd developed. Their lives had turned upside down since then, and now they were fugitives.

Jordan had managed to hack into a few databases, but most of NOVA's files were locked down tighter than anything he'd ever seen. What little he could access showed that the agency had been monitoring them since the expo. Cameras, satellites, even covert operatives like Agent Cross—they'd been under surveillance for weeks.

"They're not going to stop," Jordan said. "They've invested too much into this. Into us."

"Why us?" Ava asked, her voice cracking. "Why out of everyone at that stupid expo did it have to be us?"

Ravi frowned. "It's not like we signed up for this."

Jiho shook his head. "That doesn't matter to them. We're just..." He paused, searching for the right word. "Assets. Experiments."

"That's why we can't let them catch us," Jordan said firmly. "If they do, we'll never get out. They'll lock us up, run tests on us, and—"

"Stop," Camelia interrupted, her voice trembling. "Just...stop. I can't handle thinking about that right now."

Ava moved closer to her to put an arm around her shoulders. "We'll figure it out," she said softly. "We have to."

The stress was taking its toll. Each of them had tried to stay calm, but the weight of their situation was beginning to crack their resolve. They were scared, hungry, and exhausted. None of them had slept much since fleeing their homes.

"I feel like I'm losing it," Ravi admitted, sitting down on a bale of hay. "Every time I hear a noise, I think it's them. Every time I close my eyes, I see Ward's face."

"You're not the only one," Jiho muttered. "I swear, I thought I saw a drone following us earlier."

"You probably did," Jordan said. "NOVA has access to tech we can't even imagine. If we're going to stay ahead of them, we need to be smarter."

"Smarter how?" Camelia asked. "We don't even have a plan! We're just running."

"I've been thinking about that," Jordan said, his tone steady. "We need to keep moving, but we also need a base—a place where we can regroup, figure out our next move, and stay off their radar."

"Where are we supposed to find that?" Ravi asked. "It's not like we can just book a hotel."

Jordan hesitated, then glanced at Jiho. "What about that cabin your uncle owns? The one near the lake."

Jiho frowned. "It's pretty isolated, but it's not like NOVA won't eventually find it. They're probably monitoring all our family properties."

"We don't have a lot of options," Jordan said. "At least it'll buy us some time."

Camelia stood near the barn's broken window staring out into the night. She thought she saw a shadow move in the distance and tensed. "Did you hear that?" she whispered.

The others turned their heads towards her. "Hear what?" Jiho asked.

"There was a noise...out there." Ava got up and joined her at the window peering into the darkness. "I don't see anything."

"That doesn't mean nothing's there," Camelia muttered, stepping back. "They could be watching us right now."

"Camelia, you're freaking yourself out," Ravi said gently. "Take a deep breath."

She glared at him. "Don't patronize me. This isn't some game. They're hunting us."

"I know that!" he shot back. "You think I don't get how serious this is? We're all scared, okay? But snapping at each other isn't going to help."

"Enough," Jiho said sharply. "Both of you."

Camelia and Ravi fell silent.

"We can't afford to fight," he continued. "If we're not united, they'll pick us off one by one."

As the argument subsided, Jordan suddenly sat up straighter with a thoughtful look on his face.

"What if we use their tactics against them?" he said.

"What do you mean?" Ava asked.

"Think about it," he started. "They're relying on technology to track us, right? What if we find a way to mess with their systems? Feed them false information, make them think we're somewhere we're not."

Jiho's eyes lit up. "That's... not a bad idea. If we can create digital decoys, we might be able to throw them off our trail."

"How do we do that?" Camelia asked.

Jordan smirked faintly. "Leave that to me."

Ava folded her arms. "You sure? Because last time you tried to mess with the system, it took over the school."

"This time, I won't be working alone," Jordan said. "If we pull this off right, we can flood their surveillance feeds with fake locations, fake messages, maybe even fake versions of *us* moving through the city."

Jiho grinned. "Ghost versions of ourselves. I like it."

Ravi, who had been quietly listening, finally spoke. "And what happens when they realize it's fake?"

Jordan's smirk faltered.

"They *will* catch on," Ravi continued. "Maybe not right away, but they will. We need an exit plan for when that happens."

Silence settled over the group. He was right. Misdirection would buy them time, but not forever.

Ava exhaled sharply. "Then we make sure by the time they figure it out, we're already somewhere they can't touch us."

Jordan nodded. "Exactly. We don't just hide—we disappear."

For a moment, no one spoke. Then Jiho clapped his hands together. "Alright. Let's make some ghosts."

As they discussed the details, Ava noticed Camelia sitting quietly with a troubled expression. She scooted closer and nudged her gently.

"Hey," Ava said softly. "We're going to get through this."

Camelia gave her a weak smile. "I hope you're right."

"I am," Ava said firmly. "We've made it this far, haven't we?"

Camelia nodded, her smile growing a little stronger. "Yeah. We have."

Outside, a small drone hovered silently in the trees near the barn. The camera was focused on the dimly lit interior. From a remote location, a NOVA operative watched the live feed. "They're at the old barn near Miller's Creek," he reported into his earpiece. "Should we move in?"

A crackle of static came through his earpiece before Ward's voice responded, cool and decisive. "Not yet. Maintain visual. I want to see what they do next."

The operative adjusted the drone's angle, zooming in on the group inside. They were huddled together, speaking in hushed voices, their movements tense. He recognized the signs—they were planning something.

"They're not just hiding," he murmured. "They're strategizing."

Another voice joined the comms—Cross. "They're cornered. If we hit them now, we end this."

Ward's reply was sharp. "And risk driving them deeper underground? No. We do this right."

The operative kept his eyes on the screen as Jordan pulled out a laptop, his fingers flying across the keys. The drone's systems detected an increase in electronic activity. It was a data spike originating from inside the barn.

His stomach twisted. "They're up to something. Could be a countermeasure."

Ward's voice hardened. "Trace it. If they think they can outmaneuver us, they're about to learn how wrong they are."

The drone adjusted its sensors and scanned for signals. A warning flashed across the operative's screen.

ALERT: Unauthorized Data Interference Detected.

His blood ran cold.

"They know we're watching."

Chapter 19

Camelia was the first to wake fully. She stretched her stiff limbs and looked around at her friends, all of them still pretending to sleep or staring off into the distance. The barn, with its aged beams and scattered tools, felt safe enough for now, but she knew it wouldn't last.

Ava sat up next, rubbing her eyes. "Morning," she said quietly.

"Morning," Camelia replied, her voice subdued.

Jordan was hunched over his laptop, which he'd been glued to since dawn. The faint hum of the machine filled the silence as he typed furiously. His brows furrowed in concentration, but his movements were slower than usual—a sign of his growing fatigue.

"What are you even doing?" Jiho asked groggily. He pushed himself up on one elbow and looked over at Jordan.

"Trying to track NOVA's surveillance patterns," Jordan muttered without looking up. "I need to figure out how close they are and if they've found anything that could lead them here."

Ravi groaned as he sat up, his joints popping. "You've been at that thing all night, haven't you?"

Jordan nodded, still focused on his work. "I'm fine."

Ava frowned. "You need to sleep, Jordan. You're going to burn out, and we can't afford that right now."

"I said I'm fine," Jordan snapped, finally looking up. His eyes were bloodshot. "We don't have time to rest. NOVA's probably watching our families. If they figure out where we are, it's over."

The room went silent for a moment, the weight of his words sinking in. Ravi broke the tension by standing up and stretching.

"Okay, fine," Ravi said, his tone measured. "But you're not the only one carrying this, Jordan. We're all in this together, remember?"

"I know that," Jordan replied, his voice softer now. "But I'm the only one who can hack their systems. If I don't stay on top of this, we're sitting ducks."

Camelia crossed her arms and leaned against the barn wall. "What if you screw up because you're too tired to think straight? You're not a robot. You need a break."

"I'll rest when I'm done," Jordan said stubbornly.

Ava stepped between them, raising her hands. "Enough, okay? Let's just figure out what we're doing today. Fighting isn't going to help."

Jiho sighed and got to his feet, brushing hay off his clothes. "She's right. We've got bigger problems than his lack of sleep."

The group gathered around the bay hales in the center of the barn.

"So," Ravi began, "what's the plan? Are we just going to keep hiding here or are we actually going to do something?"

"Like what?" Camelia asked. "Run into the woods and hope they can't find us? That's not a plan; that's desperation."

"I don't know," Ravi admitted, "but sitting here isn't going to solve anything."

Jordan closed his laptop and looked at the group. "We need to stay here for at least one more day. I've been tracking their drones, and they've been circling closer to our last known locations. If we move too soon, we'll just lead them right to us."

"What if they're already watching us?" Camelia asked, her voice trembling.

"They're not," Jordan said firmly. "I've been scanning for signals. If a drone was nearby, I'd know."

"How can you be so sure?" Jiho asked.

"Because I trust my abilities," Jordan replied.

Ava shifted uncomfortably. "That's great and all, but what about the rest of us? We're not exactly trained spies. If they catch us out there, it's over."

As the conversation continued, Camelia found herself withdrawing. She felt useless compared to the others. Jordan had his tech skills, Ravi had his strength, Jiho was resourceful, and Ava always knew how to keep everyone calm. But what could she contribute?

"Camelia," Ava said, pulling her out of her thoughts. "What do you think?"

Camelia hesitated. "I don't know. I just... I feel like whatever we decide, it's not going to end well."

"Thanks for the optimism," Ravi said sarcastically.

Ava shot him a look. "Ravi."

"Sorry," he muttered.

"No, he's right," she said quietly. "I'm not helping. I don't even know why I'm here."

"Hey," Jiho said, his voice gentle. "We're all here because we're in this together. You don't have to have all the answers. None of us do." She gave him a small smile, appreciating the gesture, but the doubt lingered.

Later that morning, as the group prepared to eat the last of their meager supplies, a faint noise outside caught their attention.

"Did you hear that?" Camelia whispered, her heart racing. The others froze listening.

"There it is again," Jiho said, pointing toward the barn door.

Jordan grabbed his laptop, and Ava picked up a heavy wrench they'd found in the barn earlier. Ravi and Jiho moved toward the door cautiously, ready to defend themselves if necessary.

The door creaked open slowly, and a small figure stepped inside.

"Whoa, whoa, don't hit me!" a young brown boy with curly hair said throwing up his hands.

The group stared at him in shock. He couldn't have been more than twelve years old, with an Afro and a backpack slung over one shoulder.

"Who are you?" Ava demanded, lowering the wrench but not relaxing completely.

"Name's Ethan," the boy said, looking around at the group. "I saw you guys sneak in here last night. Thought you could use some help."

"How do we know you're not working for NOVA?" Jordan asked suspiciously.

Ethan snorted. "Do I look like a government agent to you?"

Jiho crossed his arms. "How did you find us?"

"I live around here," he said. "This barn's been abandoned for years. It's kind of my hideout. But don't worry—I'm not going to tell anyone you're here."

After some tense questioning, the group determined that he was telling the truth. He'd overheard his older brother Elijah talking about the kids on the news and recognized them when he saw them sneaking into the barn.

"I can bring you food and stuff," Ethan offered. "But you have to promise not to get me in trouble."

"Why would you help us?" Camelia asked, skeptical.

He shrugged. "You guys are kind of cool. Besides, I don't like those NOVA people. They're creepy." The group exchanged uncertain looks.

"Let's think about it," Jordan said finally.

Ethan nodded and left, promising to come back later with supplies.

As the day wore on, the group's spirits lifted slightly. The unexpected arrival had given them a glimmer of hope, even if they weren't sure they could trust him completely.

"We can't stay here forever," Jiho said as they sat around the lantern that evening. "But if Ethan can bring us supplies, we might be able to last a little longer."

Jordan nodded. "I'm still working on a plan to throw NOVA off our trail. If we can pull it off, we might have a chance to disappear for good."

"Do you really think that's possible?" Ava asked.

Jordan hesitated, then nodded. "We have to believe it is."

Camelia pulled her jacket tighter around her shoulders and glanced toward the barn door where the wind whistled through the cracks. "Even if we disappear, what then? We can't just live like fugitives forever."

"We won't have to," Jordan said. "If we do this right, NOVA won't be looking for us anymore."

Ava scoffed. "Yeah? And how exactly do we make them stop hunting us?"

Jordan exhaled. "We make them think we're not worth the effort. If we erase our digital footprints and feed them false leads, they'll eventually shift focus. NOVA doesn't waste resources on ghosts."

Ravi leaned forward with his elbows on his knees. "That's a big *if*. One wrong move, and we just make them more determined to find us."

Jiho sighed. "So we *don't* make a wrong move."

Camelia spoke. "If we're going to do this, we need to be smart. No unnecessary risks. No mistakes."

Jordan met her gaze, determination flickering in his eyes. "Agreed. We don't just survive—we win."

Ava looked around at the others, then nodded. "Then let's make sure NOVA never sees us coming."

Chapter 20

The barn was becoming unbearable. Four days of hiding had taken its toll, and the kids were beginning to crack under the weight of their situation. Tension and fear seemed to seep into every corner of the structure, clinging to them like an oppressive fog.

Jordan sat on a hay bale. His laptop was balanced on his knees as he scanned for any new information about NOVA's movements. The glow of the screen highlighted the dark circles under his eyes. "They're expanding their search radius," he said, his voice heavy. "If we stay here, it's only a matter of time before they find us."

Ava leaned against a wooden post, arms crossed tightly. "So what do we do? We can't exactly just walk out of here and disappear."

Ravi paced back and forth near the barn door. "We need a better hiding spot. This place is too exposed. If they start sweeping the area, we're done for."

Camelia sat quietly in the corner. Her usually calm demeanor was fraying. "Where would we even go? It's not like we have a lot of options."

Jiho suddenly spoke up. "I thought we decided on my uncle's cabin. Or did y'all forget?"

"I forgot you mentioned it. To be honest we were running. So it may have slipped our minds. Where is the famous cabin?" Ravi asked.

"It's in a perfect spot," he answered. "It's deep in the woods, way off the grid. No cell signal, no neighbors, nothing. If we can make it there, it might buy us some time to figure out our next move."

Ava raised an eyebrow. "And your uncle? He's just going to let us crash there?"

"He doesn't really use it. It's more of a hunting retreat. And he's out of town for the next few months, so it should be empty."

Jordan closed his laptop with a decisive snap. "It's our best shot. If we can get there without being spotted, we'll have a much better chance of staying hidden."

Leaving the barn wasn't easy. The group packed their meager supplies, stuffing everything into their backpacks. Ethan had brought them enough food to last a few days, but they knew they'd have to ration carefully.

"We'll need to move at night," Jordan said as he slung his backpack over his shoulder. "Less chance of being seen."

Jiho nodded. "It's about a two-hour walk from here, maybe longer if we're careful."

The group waited until the cover of darkness before they slipped out of the barn. The cool night air was a welcome relief from the stifling heat of the barn, but every rustling leaf and snapping twig made them jump.

"Stick together," Jordan whispered. "And stay quiet."

Ravi took the lead. He scanned the path ahead for any signs of danger. Jordan followed while Ava stayed close to the middle. In the back was Camelia and Jiho. She clung to his arm due to her frayed nerves.

After what felt like hours of trudging through the dense forest, the cabin finally came into view. It was a modest structure. It was weathered and rustic with a small porch and a tin roof that glinted faintly in the moonlight.

Jiho approached the door cautiously fishing a key from a hiding spot. "He keeps a spare hidden nearby," he explained as he unlocked the door.

The inside of the cabin was simple but cozy. A worn couch sat in the center of the room that faced a stone fireplace. A small kitchen with outdated appliances occupied one corner, and a narrow hallway led to two small bedrooms and a bathroom.

"This will work," Jordan said setting his backpack down. "It's not perfect, but it's safe."

Camelia sank onto the couch. "Safe is all we need right now."

Once they were settled, the group gathered around the small kitchen table to plan their next steps. Jiho spread out a map of the area marking their location and the surrounding terrain.

"NOVA's likely watching all the major roads," Jiho said while he traced a finger along the map. "If we need to leave, we'll have to stick to the back trails."

Jordan's mind was already racing with possibilities. "We also need to think about how we're going to survive long-term. Food, water, and supplies aren't just going to appear out of nowhere."

"Ethan can help with that," Ava said. "He's been reliable so far."

"We'll need to contact him to meet up. That also means one or two of us will need to make a trip to the barn twice a week." Ravi responded.

"Whoever goes has to be careful. He's already put himself at risk every time he comes to see us. If NOVA catches on, he's done for."

Camelia added. "We can't rely on him forever. We need to figure out a way to stand on our own."

The realization set of their circumstances. In order to get what they need for basic needs, they would have to risk being caught. They couldn't agree on if it was worth it and tensions began to build up.

"I still don't understand how we ended up here," Ravi said frustratingly. "We didn't ask for these powers. We didn't do anything wrong."

"Tell that to NOVA," Ava replied bitterly. "They don't care. To them, we're just a threat that needs to be contained."

Jordan sat in a chair. "We can't change what's happened. All we can do is focus on staying ahead of them."

"And what if we can't?" Camelia asked trembling. "What if they catch us? What happens then?"

Jiho placed a reassuring hand on her shoulder. "They won't. We won't let that happen."

Jordan replied. "No matter what happens, we stick together and we fight back."

For now, the cabin offered a fragile sanctuary. But they knew it was only a matter of time before NOVA caught up to them. And when that day came, they would need to be ready. As the first rays of dawn filtered through the trees, the group settled into an uneasy sleep, their thoughts heavy with the challenges ahead.

Jiho was the first to wake up. He shuffled into the small kitchen glancing at the ancient appliances with a mix of amusement and skepticism. "This fridge might be older than all of us combined," he muttered as he opened it to check for anything useful. Predictably, it was empty except for— "A bottle of mustard and a few cans of soda. How delicious," Jiho said sarcastically.

The creak of floorboards announced Ravi's arrival. He yawned and stretched his arms as he looked around. "Morning, chef. What's on the menu?"

Jiho smirked. "Unless you're into mustard sandwiches, we're out of luck until Jordan shows up."

"Great," Ravi said and grabbed a can of soda. "Breakfast of champions."

One by one, the others woke up. Ava groggily rubbed her eyes and sat at the small kitchen table, while Camelia gravitated toward the couch. Jiho walked over to her and gave her his sketchbook. She held onto it like it was a lifeline. Jordan came in with a backpack of supplies and his tablet tucked under his arm.

"So, what's the plan for today?" Ava asked.

"First, we get organized," Jordan said as he set the backpack on the table. "We need to figure out what we have, what we need, and how to make this place livable."

Jiho nodded. "There's a shed out back with some tools and supplies. We can check that out."

"I'll go with you," Ravi offered.

"I'll take stock of what Ethan left us," Ava added. "We need to ration everything carefully."

Jordan glanced at Camelia, who was still seated on the couch. "And you?"

Camelia shrugged. "I'll... help wherever I can."

He didn't press her. "Okay. Let's get to work."

Jiho and Ravi headed outside. The crisp morning air was invigorating after the stuffy confines of the cabin. The shed was a short walk away nestled under a towering oak tree. Jiho unlocked the door and the two stepped inside, coughing as a cloud of dust greeted them.

"Well, this is a treasure trove," Ravi said as he surveyed the assortment of tools, camping gear, and random odds and ends.

Jiho picked up a rusted hatchet and tested its weight. "It's not much, but it's better than nothing."

Ravi found an old fishing pole in the corner and held it up with a grin. "Think there's a lake nearby? We could try catching dinner."

"Let's focus on not starving today before we start planning fishing trips."

Back inside, Ava and Camelia were going through the supplies.

"Okay, we've got canned beans, a loaf of bread, some granola bars, and a few bottles of water," Ava said, ticking items off on her fingers. "Not exactly gourmet, but it'll keep us alive."

Camelia nodded absently. Her eyes drifted towards the window. She hadn't said much since they arrived.

"You okay?" Ava asked softly.

"I'm fine," she replied quietly.

Ava decided not to push. "Let me know if you want to talk, okay?"

Camelia gave her a small, grateful smile.

By mid-afternoon, the group had settled into a rhythm. Jiho and Ravi worked on fortifying the cabin using the tools from the shed to secure the windows and doors. Ava organized their supplies into neat piles ensuring they could easily track what they had.

Jordan, meanwhile, was glued to his laptop, scanning for any signs of NOVA activity. His expression grew darker as he read through the data. "They're getting closer," he said grimly during a break. "Director Ward is furious, and they've started questioning our families more aggressively."

Camelia's head shot up. "What do you mean, aggressively?"

"They haven't taken anyone into custody yet," Jordan said choosing his words carefully. "But they're not ruling it out."

Ava swore under her breath. "This is bad. If they go after our families..."

"We won't let it come to that," Jiho said firmly as he returned from the shed with Ravi. "We'll figure something out."

Camelia tightened her grip on her sketchpad. "We have to do more than *figure something out*. We need to stop them before they get that far."

Jordan nodded. "I know. That's why we need to act fast." He turned his laptop toward them. "I managed to intercept more of their internal chatter. NOVA's stepping up surveillance on our families, but they're being careful about it—no direct action yet. That means we still have time to disrupt their plans."

Ava crossed her arms. "And how do we do that? Hack into their system *again*? We barely got away last time."

Jordan's jaw tightened. "We don't just hack them. We *cripple* them."

Jiho raised an eyebrow. "I like the sound of that. Got a plan?"

"I found something interesting while digging through their files. NOVA relies on a secure communication network to coordinate their teams. If we can take that down—even temporarily—we can create chaos on their end. Confuse their operatives, and delay their response times. Basically, throw a wrench in everything they're doing."

Ravi leaned against the wall. "And how do we pull that off? Please don't say 'just leave it to me,' because I've seen what happens when you wing it."

Jordan smirked despite himself. "I don't plan on winging anything. But we'll need to get closer to one of their relay points. These communication hubs aren't just satellites. They use ground stations to boost their signal. If we can shut down one of those, even for a few hours, we can give our families time to get somewhere safe."

Ava narrowed her eyes. "You mean sabotage."

"Exactly."

Jiho let out a low whistle. "Man, you've got a death wish."

Camelia shook her head. "He's right, though. If we just sit here, NOVA will come for us *and* the people we care about. We can't let that happen."

Chapter 21

That night, as the others drifted off to sleep, Camelia opened up the sketchbook. She drew quietly. The only sound in the cabin was the scratching of her pencil.

Jiho glanced over at her. "Can't sleep?"

Camelia shook her head. "Too much on my mind."

"We'll get through this," he said. "One step at a time."

Camelia managed a small smile. "I hope you're right."

"I usually am," he said with a smirk. He glanced at the sketchbook. "What are you working on?"

Camelia hesitated, then turned it slightly so he could see. The page was filled with rough sketches—faces, shadows, and outlines of figures in motion. But at the center was something more detailed: a depiction of the barn, their first temporary refuge, surrounded by the dense woods. The figures of their group stood at the edges, half-formed as if she hadn't quite decided where they belonged.

Jiho studied it for a moment. "Looks like a plan."

Camelia let out a breath. "It's... I don't know. Maybe I just need to see it. Where we are. What we're up against."

Jiho nodded. "Makes sense. Sometimes putting things down on paper makes them real. And sometimes it helps us figure out what to do next."

"That's what I'm hoping for."

"You ever think about what you'll do after all this?"

Camelia blinked. "After?"

"Yeah." He turned his head toward her. "When we're not running. When NOVA's not hunting us down. What do you want?"

She was quiet for a long moment. "I don't know," she admitted. "I guess I never really let myself think that far ahead."

Jiho nodded slowly. "Yeah. Me neither." He sighed. "But I think we should."

Camelia looked at him. "Why?"

"Because if we don't believe we'll make it through this, who else will?"

"Then I guess we better make sure we do."

Jiho grinned. "Now that's the spirit."

Jiho lay restless on his cot. He couldn't sleep because his mind was spinning about their precarious situation. The cabin had become their sanctuary, but its isolation felt like a double-edged sword. As he shifted to a more comfortable position, his hand brushed against something unfamiliar under his pillow. Startled, he sat up and pulled out a small, folded piece of paper. The moonlight streaming through the window revealed hastily written words:

"Meet me outside by the old oak tree. Midnight. Come alone."

His first thought was that it could be a trap, but his gut told him otherwise. He carefully unfolded the paper again searching for any clue about its source, but there was no signature. Glancing at the kitchen clock, he saw the time: 11:47 p.m. He had barely over ten minutes.

Quietly, he slipped on his jacket and moved discreetly to avoid waking the others. Ava and Camelia were huddled together on the couch, Ravi snored softly by the fire, and Jordan's cot in the corner was empty. He assumed he was in the backroom tinkering with his devices.

Pushing the cabin door open, he stepped into the crisp night air. The cold seeped through his jacket and the hairs on the back of his neck stood on end. The old oak tree stood like a sentinel at the edge of the clearing, its twisted branches clawing at the night sky. He approached cautiously as his eyes were scanning the shadows.

"Hello?" he slightly whispered.

A figure emerged from the darkness and stepped into the soft glow of the moonlight. He tensed up when he recognized the tall lean frame and the familiar sharp features. He was one of the agents in the library.

"I remember you!" Jiho said, his voice a mix of surprise and confusion.

The man casually tucked his hands into the pockets of his black jacket. "My name is Agent Petersen."

Jiho's mind raced. "What are you doing here? And how did you even get the note into the cabin without us noticing?"

"You'd be surprised how easy it is to stay unnoticed when people think they're safe. Let's just say I've been... monitoring the situation."

Jiho frowned. "Monitoring us? Since when?"

"Since the day you ran away from the school," he admitted. "I've been keeping tabs on all of you and making sure you didn't get yourselves into even deeper trouble."

"If you've been watching us, then why haven't you turned us in? What's your game?"

He sighed and stepped closer. "My job isn't as black-and-white as you think. Yes, I work for NOVA, but that doesn't mean I agree with everything they do. There are people within the agency, Director Ward included, who view you as a threat. But there are others, like me, who believe you're just kids caught in a bad situation."

Jiho narrowed his eyes. "So what? You're here to give me some kind of warning?"

"Exactly," he said seriously. "Ward is losing her patience. Her team hasn't found you and the higher-ups are pressuring her to take extreme measures. If they don't locate you soon, they're going to start targeting your families to force you out of hiding."

Jiho's stomach churned. "We already knew that was a possibility."

Petersen shook his head. "You don't understand. This isn't just about surveillance or questioning. They're preparing to take your parents into custody as leverage. Once that happens things will escalate fast. You and your friends need to act before it's too late."

Jiho took a step back. "What do you expect us to do? We're not exactly equipped to fight off a government agency."

"I'm not saying you should fight," he continued. "But you need to think strategically. Staying in one place too long makes you an easy target. And splitting up might actually be your best option."

Jiho frowned. "Splitting up? There's no way we'll agree to that. We're stronger together."

"Maybe. But you're also easier to find together. If you split up, it'll be harder for NOVA to track all of you. It's a risk, but it might buy you time."

Jiho crossed his arms. "And why should I trust you? You're still one of them."

"Because I'm the reason they haven't found you yet. I've been feeding them just enough misinformation to keep them off your trail. But I can only do so much without blowing my cover."

Jiho studied him searching for any hint of deceit. "Why are you helping us? What's in it for you?"

"Let's just say I've seen what happens when NOVA gets too much power. I don't want to see you and your friends become casualties of their ambition."

"I need to talk to the others about this."

"Not yet," he said firmly. "You need to think this through first. If you go to them now, you'll just stir up more panic. You're the level-headed one. If anyone can convince them to make the right choice, it's you."

Jiho glared at him. "This isn't just about me. We're a team. We make decisions together."

Petersen stepped back with his hands raised in a placating gesture. "I get it. I'm not asking you to decide right now. Just... consider what I've said. Time is running out." Then he melted back into the shadows leaving Jiho alone under the old oak tree.

The weight of their conversation pressed down on Jiho as he made his way back to the cabin. Inside, the others were still asleep, their faces peaceful in the faint glow of the dying fire. He slipped back onto his cot with the note still clenched in his hand. Sleep didn't come easy that night. As much as he wanted to dismiss Petersen's warning, he couldn't shake the feeling that their time was running out.

The next morning Ava stirred first. She sat up, rubbing her eyes, and glanced around. Jordan was sprawled on a tattered cot, one arm dangling off the side. Ravi was curled up in a sleeping bag on the floor, snoring lightly. Camelia had somehow managed to cocoon herself in a mountain of blankets.

But Jiho was already up. She noticed him immediately sitting by the small dining table with his back to the group. He was hunched over with his elbows on the table and his head resting in his hands.

"Jiho?" Ava called softly, careful not to wake the others. He didn't respond, didn't even flinch. She climbed out of her blankets and tiptoe across the creaky wooden floor until she was closer to him. He was staring at a folded piece of paper in his hands. His brow was furrowed and his lips pressed into a thin line.

"Jiho, are you okay?" Ava asked again.

He startled slightly, as though he hadn't realized she was there. Quickly, he crumpled the paper in his fist and shoved it into his pocket before turning to face her.

"Yeah," he said, but his voice was strained, and his eyes didn't meet hers.

Ava frowned. "You don't look okay. Did something happen?"

"Nothing," Jiho replied too quickly. "Just couldn't sleep."

Ava crossed her arms and gave him a skeptical look. "You're a terrible liar, you know that?"

He sighed. "It's nothing. Really."

But Ava wasn't buying it. Jiho was one of the most even-keeled people she knew; calm, collected, and rarely rattled. Whatever was bothering him now had to be serious. By the time the others started to wake up, she had retreated to her spot by the fireplace. She decided to keep a watchful eye on him. He moved around the cabin with almost mechanical precision, even helped Ravi start a small fire to heat water and made breakfast without saying much of anything.

"Morning," Jordan mumbled as he joined them at the table. He immediately noticed the shift in the atmosphere and raised an eyebrow. "What's with the gloomy vibes?"

"Ask him," Ava said pointedly.

Jiho shot her a pleading look, but she ignored it.

"Hey man?" Jordan prompted. "What's going on?"

"Nothing," Jiho said again, this time with a bit more force. "Can we just eat?"

Jordan glanced at Ava, who gave a slight shake of her head. Ravi and Camelia exchanged confused looks but didn't press further. They also sensed that something was off. The group ate in near silence, the only sounds coming from the occasional scrape of utensils against plates and the soft crackling of the fire. Jiho barely touched his food. Instead, he picked at the edges of his toast and stared into space.

"Okay, seriously," Ravi said, breaking the silence. "What's going on with you? You've been acting weird all morning."

"Maybe he's just tired," Camelia offered.

"It's not just that," Ava said. "Something's bothering him, and he won't tell us."

Jiho's head snapped up, and he glared at her. "Can you drop it?"

"No," she shot back. "Because whatever it is, it's important. And if it affects us, we deserve to know."

Jordan crossed his arms. "She's right. If something's going on, now's not the time to keep it to yourself."

Jiho looked around the table, his face a mixture of frustration and guilt. He opened his mouth to say something, then closed it again, as though the words were too heavy to speak.

The tension reached its peak when Camelia placed a gentle hand on his arm. "I'm your friend," she said softly, "and they're your friends. You can trust us."

Something in her voice seemed to break through his defenses. He didn't know if it was her abilities or if her words had gotten to him. He felt something in him shift and his shoulders sagged. He slumped back in his chair and started talking.

"I... I don't know how to say this," he began barely above a whisper. "But I think there's something we need to talk about. All of us."

"You think?" Ravi said sarcastically.

"Ravi," Ava shot him a glare.

Jiho took a deep breath and stood. "Give me a minute. I need to get something."

The others watched as he walked to the corner of the cabin, where his backpack rested against the wall. He rummaged through it for a moment before pulling out the crumpled piece of paper he had hidden earlier. When he returned to the table, he placed the paper in the center and smoothed it out. It revealed the note that had been haunting him all morning. "I have something to tell you."

Chapter 22

Jiho had finally told them about his late-night meeting with Agent Petersen and the revelation hit like a storm. Jordan leaned back in his chair visibly frustrated. Ravi gripped the edge of the table, while Camelia and Ava exchanged nervous glances.

"Are you kidding me?" Jordan finally spoke in a sharp tone. "You met with a NOVA agent? Alone? Again without telling us?"

"I didn't have much of a choice," he replied evenly. "The note was under my pillow. I had to find out what it was about."

"And you thought keeping it to yourself was a good idea?" Ravi snapped. "This isn't just about you. We're all in this mess together!"

"I'm aware of that. That's why I'm telling you now. Petersen gave me information we need to consider."

"Like what?" Ava asked apprehensively.

"He said Ward and the others are running out of patience. They're planning to take our parents into custody if they can't find us soon."

Camelia gasped and her hand flew to her mouth. "They wouldn't really do that, would they?"

"Petersen seemed pretty sure," Jiho said grimly.

"So what?" Jordan said, his voice cold. "We're just supposed to trust him? He's one of them, Jiho. NOVA doesn't exactly have a great track record when it comes to telling the truth."

"I don't think he's lying," Jiho said quietly.

Jordan let out a humorless laugh. "Wow. That's rich. You're willing to take the word of some agent over the people you've been through everything with?"

"That's not what I'm saying," Jiho said frustratingly. "I'm saying we need to consider all our options. If he is right, then sitting here doing nothing isn't an option anymore."

Ravi slammed his fist on the table, making everyone jump. "What options do we have? Trusting him and walking into a trap? Splitting up like he suggested? That's insane!"

"Splitting up might actually buy us time. It's harder to track all of us if we're not together."

"No way," Camelia said firmly. "We've stuck together this long. I'm not going off on my own."

"And I'm not leaving," Ava added. "We're stronger together. If we split up, we're just giving them an advantage." She stood up. "Listen to yourselves. We're arguing about trusting some stranger when we should be focusing on what we've always done, trusting each other. We've gotten this far because we've worked together. If we let fear pull us apart now, NOVA's already won."

"I get what you're saying," Jiho said softly. "But if we don't do something, our parents are going to pay the price. Do you really want that on your conscience?"

"I don't want any of this," Ava shot back. "But running off in different directions isn't the answer."

Jordan stood abruptly making the chair scrape against the floor. "You know what? Jiho's right about one thing. Sitting here isn't going to solve anything. But trusting that agent? No way. If he really wanted to help us, he wouldn't still be working for NOVA."

"You think I didn't consider that?" Jiho replied as he stood up. "But what if he's telling the truth? What if ignoring him puts our families in even more danger?"

Jordan glared at him. "And what if trusting him gets us all captured? Or worse?"

"Guys, stop," Camelia said. "This isn't helping."

Her words brought both boys to a halt. She looked at each of them. "I don't want to lose any of you. I also don't want my parents to get hurt either. But I'm scared. I'm scared of what's going to happen if we make the wrong choice."

Jiho sighed. "I'm scared too, Cam. But that's why we have to think this through. Petersen said we should think strategically. If we just keep reacting to what NOVA does, we're always going to be one step behind."

Jordan exhaled sharply, crossing his arms. "Thinking strategically doesn't mean walking into a trap." His voice was tight with frustration. "We don't even know if Petersen is telling us everything."

Jiho met his glare but kept his tone measured. "And we don't know if he's lying either. We need information, and right now, he's the only one offering us any."

Camelia asked. "What if this is our only chance?" she asked quieter now. "If we don't act, we might not get another shot."

"I just don't want to be the idiot who trusts the wrong person and gets everyone killed." Jordan remarked.

"Wait. Who are you calling an idiot? Did you forget that if it wasn't for you and your Nexus, that we would be home with our families right now?" Jiho said firmly.

"I made one mistake. How many times are you going to throw it in my face? Some friend you are."

"Technically it's a series of the same mistakes. The drone at the park, Nexus deleting the videos ...."

"Ravi, now is not the time," Ava said.

A heavy silence settled between them. Jiho rubbed the back of his neck. "And that's why we can't rush. We figure out how to confirm if he's telling the truth before we commit to anything."

"So what do we do?" Ravi asked.

Jiho looked around the room in a steady gaze. "We don't trust him blindly, but we use the information he gave us. We come up with a plan to protect our parents and keep ourselves safe."

"What about splitting up?" Ravi asked.

"For now, we stay together. But if it comes to it... we'll have to consider it."

Jordan crossed his arms. "Fine. But if Petersen shows up again, we're all going. No more secret meetings."

"Agreed," he said.

"We'll figure this out," Jordan said firmly. "But we have to stay united. That's the only way we stand a chance."

Camelia took a deep breath. "Then we start now. We go over everything we know—every detail, every weakness NOVA might have."

Jiho walked to the table and grabbed a notepad. "We list everything Petersen told us, then compare it with what we've seen for ourselves. If anything doesn't add up, we rethink our approach."

Ravi leaned forward. "And if we find a hole in his story?"

"Then we assume he's playing us," Jordan said. "And we plan for that too."

Chapter 23

The following week, they were gathered at the table one morning. Jordan had just came back after picking up the supplies. Ethan also left news about NOVA's increasing efforts to locate them.

"We can't just sit here forever!" Ravi exclaimed, slamming his fist on the table. The sound echoed through the room which caused Camelia to flinch.

"We're not sitting here forever," Ava shot back. "We're trying to figure out the best plan that doesn't get us caught or worse."

"Yeah? And how's that going so far?" Ravi stood up. His towering frame made him seem even more intimidating. "Because all I see is us hiding while NOVA's closing in!"

"Would you calm down?" Jordan interjected. "Shouting isn't helping anyone."

"It's better than doing nothing," Ravi growled.

"Stop it," Camelia said trembling. "Please, don't fight."

"Maybe if people actually listened to me, I wouldn't have to fight," Ravi muttered.

Jiho finally stood up. "*Enough*!" he snapped. His voice was so uncharacteristically loud, that it startled everyone into silence. "We're all on edge, but fighting each other isn't going to solve anything!"

Ravi turned on Jiho. "Easy for you to say. You've been acting all high and mighty since we got here, like you're the one in charge."

"I'm not trying to be in charge," he replied. "I'm just trying to keep us from tearing each other apart."

"Well, you're not doing a great job of that," Ravi shot back.

Ava stood between the two boys. "Ravi, back off. He's right. We need to work together, not against each other."

"Of course, you'd take his side," he sneered. "You always think you know better than everyone else."

"Don't put this on me," she snapped.

The argument escalated quickly, with everyone talking over each other. Accusations flew, tempers flared, and the air seemed to hum with a strange energy. In the heat of the argument, Ravi's anger got the better of him. Without thinking, he slammed his fist into the table again. But this time the table cracked under the force and split down the middle.

"Ravi!" Camelia cried jumping back.

"Nice going," Jordan said sarcastically. "Maybe you can punch through the walls next and really make us easy to find."

"Shut up, Jordan!" Ravi shouted.

Before anyone could react, Ava stepped forward. "Enough!" she yelled. Everyone in the room froze, their emotions hitting a boiling point.

Jordan cracked. "You think you're the only one with an issue? Maybe if you stopped trying to control everything—"

"I'm trying to keep us alive!" She interrupted.

The room erupted into chaos as their powers, fueled by their emotions, began to manifest uncontrollably. Ravi's strength surged and the floorboards beneath him groaned as he took a threatening step forward. "You think you're better than me? Say it to my face!"

"Stop it!" Camelia screamed as she accidentally triggered her hypnotic influence. For a brief moment, Ravi froze mid-step with a vacant expression.

Ava noticed the shift and glared at Camelia. "What are you doing?"

"I didn't mean to!" She cried. "I'm scared and I couldn't control myself."

Meanwhile, new abilities kicked in Jordan. His eyes now glowed faintly as he scanned the situation. "Everyone needs to calm down," he said. No one heard him because his voice was drowned out by the chaos.

Jiho instinctively activated his powers. The cabin's interior shimmered and warped. It momentarily turned into a disorienting simulation of a swirling void.

"Jiho, stop!" Ava shouted through the illusion.

"I'm trying!" Jiho yelled back. His hands trembled as he struggled to regain control.

The powers clashed violently and created a cacophony of sights and sounds that made it impossible to think. All of their powers collided in a chaotic storm. In the midst of it all, Ravi swung his arm in frustration and the motion sent a nearby chair flying across the room. It narrowly missed Camelia, who ducked just in time.

"Stop it, Ravi!" Ava screamed.

"I can't!" Ravi shouted back. He started to panic as he realized how out of control he was. Finally, Jordan managed to send out a pulse that temporarily disrupted everyone's powers. The room went still. The chaotic energy dissipated as quickly as it had come. The friends stood in the wreckage of the cabin. Their breaths were heavy and their bodies felt drained. The cracked table, broken chair, and warped floorboards bore silent testimony to the damage they had caused. Not just to the cabin, but to each other.

"What... just happened?" Camelia whispered as tears streamed down her face.

"We lost control," Jiho said quietly.

"No kidding," Jordan muttered.

Ravi sank to the floor with his head in his hands. "I'm sorry," he said barely audible. "I didn't mean to... any of it."

Ava sighed and sat down beside him. "We all messed up," she admitted. "This... this isn't who we are."

"We can't let this happen again," Jiho said firmly, looking around at the others. "If we're going to make it through this, we have to figure out how to control our powers."

The group exchanged hesitant glances, the weight of their actions settling heavily on their shoulders. They realized just how dangerous their powers—and their disagreements—could be. The shattered table and broken furniture were evidence of their inability to control their powers, but the real damage wasn't the splintered wood or warped floorboards. It was the fracture in their trust and the toll on their hearts.

Camelia sat on the edge of the couch, her knees pulled to her chest. Her hands trembled and her breathing was shallow. She couldn't stop replaying the moment in her mind: Ravi's arm swinging wildly, the chair flying across the room, and how close it had come to hitting her.

"It wasn't his fault," she whispered to herself. But she couldn't help but wonder if that was even true.

Jiho, perched by the window, glanced over at her. He hadn't said much since the incident, but he'd been keeping an eye on everyone. Her pale face and shaky demeanor worried him more than he wanted to admit.

"Cami," he called as he softly walked over and sitting down beside her. "Are you okay?"

She didn't answer right away. Instead, she stared at the cracked floorboards as if they held the answers to the questions swirling in her mind. "I don't know," she finally said.

He leaned closer. "Talk to me. What's wrong?"

"What's wrong?" She repeated almost breaking. She turned to look at him on the verge of crying. "I almost got hit. That chair... it could've..." She couldn't finish the sentence.

He stretched his arm out and motioned for her to lean in. "But it didn't. You're okay now."

She shook her head violently. "No, I'm not okay! Don't you get it? This isn't okay! We're dangerous! I'm dangerous!"

Across the room, Ravi had been sitting against the wall with his head buried in his hands. At her outburst, he looked up. "Camelia... I'm sorry," he said hoarsely.

She didn't respond to him. She just kept her gaze fixed on the floor.

"I didn't mean to lose control," Ravi continued, standing up slowly. "I... I didn't mean to scare you."

She finally looked up at him with fear and sadness. "It wasn't just you. It was all of us. I... I used my power without meaning to. I froze you. What if I'd made things worse? What if someone had gotten hurt because of me?"

"You didn't hurt anyone," Jiho spoke gently.

"But I could have!" She shouted. "Don't you see? We're not ready for this. We don't know how to control what we can do, and we're going to get someone hurt—or worse."

Ava, who had been sitting silently by the fireplace, finally stood. "Camelia, you're right," she said. "We're not in control, and that's terrifying. But that's why we have to stick together. We have to figure this out."

Tears streamed down her cheeks. "And what if we can't? What if it's too late by the time we do?"

"It won't be," Ava said firmly as she walked closer. "Because we won't let it be. We're in this together. You're not alone."

Jordan finally spoke up. "She's not wrong, though," he stated seriously. "We're playing with fire here. We've already gotten close to exposing ourselves more than once. If NOVA finds us before we figure this out, it's game over."

"Then we need to focus," Jiho replied. "We can't keep letting our emotions control us. We have to train and learn how to manage our powers."

"And how do we do that when we can't even have a conversation without it blowing up in our faces?" Ravi asked bitterly.

The room fell silent again, the weight of the situation pressing down on all of them. "I don't know if I can do this," Camelia whispered. "I don't even want these powers anymore. I want to be with my family."

"I know it's hard," Ava said softly. "I know it feels like too much. But we can't give up. If we don't figure this out, no one else will."

She didn't respond, but she leaned into Jiho's embrace as her body shook with silent sobs.

Ravi stood awkwardly across the room. "I'll do better," he said quietly. "I'll make sure this doesn't happen again."

Jordan responded. "We all need to do better. No more excuses, no more losing control."

Jiho looked around at his friends. "We can get through this. But only if we trust each other. Can we do that?"

As they began cleaning up the damage in the cabin, a sense of quiet unity settled over them. They weren't out of the woods yet, but they were beginning to understand the weight of their powers—and the responsibility that came with them.

Camelia wiped her eyes. "I'll try. For all of us."

Ava smiled softly. "That's all we need."

Jiho picked up a piece of broken furniture, his lips quirking into a faint smile. "Guess this is just another part of the adventure, right?"

Ravi chuckled despite himself. "Some adventure."

Jordan's eyes flickered with a faint glow as he powered down his interface. "Let's make it one worth surviving."

Chapter 24

The next day, Camelia had been quieter than usual. Her friends noticed, but it was Jiho who took it upon himself to try and lift her spirits.

"Camelia, look!" He called as he balanced a broom on his fingertip in the middle of the cabin. His face twisted in mock concentration. His tongue stuck out as he staggered dramatically and pretended it was some kind of monumental feat.

She sat at the couch tracing circles in her sketchbook. She glanced up briefly and offered him a faint smile. "Nice trick, Jiho."

"Nice trick?" he gasped, letting the broom clatter to the floor. "That was an ancient balancing art passed down for generations!"

Ava snorted from her seat by the window. "Generations of clowns, maybe."

"Thank you for your support, Ava," Jiho said, feigning hurt before turning his attention back to Camelia. "Okay, I get it. You're not impressed by my incredible broom skills. How about... this!"

He grabbed an old deck of cards from the counter and fanned them out with an exaggerated flourish. "Pick a card, any card. Prepare to be amazed."

She sighed softly and pulled a card. Jiho made a big show of shuffling the deck. His hands moved with an exaggerated clumsiness. "Now, was your card..." He dramatically revealed the Queen of Hearts. "This?"

She shook her head. "Nope."

Jiho frowned and flipped over another card. "This?"

"Nope."

Ava leaned over. "Jiho, maybe quit while you're behind."

She giggled quietly at that, but it was fleeting. Her smile faded almost as quickly as it appeared. His heart sank. He'd spent the entire day cracking jokes and trying to distract her, but he couldn't shake the feeling that whatever was weighing on her was something she needed to process on her own.

That night Camelia laid in her makeshift bed and stared at the ceiling. Her chest felt tight with the events of the past few days replaying in her mind. No matter how hard she tried to distract herself, the memories clung to her like a shadow. She glanced toward the others, their sleeping forms barely visible in the dim light. Guilt pricked at her. They have been so kind, so supportive, but she couldn't shake the feeling that she was dragging them down.

Quietly, she slipped out of bed, being careful not to wake anyone. She grabbed her hoodie and boots and eased the cabin door open just enough to step outside. The crisp night air greeted her. The dark and endless forest stretched out before her, but it didn't feel as threatening as it once had. She walked slowly with her hands tucked into her hoodie pockets. The moonlight filtered through the trees and casted silver patterns on the ground. Each step seemed to echo in the silent night, but it didn't bother her. The solitude felt comforting to her. Like it understood the storm that was swirling inside her.

She stopped by a small clearing where the sky opened up. The stars speckled the inky blackness with their distant light. She tilted her head back and took a deep breath.

"Why does it feel like this is all my fault?" she whispered to the night.

She thought back to the fight. The way her powers had surged uncontrollably which froze Ravi in place. She remembered the fear in his eyes and the way everyone had looked at her afterward. Even though they'd reassured her that it wasn't her fault, she couldn't shake the feeling that she'd caused the chain reaction that nearly tore them apart.

"I didn't ask for any of this," she said.

The trees around her swayed gently in the breeze, as if offering their silent agreement. She sat down on a fallen log and wrapped her arms around herself. She wasn't sure how long she'd been sitting there when she heard the faint crunch of footsteps behind her. Her heart jumped as she whirled around and scanned the shadows.

"It's just me," Jiho's voice called softly.

She exhaled. "What are you doing out here?"

He stepped into the clearing. "I could ask you the same thing."

She turned back to the stars. "I just... needed some air."

He sat down beside her on the log, leaving a comfortable distance between them. "You could've woken me up, you know. I'm a great midnight air-getting buddy."

She smiled faintly. "I didn't want to bother anyone."

"You're not a bother," Jiho said firmly but reassuring. "Don't ever think that."

They sat in silence for a moment. "Jiho," she said quietly. "Do you ever think... maybe we're not supposed to have these powers?"

He considered her words. "Honestly? Yeah, I've thought about it. A lot. But I don't think it's about whether we're 'supposed' to have them. It's about what we do now that we do."

She frowned. "What if we can't handle it? What if I can't handle it?"

He rested his elbows on his knees. "You're one of the strongest people I know. And I'm not just talking about your powers. You care about people. You care about us. That's why this is so hard for you."

She looked at him with unshed tears. "What if caring isn't enough?"

"It is. Because it's what's going to keep us together, keep us from losing ourselves. You're not alone in this. We're all figuring it out together."

Camelia exhaled deeply and looked over at him. His quiet presence was comforting, but she wasn't ready to share everything she was feeling, not yet.

"Jiho," she said softly.

"Yeah?" he replied, his voice warm but subdued.

"I appreciate you coming out here. I really do." She hesitated. "But I think I need some time alone."

"Are you sure? I can stay. You don't have to go through whatever this is by yourself."

"I know you mean that, and it means a lot to me. But I just... I need to sort through some things on my own. I promise I'll come back soon."

He didn't answer right away. His dark eyes searched hers for any hint of hesitation. Finally, he nodded reluctantly. "Okay," he stood up and brushed off his jeans. "But if you're not back in an hour, I'm coming to find you. Deal?"

"Deal," she said, her smile growing a little.

Jiho turned to leave, but he paused after a few steps, looking back over his shoulder. "And Camelia?"

"Yeah?"

"We're here for you. No matter what, okay?"

Her throat tightened, but she managed a quiet, "Okay."

Satisfied he made his way back toward the cabin, his footsteps fading into the distance. With him gone, the forest felt larger, quieter, and more profound. Camelia tilted her head back to look at the stars again. The weight on her chest didn't feel as suffocating now. She couldn't stop replaying everything in her mind: the fight, the chaos, the way her powers had surged without her meaning to. She clenched her fists, her nails biting into her palms.

Why did it have to be me?

Camelia stood and started walking again, her steps slow and deliberate. The crunch of leaves and twigs beneath her boots filled the quiet, grounding her. She wasn't sure where she was going; she just needed to move, to let her thoughts flow freely.

She found herself back at the clearing, the one she and Jiho had passed through a moment earlier. The open sky above was like a vast, blank canvas, and for a moment, she just stood there, letting the stillness wash over her. Sitting down in the center of the clearing, she pulled her knees to her chest and rested her chin on them. *What if Jiho's wrong?* she thought. *What if I can't control this? What if I'm the one who ends up hurting everyone I care about?*

Her thoughts spiraled, each one darker than the last. She closed her eyes tightly, trying to push them away, but they clung to her like shadows. Without realizing it, her powers began to stir. These weren't the same as before. They felt different. The ground around her frosted over as thin tendrils of ice crept outward in jagged patterns. She opened her eyes and saw her breath puffing out in the cold air.

"No," she whispered, holding her hands out in front of her. "This can't be real. I already have one set that I can't control. Stop!"

The frost hesitated, then continued spreading, as if defying her command. Frustration bubbled up inside her, and she slammed her fists against the ground. The frost surged forward in response, encasing nearby blades of grass and leaves in crystalline ice.

Tears welled in her eyes. "I can't control these either!" she cried, her voice breaking.

She stayed there for what felt like hours, her powers slowly calming as her emotions ebbed. When she finally stood, the clearing shimmered under a thin layer of ice, the moonlight making it shine like a frozen lake.

Chapter 25

The next night, she slipped out the cabin to take another walk. Her boots crunched softly against the forest floor as she wandered deeper into the woods. She had told herself the walk was to clear her mind, but the truth was more complicated. The burden of the past few days pressed down on her shoulders, and no matter how much Jiho or the others tried to reassure her, she couldn't shake the doubt stabbing at her chest.

The frost incident had rattled her. She wasn't just scared of herself; she was terrified of what they all could do. Her feet carried her instinctively toward the clearing she'd discovered the night before. But as she approached, a soft sound caught her attention—a branch snapping underfoot. She froze, heart pounding. The others were back at the cabin. *Who else would be out here?*

"Camelia."

Her name came softly but clearly, and she spun around to see a figure stepping out from the shadows. Her breath caught.

"Let me guess. Agent Petersen?" she whispered, disbelief lacing her tone.

The man raised his hands in a gesture of peace. "I didn't mean to startle you."

"What are you doing here?" she demanded.

"I'm here because of you," Petersen said calmly. "I know what you've been going through. All of you. I want to help."

She narrowed her eyes. "Help? By dragging us into some government experiment or arresting and locking us up?"

He sighed with a softening expression. "I understand why you're suspicious. After everything you've been through, I would be too. But I'm not your enemy. I came to offer you a way out of this chaos."

She didn't respond immediately. Her mind was racing with thoughts of her friends. Thoughts of Jiho trying to cheer her up earlier, of Ava's sharp intuition, of Jordan and his growing attachment to Nexus and of Ravi's steady presence and how the group had fought so hard to stay together. But she also thought of the constant fear, the tension, the way their powers seemed to spiral out of control more often than not.

"What kind of way out?" she asked cautiously.

He took a step closer. "I've been watching you. Not just tonight, but over the past few days. You're struggling with your powers, aren't you? Struggling to feel in control."

Her stomach churned. "How do you know that?"

"It's my job to know," he replied. "You're not alone in this. But trying to figure it out on your own, without guidance, well it's dangerous. For you and for everyone around you."

She crossed her arms. "And you think your organization can 'guide' us? Like NOVA has any idea what it's like to be us."

He tilted his head slightly. "Maybe not. But we have resources. Technology. Experts who've studied cases like yours. We can help you control your abilities, Camelia. We can keep your friends safe. And your families."

The mention of their families hit like a gut punch. she thought of her parents and the fear they must be feeling after being questioned by NOVA agents.

"And what's the catch?" she asked, her voice hard.

"No catch," he said though his tone grew more serious. "But I'll be honest with you. This situation can't go on much longer. Director Ward is under immense pressure to contain it. If we don't act soon, others will. People who won't be as understanding as me."

"Are you threatening me?"

"No," he said quickly. "I'm trying to protect you. But I can't do that unless you trust me."

Camelia's mind whirled. Every instinct screamed at her to walk away, to go back to the cabin and tell the others. But another voice whispered doubt. *What if he was right? What if staying hidden only made things worse? What if their powers really were too dangerous to leave unchecked?* She thought of the frost spreading uncontrollably in the clearing, of Ava's emotional manipulation during arguments, of Jordan's AI spiraling beyond his control.

"What happens if I agree?" she asked hesitantly.

"You and your friends would come with us," he said. "We'd provide you with the tools and support you need to master your abilities. You'd be protected. No more running, no more hiding."

"And if I don't agree?"

His expression darkened slightly. "Then the situation escalates. And I can't promise it'll end well for anyone."

She felt a lump rise in her throat. "I need time to think."

He nodded. "Take the time you need. But not too long. Things are moving fast, and decisions need to be made." He stepped back into the shadows, his figure disappearing as quickly as it had appeared.

Camelia didn't move for a long time. Her thoughts were a tangled mess. When she finally made her way back to the cabin, the others were still asleep. She climbed into her sleeping bag and stared at the ceiling. *What am I supposed to do?* She couldn't sleep. The weight of her encounter with Petersen bore down on her. And for the first time she wasn't sure if she could keep this secret from her friends.

She spent the entire day wandering the edges of the forest, her sketchbook untouched in her hands. The others were too focused on planning to notice the way her thoughts drifted elsewhere and how every step she took felt heavier. She replayed NOVA's threats over and over: the surveillance, the pressure on their families, and the inevitable outcome if they kept running. Maybe there was another way. Maybe if she turned herself in, she could buy the others time and keep their families safe.

By nightfall, her decision was made. All she needed was to wait until everyone is asleep so she could slip out again. Her breath formed clouds in the cool night air as she walked deeper into the woods, her mind replaying the words Agent Petersen had said earlier. *We can help you. We can keep your family safe.*

Her steps slowed as she reached the clearing where he had promised to wait. She had agonized over the decision, turning it over in her mind a hundred times. Every instinct told her this was wrong and that her friends would see it as betrayal. But the memory of her parents' worried faces when she'd called them haunted her. As she approached he stepped out from the shadows, just as he had the first time. He looked the same - calm and controlled,\ with a hint of urgency in his eyes.

"You came," he said softly.

Camelia stopped a few feet away. "I came to tell you I've made my decision."

"And?"

She took a deep breath to steady herself. "I'll align with NOVA—but only me. My friends don't want this, and I'm not going to force them into it. But I can't keep risking my family. They've already been questioned. If I can protect them by working with you, I will."

For a moment he said nothing. Then he gave a slow nod. "You're making the right choice. This is about more than just you and your friends. It's about everyone your powers could affect."

Her jaw tightened. "I'm not doing this for you. Or for NOVA. I'm doing this for my parents. And if I find out you're lying to me, if you hurt them in any way, I'll make you regret it."

Petersen didn't flinch at her words. Instead, his lips curved into a small approving smile. "Understood. Your family will remain safe, I promise you that."

"Before I agree," she said crossing her arms, "I have some conditions."

He raised an eyebrow intrigued. "Go on."

"First, you leave my friends alone. They've been through enough. I'll come with you, but only if you guarantee their safety. No more agents showing up at their houses and no more surveillance."

Petersen's smile faded slightly. "You're asking a lot. Your friends' powers—"

"Are *their* responsibility," she interrupted sharply. "I'm only responsible for myself. Take me, and you get what you want—a cooperative subject. But my friends are off-limits."

Petersen considered her for a long moment before agreeing. "Fine. We'll redirect our focus. But you should know your friends' powers aren't just going to disappear. If they cause harm—"

"They won't," she said firmly.

"And your second condition?"

Camelia hesitated. "You keep my family safe. No questioning them, no surveillance, no threats. They don't even need to know I'm involved with NOVA. As far as they're concerned, I'm safe and sound."

His expression softened slightly. "Done."

Her shoulders sagged with relief, though the weight of what she was agreeing to still pressed heavily on her.

"We'll need to move quickly," he said glancing at his watch. "I'll arrange for transport to our nearest facility. We can be out of here before morning."

Camelia shook her head. "I can't leave tonight. If I disappear, my friends will know something's wrong. Give me one more day. I'll tell them I'm leaving on my own terms."

He frowned. "You're asking for a lot of trust."

"I'm risking everything by trusting you," she shot back.

That seemed to placate him. "Fine. But tomorrow night, no excuses. We'll meet here, and you'll come with us."

She nodded, a knot forming in her throat. "Tomorrow night." She walked back to the cabin with a heavy heart, her thoughts tangled. She knew her friends would never forgive her if they found out. But how could they understand? When she reached the cabin, the others were still asleep. Jiho had moved his sleeping bag closer to the door, as if trying to block anyone from sneaking out again. She stepped over him carefully, settling into her spot near the window. The quiet of the cabin pressed down on her as she stared at the ceiling, unable to sleep. She could still feel Petersen's eyes on her, his words echoing in her mind.

This is the right choice. It has to be.

But as the hours dragged on, doubts crept in, and she couldn't shake the feeling that she was making a grave mistake.

Chapter 26

For the first time in a while there was laughter. Camelia sat at the small kitchen table with a steaming mug of tea in her hands. She watched as Jiho and Ava teased each other about the previous night's card game.

"You cheated," Jiho pointed a finger at Ava.

Ava smirked. "If by 'cheated,' you mean 'outsmarted,' then sure."

Jordan rolled his eyes from the corner where he sat with his laptop. "Can you two argue a little quieter? Some of us are trying to monitor for NOVA chatter."

"Chatter? You mean playing Minesweeper?" Ravi joked.

"I'm multitasking," Jordan shot back with a grin.

Camelia smiled as she sipped her tea. She let their banter wash over her, but her mind was elsewhere. Last night's conversation with Petersen lingered like a shadow. *Tomorrow night, no excuses.* Her smile faltered for a brief moment before she quickly corrected it. Jiho caught the flicker of emotion and tilted his head.

"You okay, Camelia?"

She blinked and then nodded. "Yeah, just tired. Didn't sleep well." His eyes lingered on her for a second longer than she liked, but he seemed satisfied with her answer.

The group spent the day reinforcing their plans. They took shifts patrolling the perimeter of the cabin even though it was unlikely NOVA would find them so soon. Jordan updated them on the digital measures he'd implemented to keep them off the radar.

"We're ghosts," he announced proudly holding up his laptop. "NOVA's search patterns show they're still focusing on the barn and surrounding areas."

"Ghosts who are running out of food," Ravi peered into the pantry. "When is the next time we're getting supplies?"

"Ethan said he'd drop off more supplies tomorrow," Ava reminded him.

Camelia listened to it all but her thoughts were distant. Every laugh and smile from her friends felt like another twist of the knife. They were trusting and relying on her and she was about to abandon them. As the sun dipped below the horizon, the group gathered around a small fire outside the cabin. The flames crackled, casting flickering shadows on their faces. Jiho brought out an old guitar he'd found in a closet and strummed a few awkward chords.

"Didn't know you could play," Ava teased.

"I can't," Jiho admitted. "Picked up a few things from an old game called Guitar Hero. But hey, it's better than nothing."

The off-key music and laughter filled the chilly night air and for a moment, Camelia let herself enjoy it. She leaned back against a log to stare up at the stars and memorized the sound of her friends' voices. *This is the last time,* she thought. *I have to do this.* When the fire died down and everyone began heading inside, she lingered a little longer. Jiho noticed and waited for her.

"You sure you're okay?" he asked quietly.

She forced a smile. "Just need a few more minutes out here. Clear my head."

Jiho hesitated but eventually nodded. "Don't stay out too long. It's freezing."

"I won't," she promised.

Hours later, the cabin was silent. The only sounds were the steady breathing of her sleeping friends. Camelia was awake counting down the minutes. Her packed bag sat hidden beneath her cot. *It's time.* She slipped out of her blanket as quietly as she could. Every creak of the floorboards sounded deafening in the stillness. She paused to hold her breath as Jiho shifted in his sleep.

When he didn't wake, she grabbed her bag and tiptoed toward the door. Her hand hovered over the doorknob as guilt threatened to consume her. *They'll be fine without me. This is the only way to keep my family safe.* She opened the door slowly. The cool night air hit her face as she stepped outside. The forest was dark, but she had memorized the path to the clearing where Petersen had promised to meet her. She saw him waiting as he leaned against a black SUV parked at the edge of the clearing. The vehicle's headlights were off, but the faint glow from the interior light illuminated his face.

"You're on time," he straightened as she approached.

Camelia nodded as she gripped the strap of her bag tightly. "Let's get this over with."

"Do you have everything you need?" He asked gently.

She nodded but didn't say anything.

He opened the passenger door for her, but she paused before she got in.

"This deal still stands, right?" she said slightly trembling. "My family stays safe. My friends are off-limits."

"It stands. You have my word."

With a deep breath, she climbed into the SUV. The door shut behind her with a finality that made her stomach churn. The ride was silent for the first couple of miles. She stared out the window as she watched the dark forest blur into open fields.

"Do they know you're gone?" he asked suddenly.

"No," she said quietly. "I didn't tell them."

"Probably for the best," he replied. "Goodbyes can be messy."

She didn't respond. She couldn't shake the image of her friends waking up to find her gone. She could almost hear Ravi's voice accusing her of abandoning them. She also couldn't bear to see Jiho's face. He was so close to her and she didn't want to see him hurt.

Petersen glanced at her. "You're doing the right thing. You're protecting the people you care about."

"I hope so," she murmured.

A few minutes later, the SUV pulled up to a sleek modern building surrounded by tall fences and security cameras. The NOVA facility loomed in the night light. Its stark design was a sharp contrast to the natural beauty of the forest they had just left.

Camelia clutched her bag as she stepped out of the vehicle.

"This way," he said as he led her toward the entrance.

Inside, the facility was cold and sterile with white walls and bright lights. The sound of their footsteps echoed as they walked down a long hallway. A young woman in a lab coat approached them with her clipboard in hand. She gave Camelia a polite smile. "Welcome Miss Suarez. We'll get you settled in shortly."

Camelia glanced at Petersen, who gave her an encouraging nod.

"This is your new beginning," he said.

Camelia swallowed hard. But as she followed the woman deeper into the facility, she couldn't shake the feeling that she had just made the worst mistake of her life. The further they walked, the more the air seemed to press in around her. The fluorescent lights buzzed faintly overhead which casted a harsh glow on the pristine floors. Everything smelled of antiseptic—too clean and too controlled. She tightened her grip on the strap of her bag.

Doors lined the hallway. Each one were identical. Their small observation windows revealed glimpses of stark white rooms beyond. Some were empty. Others weren't. She caught sight of a man sitting on the edge of a narrow cot, staring at the wall. Another door showed a young girl no older than twelve with her arms wrapped tightly around herself.

Camelia's stomach twisted. *What have I done?* The woman in the lab coat stopped in front of a reinforced door and scanned her ID badge. The lock clicked open. "This will be your room," she stepped aside to let her in. She hesitated. Petersen's voice was calm but firm. "Go on."

Slowly, she stepped inside. A single camera in the corner blinked red. She turned to protest, to demand answers, but before she could speak the door shut behind her with a final echoing *click*. She was alone. And she had just handed herself over to the enemy.

Chapter 27

The next morning, Ravi groaned as he stretched out on the couch.

"Where's breakfast?" he mumbled groggily.

Ava, already up and staring out the window, turned sharply. "Where's Camelia?"

Ravi sat up straighter. "I don't know. Isn't she still in her little funk?"

Ava glanced at Jiho, who had been unusually quiet since waking up. He was perched on the edge of the dining table, staring at the floor as if lost in thought.

"Jiho?" Ava pressed.

Guilt flickered across his face. "She wasn't here when I woke up."

"What do you mean she wasn't here?" her tone sharpened.

"Last night, she wanted to stay outside a little longer to think. I didn't think much about it since she did come back inside. But when I got up this morning, I didn't see her so I assumed she wanted some alone time again."

"It has to be more than that. Did she say anything about what she was feeling?"

He sighed. "Not last night. But we did have a long talk a couple of nights ago. She seemed... conflicted."

"You knew she was having doubts?" Ava asked incredulously. "And you didn't think to tell us this before now?"

"I thought she just needed some space," he defended himself. "This was right after the blowout. I didn't think she'd... disappear."

"Disappear?" Ravi echoed sitting up fully. "She's probably just outside. Maybe she went for a walk."

"Then why hasn't she come back yet?" Ava shot back.

"Let's not jump to conclusions," Jordan interjected from the corner where he had been quietly observing. "She could be nearby. Let's check the area before we start panicking."

157

The group split up into pairs to scour the woods surrounding the cabin. One pair headed north, while the other moved south.

"This is why we don't keep secrets," Ava said, not bothering to mask her irritation.

"I didn't think it was a big deal," Jiho muttered.

"Not a big deal?" Ava stopped walking and turned to face him. "She's gone. What if NOVA found her? What if—"

"Don't say that," Jiho interrupted. "We don't know that. Let's just keep looking." He hated the uncertainty gnawing at him. *She couldn't be gone. She wouldn't just leave.*

Meanwhile, Ravi and Jordan followed a faint path leading toward a clearing.

"You think she's okay?" Ravi asked.

"I hope so," Jordan replied. He was scanning the ground for any signs of her.

They reached the clearing and Ravi's gaze fell on a set of tire marks in the dirt. "Hey, look at this."

Jordan crouched down to study the tracks. They were fresh and the dirt was still soft and disturbed.

"These aren't old. Someone was here recently."

"You don't think..." Ravi trailed off.

He didn't answer immediately. He closed his eyes and focused on the faint hum of information surrounding him. He began to piece together data from the scene: the type of vehicle, the direction it had gone, and a faint trace of Camelia's presence.

"She was here," he said finally as he opened his eyes. "She got into a car."

Ravi's expression darkened. "With who?"

"I don't know yet. But I can find out."

Back at the cabin, the group reconvened. Ravi and Jordan explained what they had found, and they began processing the details.

"The tracks lead southeast," Jordan said. "It's a black SUV, late model. Whoever picked her up didn't stay long. They were in and out."

"You're sure it was her?" Ava asked.

"I'm positive. I can trace her signal. Her phone must have been on when she got in."

"Wait, you can do that?" Jiho asked surprised.

"I can't access everything, but I can follow enough breadcrumbs to get an idea of where she went."

"So where is she now?" Ava pressed.

Jordan closed his eyes again to focus. The information flowed to him in fragmented bursts—coordinates, timestamps, faint echoes of activity.

"NOVA," he said finally, his voice barely above a whisper.

The room fell silent.

"They have her," Ava said.

"How do you know?" Ravi asked Jordan.

"The signal ends at one of their facilities," he explained. "It's not far from here, but it's heavily secured."

Ava paced the room. "This is bad. If they have her, they probably know about us, too. It's only a matter of time before they come for us."

"We don't know that," Jiho said.

"She wouldn't just leave with them," Ravi said. "Not without a reason."

"Maybe she didn't have a choice," Ava said. "Or maybe..." She trailed off, unable to finish the thought.

"Maybe what?" Jiho asked defensively.

"Maybe she told them about us," Ava said bluntly.

"She wouldn't do that," he stated firmly.

"You don't know that," Ava argued back. "She's been distant for while. We all saw it."

"Do you blame her? Anyone else accidentally use their powers and we're all 'just let it go and move on.' She accidentally did it and everyone was down her throat telling her she's dangerous. Truthfully I don't blame her. We haven't been good friends to her and you know it."

"Enough," Jordan said, his voice cutting through the argument. "Fighting won't help us figure this out."

"So what do we do?" Ravi questioned.

"We have to get her back," Jiho said.

"And walk right into their trap?" Ava countered. "That's suicide."

"We can't just leave her there!" Jiho exclaimed.

"We won't," Jordan said calmly. "But we have to be smart about this. If we're going to go after her, we need a plan."

The group spent the rest of the day debating their options. Ava remained skeptical about a rescue mission while Jiho was adamant about not abandoning Camelia. Jordan worked silently in the background to map out the facility and gather as much information as he could.

"Time is running out," Jiho said finally. "If we don't act soon, it might be too late."

"And if we act recklessly, we'll all end up captured—or worse," Ava argued.

Jordan looked up from his makeshift workstation. "I've got enough data to get us in. It won't be easy, but it's possible."

"Then let's do it," Jiho said.

"Are we sure about this?" Ravi asked, his voice uncertain.

"No," Ava said, crossing her arms. "But what choice do we have?"

Jordan nodded, determination flashing in his eyes. "We'll get her back. No matter what it takes."

As night fell over the cabin, the group braced themselves for what lay ahead. Jiho sat at the dining table staring blankly at the map Jordan had spread out earlier. His fingers were idly tracing a line that led to the NOVA facility. Ravi leaned against the door frame with a heavy scowl. Ava paced the room and Jordan was typing furiously on his laptop.

None of them spoke about Camelia's absence, but it hung over them like a storm cloud, suffocating and relentless.

"We're falling apart," Ava said suddenly. "We can't keep doing this."

Jiho looked up. "Doing what?"

"This!" Ava gestured wildly. "Blaming each other, second-guessing everything. We're wasting time, and it's getting us nowhere."

"You think I don't know that?" Jiho snapped, his voice sharper than he intended.

"Guys, stop," Ravi interrupted, stepping between them. "This isn't helping."

"She started it," Jiho muttered under his breath earning a glare from Ava.

"Enough," Jordan said, his voice quiet but firm. "This isn't about whose fault it is. It's about what we do next."

Ava sat down on the couch. "Do you even think we can trust her anymore?"

"Of course we can," Jiho replied immediately.

"How do you know that?" Ava pressed. "She left, Jiho. She didn't tell anyone. For all we know, she could've—"

"She wouldn't betray us," Jiho slammed his fist hard onto the table.

"Then why did she leave?" Ava questioned back.

"Because we pushed her away!" Jiho shouted. "All of us. She felt like she didn't belong, like we didn't trust her."

Ava's mouth opened as if she was going to argue, but she remembered how they treated her.

"We didn't mean to," Ravi said quietly. "We were all just... stressed."

"That doesn't change what happened," Jiho said bitterly.

"Okay," Jordan interjected. "This isn't about what we meant or didn't mean. What's done is done. The question is, what do we do about it?"

"I hated the way we've been acting," Ravi admitted after a long pause. "Fighting all the time and pointing fingers. It's not us."

"I know," Ava said, her voice barely above a whisper. "I've been so scared of losing everything that I didn't stop to think about how I was treating you all. Especially Camelia."

Jiho looked at her, surprised. "You're admitting you were wrong?"

She gave him a weak smile. "Don't get used to it."

Jordan leaned back in his chair. "She might be gone, but that doesn't mean we're powerless. If anything, we need to be stronger now—for her and for ourselves."

"But how do we fix this?" Jiho asked. "How do we even begin to make it right?"

"We start by being honest with each other," he said firmly. "No more secrets. No more assumptions. If we're going to survive this, we have to trust each other completely."

Ava added. "Agreed. And that means listening to each other, even when we don't like what we're hearing."

"Fine," Jiho said reluctantly. "But that works both ways. If I say something, I don't want you all jumping down my throat."

"Deal," Ravi said, extending his hand toward Jiho.

He hesitated before shaking it.

"And we need a plan," Jordan pulled their attention back to the map on the table. "NOVA isn't going to stop looking for us, especially now that they have Camelia. We have to figure out our next move."

"What about going to get her?" Jiho asked.

"Too dangerous," Ava said immediately.

"But we can't just leave her there!" Jiho argued.

"We're not," Jordan said calmly. "But rushing in without a strategy will only get us all captured—or worse."

Ravi tapped a spot on the map. "Then let's get a strategy. We know where NOVA took her, right?"

Jordan nodded. "I've been monitoring their encrypted channels. They moved her to one of their research facilities. It's not their main headquarters, but security's still tight."

Jiho exhaled sharply. "Of course it is."

Ava crossed her arms. "How tight are we talking?"

Jordan pulled up a new screen on his laptop. It displayed satellite images of the facility. "Perimeter fencing, surveillance towers, and armed guards at the main entrances. It's designed more like a containment center than a lab."

Jiho muttered a curse. "They don't want her leaving."

"They don't want *anyone* leaving," he corrected grimly. "And if they're keeping her there, they have a reason."

Ava frowned. "Meaning?"

He hesitated before answering. "They want something from her—whether it's cooperation, testing, or worse. We don't have time to wait this out."

A heavy silence settled over the group.

Ravi broke it first. "So we break her out."

Ava shot him a look. "You just said it's a fortress."

"And?" he shrugged. "No place is impenetrable. There's always a way in. We just have to find it."

Jiho grinned. "Now you're talking."

Jordan was deep in thought. "If we do this, it has to be *perfect*. We'll need distractions, an escape route, and a way to get in without triggering every alarm in the place."

Ava sighed. "Great. A simple rescue mission."

Jordan smirked slightly. "When have we ever done 'simple'?"

"And we'll make NOVA regret ever messing with us," Jiho added

"We do this right," Jordan said, his voice firm. "And we bring her home."

Chapter 28

Ava was the first to stir. Her footsteps were quiet as she moved toward the small kitchen area. The others gradually followed and gathered around the table. Jiho leaned against the wall. Jordan sat with his laptop open projecting a holographic map of the NOVA facility above the screen. Ravi fidgeted with an old pen he'd found twirling it between his fingers.

"We need to finalize the plan," Jordan said, his voice cutting through the quiet.

Ava set down the cup of tea she'd made and joined the group. "Before we do anything, we need to make sure we're prepared. This isn't just sneaking out to avoid a teacher. We're up against professionals."

"They've already got Camelia," Jiho declared. "If we wait too long, who knows what they'll do to her?"

"We're not waiting," Jordan replied firmly. "But rushing in without the right tools or information will only get us all caught—or worse." He gestured to the map hovering above his laptop. "I've been analyzing the facility's layout. NOVA's systems are advanced, but I've managed to get into their public-facing security feeds. These are the entry points."

He tapped on three spots that lit up red. "The main gate is heavily guarded, but there's a secondary entrance near the northwest side. It's used for deliveries, so it's not as secure. We could use that."

"Could?" Ravi raised an eyebrow.

"There's no guarantee it'll be clear," he admitted. "But it's our best shot at getting close without being seen."

"What about getting inside?" Ava asked. "Even if we get to the gate, they'll have cameras and guards."

"That's where I come in," Jordan said. "I can loop their camera feeds long enough for us to get through."

"And the guards?" Jiho asked.

"That's... trickier."

"I'll handle them," Ravi said cracking his knuckles.

"No offense, but I don't think brute force is the answer," Ava remarked.

"It's not brute force," he countered. "It's precision. I can disarm them before they even know what hit them."

"Let's not get ahead of ourselves," Ava glanced at Jiho. "What do you think?"

Jiho met her gaze with a conflicted expression. "I think... I think we're doing this for the right reasons, but we have to be smart. If something goes wrong, it's not just Camelia—they'll come after all of us. And if they know where our families are..."

"That's why we have to make this work," he said. "The longer we wait, the more dangerous it gets—for us and for our families."

Ava nodded slowly. "Okay. So we use the northwest entrance. Jordan handles the cameras, and Ravi deals with the guards if it comes to that. What about Jiho and me?"

"Jiho's speed could be crucial if we need to grab something or someone quickly," he said. "And you, Ava... your ability to manipulate emotions could help keep things under control if anyone panics."

Ava frowned. "You want me to brainwash people?"

"Not brainwash," he said carefully. "Just... influence. If it keeps us safe, isn't it worth it?"

She didn't respond immediately, but the conflicted look on her face spoke volumes. As the group continued hashing out the details, Ravi stood up. "All this planning is great, but what if something unexpected happens? We need a backup plan."

"Agreed. If anything goes wrong, we fall back to the woods near the cabin. There's enough cover there to hide while we regroup."

"And if we get separated?" Jiho asked.

"Head to the fallback point," he said. "No exceptions. We can't risk anyone else getting caught."

Ava exhaled, arms still crossed. "Fine. But we need a way to communicate if things go sideways."

Jordan tapped a few keys on his laptop. He brought up a schematic. "I've been working on something. Encrypted comms—short-range earpieces that should keep us off NOVA's radar, at least for a while."

Jiho grinned. "Now *that* is what I'm talking about."

Ravi stopped pacing. "And weapons? I don't plan on fighting an army with just my fists."

Ava gave him a sharp look. "We're not looking to fight—we're looking to *get Camelia out*."

"Yeah, well, if NOVA catches us, I doubt they'll care about our intentions," he shot back.

Jordan sighed. "He's not wrong. We need a way to defend ourselves if things go south. I have a few ideas, but nothing lethal."

Ravi rolled his eyes but didn't argue.

Ava turned back to the map. "Okay. We go in, we get Camelia, we get out. No unnecessary risks. No getting caught up in anything we can't handle."

Jordan glanced around the group, meeting each of their eyes. "Then it's settled."

A heavy silence fell over them. This was it. No more talking—only action.

Ravi cracked his knuckles. "Let's bring her home."

The next morning the group packed their supplies. Ravi carried a small bag of makeshift weapons he'd put together, just in case. Ava double checked the map, committing every detail to memory. Jordan closed his laptop. His fingers hovered over the keyboard for a moment before he finally powered it down. "Ready?" he asked, looking up at the others.

They all nodded, though none of them looked entirely confident. As they stepped out of the cabin, the forest seemed to close in around them.

"This is it," Jiho said, his voice barely above a whisper.

"For Camelia," Ravi said.

"For all of us," Ava added.

Jordan led the way, the map glowing faintly on his tablet as they disappeared into the woods. They made the three mile trek faster than they 'd expected. They crouched behind a thick cluster of trees. They could see the massive steel-and-glass NOVA facility looming in the distance.

It was quiet except for the occasional rustling of leaves in the wind and their shallow breaths as they took in the sight before them. Jordan glanced at his tablet. "The northwest entrance is the weakest spot. We'll cut through the tree line here and move fast. If we time it right, we can avoid the cameras."

Jiho frowned as he scanned the facility's perimeter. "This place is a fortress. Are we sure about this?"

Ravi gripped a makeshift baton. "No, but we're here, aren't we?"

Ava adjusted her scarf. "Let's just stay focused. Camelia's in there. We're not leaving her behind."

As they approached the tree line, a low whirring noise made them freeze. Jordan raised a hand, his eyes darting upward. A sleek black drone hovered above them, its camera lens reflecting the sunlight.

"Uh-oh," Ravi muttered.

"Move," Ava hissed.

The group scattered and dived for cover beneath the thick foliage. Jordan watched as the drone adjusted its position to scan the area. *It's searching for us.*

Jiho pressed himself against a tree trunk. His eyes were locked on the hovering machine. "Tell me you've got a way to shut that thing down," he whispered.

Jordan's fingers flew over his phone screen. "I can try to jam its signal, but it'll only be temporary."

Ravi gritted his teeth. "Do it. Fast."

Before anyone could react, a sharp, authoritative voice crackled through the drone's speakers, making them jump.

"I wouldn't do that if I were you."

The group exchanged panicked glances.

"Who's that?" Ava whispered.

The voice continued calmly. *"Step away from the facility. You've already made a mistake coming this far. Don't make it worse."*

"Is that... Director Ward?" Jiho asked, his voice barely audible.

Jordan's fingers flew across his tablet as he tried to scramble the drone's signal. "She's got to be watching us through this thing. If I can just—"

The voice cut in again. *"Jordan, don't even try. You think you can outmaneuver us? You're smart, but we're smarter. All of you, turn around now, or there will be consequences."*

Ava's breathing quickened, her hands trembling. "What do we do? She knows we're here!"

Jiho looked toward the facility, then back at the drone. "We retreat. Now."

"Retreat?" Ravi snapped. "We're right here! Camelia's in there, and we're just going to run away?"

Jiho clenched his jaw. "This isn't the time to argue. She has the upper hand. We're not equipped to fight them."

Ravi tightened his grip around his baton so hard that it almost broke. "So, what? We just leave her? Let them win?"

Jordan stepped in. "No one's saying we give up. But he's right—we can't do this head-on. Let's fall back, regroup, and come up with a better plan."

Ava grabbed Jiho's arm. "Can you get us out of here without them following us?"

"Hold on to me. All of you."

The group huddled around Jiho as he closed his eyes and intensely focused. A faint blue glow surrounded him, and the air shimmered as though reality itself was bending. Within seconds, the forest around them shifted and blurred and was replaced by the familiar surroundings of the cabin.

"Wait... are we actually here?" Ava asked.

"No," Jiho said, his voice strained. "It's a virtual projection. The drone won't be able to track us, but we need to move quickly. The illusion won't last long."

Ravi looked skeptical but didn't argue. "Fine. Let's go."

They moved swiftly through the woods, their nerves on edge. The drone was nowhere to be seen, but Ward's voice lingered in their minds.

"What does she want with us?" Ava asked, her voice barely above a whisper.

"Control," Jordan said without hesitation. "She doesn't want us out here making our own decisions. She wants to put us in a box, run tests, and use us for their agenda."

"Camelia's already in that box," Jiho said, his tone heavy with guilt. "We can't let them do the same to us."

When they reached the cabin, they hurried inside and locked the door behind them. Jiho sank onto the couch. His hands trembled from the effort of maintaining the virtual projection. Ava handed him a bottle of water.

"Are you okay?" she asked softly.

"I'm fine," Jiho muttered, taking a sip. "Just tired."

Jordan set his tablet on the table. "Ward's playing games with us. She wants us scared and disorganized."

"It's working," Ravi admitted. "She knew exactly where we were and what we were doing. How do we fight someone like that?"

Jiho straightened. "We don't give her what she wants. We stay one step ahead.".

"We need to figure out how she's tracking us," Jordan said. "There's no way that drone just stumbled across us by chance."

"She might have trackers on us," Ava suggested. "Something we don't know about."

"Or she's monitoring our devices," Jiho added. "That drone was too precise."

Ravi slammed his fist on the table. "Great. So what do we do? Toss everything and live off the grid?"

Jordan gave him a sharp look. "If that's what it takes, yes. But first, we need to find a way to disable whatever she's using to watch us."

Ava frowned. "We can't just assume it's our phones. We barely cut them on now and when we do it's for a few seconds. What if it's something else? Something we're not even thinking about?"

Jiho ran a hand through his hair. "Like what? Hidden transmitters? Bugs in our clothes?"

Jordan's expression darkened. "It's possible. NOVA's tech is advanced—they could've planted something without us even noticing."

Ravi exhaled sharply. "So how do we find them?"

Jordan stood and walked towards his laptop. "There's a way. I can scan for unauthorized signals—if there's a tracker or a hidden transmitter, I'll find it."

Ava nodded. "Good. Do it. Because if they know where we are, we're already out of time."

Jordan sat down and his fingers flew over the keyboard. The others watched in tense silence as lines of code scrolled across the screen. After a few seconds, he froze.

"There," he said grimly. "Something's piggybacking off our devices."

Jiho leaned over. "What is it?"

Jordan's jaw tightened. "It's not our phones. It's *everything else.* Our watches, Ava's earpiece, even Ravi's jacket."

Ravi's eyes widened. "What? My *jacket*?"

"They've been tracking us with micro-emitters. Probably activated remotely when Camelia turned herself in," he explained.

Ava's face hardened. "She didn't just turn herself in. She led them to us."

A heavy silence settled over the room.

Ravi was the first to speak. "So we burn it all?"

Jordan nodded. "We get rid of everything. Now."

Chapter 29

Camelia sat on the edge of the cot in the room they'd assigned her. It was a cross between a dorm and a high-tech holding cell. She hadn't slept much since arriving. The door slid open with a soft hiss and Director Ward stepped in. She carried a tablet tucked under one arm. Her expression was as calm and collected as ever, though her sharp eyes seemed to study Camelia carefully.

"Good morning, Miss Suarez," Ward said. "I hope you've found your accommodations... sufficient."

She didn't look up right away. "They're fine," she replied flatly.

Ward stepped closer and placed the tablet on the small table between them. She gestured for her to look. "I thought you should know what's been happening. Your friends... well, they've been busy."

Camelia's heart skipped a beat as she glanced at the tablet. Footage played across the screen showing the forest surrounding the NOVA facility. Her friends moved cautiously through the trees. Their faces set with determination.

"They came here last night," Ward said matter-of-factly. "I suppose they thought they could rescue you."

"What did you do to them?"

Ward raised a hand. "Relax. We didn't harm them. In fact, we allowed them to retreat. But only because of the arrangement we have with you."

"Arrangement?"

Ward met her gaze. "You came here willingly, Miss Suarez. You said you wanted to protect your family and your friends. That decision showed maturity and foresight. But your friends... they don't share that same ideal. They're reckless, impulsive, and are putting everyone, including their families, at risk."

Camelia felt guilty. "They were just trying to help me."

172

Ward leaned forward and spoke in a firm voice. "Help you? By endangering themselves, their families, and the public? Let me remind you, that you came here on your own. You made a choice to protect the people you care about. You're being mature about this. They are not."

Camelia opened her mouth to argue, but Ward cut her off.

"They think they're invincible. That their powers give them the right to do whatever they want, regardless of the consequences. But they're wrong. Their behavior isn't just reckless; it's dangerous." Ward's gaze bore into her. "If they continue like this, they'll force my hand. And trust me when I say, none of you want that."

Camelia felt the weight of Ward's words pressing down on her. She wanted to yell, to defend her friends, but she couldn't deny the truth in what Ward was saying.

"What happens now?" she asked quietly.

Ward tapped on the tablet and continued scrolling through the footage. "That depends on them. If they come back, and I'm sure they will, they won't get the same leniency. The only reason they were allowed to retreat this time is because of you."

"So you're using me to control them."

Ward's expression softened. "I'm giving you the chance to protect them. To keep them from making mistakes that could cost them everything."

She looked away. "They don't trust you. They think you're the enemy."

Ward sighed. "And what have I done to earn their trust? From the moment NOVA identified your group, they've lied, evaded, and actively worked against us. Meanwhile, we've done nothing but exercise patience. More patience than they deserve."

Her voice began to rise. "You're treating us like criminals! We didn't ask for these powers. We're just trying to figure things out."

Ward's gaze hardened. "And while you're 'figuring things out,' innocent people could get hurt. These powers aren't toys, Miss Suarez.

They're dangerous. If your friends can't see that, it's up to you to make them understand."

Camelia stood abruptly. "They're not bad people. They're scared. We all are."

Ward stepped closer. "I understand that. But fear doesn't excuse recklessness. It doesn't excuse putting others at risk."

"So what? You want me to betray them?"

"I want you to continue to make the right choice."

"And what exactly is the 'right' choice? Turning on the only people who have ever had my back? Handing them over to you?"

"I'm not asking you to betray them. I'm asking you to open your eyes. If they lose control, if they make one wrong move, innocent people could die. You know that as well as I do."

Camelia swallowed hard. She did know. She'd seen firsthand what could happen when powers spiraled out of control. But that didn't mean she could just turn her back on her friends.

Ward continued. "I want you to guide them. To help them see reason. You're the only one who can. This isn't just about you or your friends. There are bigger forces at play here. Forces that don't care about your feelings or your intentions. NOVA exists to protect the public and that means taking action when necessary. If your friends keep pushing, they'll leave us no choice."

She sank back onto the cot, with her head in her hands. She hated the position she was in. She was caught between her loyalty to her friends and the cold reality of their situation. Her fingers tightened in her hair as doubts swirled in her mind. Had she made the right choice? She had told herself this was the only way to keep them safe and to stop NOVA from tearing apart their lives. But sitting here, in this sterile, silent room, she couldn't shake the sinking feeling in her gut.

Ward's voice softened. "You've already made a brave choice by coming here. Don't let it be for nothing. Use your influence. Help them before it's too late." Ward turned to leave but paused at the door.

"Think about what I've said. And remember your decision to come here was the right one. It's up to you to make sure your friends don't undo everything you've tried to protect."

The door slid shut behind her, leaving her alone in the quiet room. She stared at the tablet on the table and the footage of her friends frozen on the screen. They had risked everything to come for her, and now they were in even more danger because of it. Her mind swirled with questions and fears. *Was Ward right? Were they being reckless? Or was this all just a manipulation to keep her in line?* One thing was certain: she had to make a decision. And this time, it wasn't just about her friends. It was about their survival - and their future.

Camelia exhaled shakily, her fingers hovering over the tablet's screen. Ward's words echoed in her mind, twisting with her own doubts. She wanted to believe her friends were doing the right thing—that they weren't a threat, that they could stay ahead of NOVA. But what if they weren't? What if Ward was right, and their desperation was leading them toward disaster?

Her chest tightened. No. She couldn't think like that. Not without proof. She tapped the screen to replay the footage. The grainy video showed Jiho pacing, Ravi muttering something under his breath, and Ava scanning their surroundings. They weren't reckless. They were fighting—for her, for each other, for something bigger than themselves.

But Ward wasn't entirely wrong, either. Power without control was dangerous. And if they weren't careful, NOVA wouldn't need to take them down. They'd do it to themselves. Her hand clenched into a fist. I have to warn them. But I won't turn on them.

She grabbed the tablet and stood solidifying her decision. If Ward wanted her to use her influence, fine. But she wasn't going to be her pawn. She was going to make sure her friends survived—on their own terms.

Chapter 30

Jiho paced back and forth near the door in a grim expression. Ravi sat at the table drumming a restless rhythm. Ava and Jordan leaned against the counter in equally tense postures. They had barely managed to retreat from the facility. The drone's message still echoed in their minds carrying Director Ward's voice.

"I wouldn't do that if I were you."

It wasn't just a warning. It was a reminder of the power Ward held over them.

"We can't keep doing this," Jordan finally said, breaking the silence. "They're always one step ahead of us. We need a better idea."

"Or any idea at all," Ava muttered. "Right now, all we're doing is reacting."

Ravi exhaled and pushed back from the table. "Okay, so what do we do? Ward's not bluffing. She could turn our families against us or worse. And Camelia..." He trailed off. "She's in there. With them. Voluntarily."

"We don't know that," Jiho argued. "Maybe they forced her. Maybe they threatened her family."

"She left on her own," Ravi shot back. "She didn't even tell us."

"We don't know what they said to her," he countered. "Cami wouldn't just abandon us. She wouldn't."

Ava stepped between them before the argument could escalate further. "Stop. Fighting each other isn't going to solve anything." She turned to Jiho. "You're right, we don't know why she left. But that doesn't change the fact that she's with NOVA now. We need to figure out our next move."

Jordan nodded. "And fast. Ward's probably already planning her next move. We need to stay ahead of her, or at least stop playing right into her hands."

Ravi frowned. "Staying ahead of a government agency? Yeah, that's easy."

Jiho's eyes flicked toward the window. "It's not impossible," he said quietly. "We've got powers. We just need to use them smarter."

"Smarter how? Every time we try something, they're already prepared for it. It's like they know what we're going to do before we even do it."

"That's because they probably do. They've been watching us since the expo. Ward said it herself—they know us. They've been studying us, our powers, everything."

A heavy silence fell over the group as the weight of his words sank in.

"So what?" Ravi asked, his voice low. "We just give up?"

"No," Jiho said firmly. "We adapt. If they know us that well, then we need to change the game. Do something they can't predict."

Ava raised an eyebrow. "And what does that look like?"

Jiho glanced around the room. His gaze lingered on the small stack of supplies they had left. "I don't know yet. But if we're going to figure it out, we need to be on the same page. No more secrets. No more arguments."

Jordan sighed. "Agreed. We can't afford to be divided. Not now."

Ava added. "We're in this together. No matter what."

Ravi said. "Fine. But we need more than just teamwork. We need answers. And the only person who might have them is Camelia."

Jiho responded. "Then we get her back."

Jordan glanced at him. "How?"

"We find a way to contact her. If she's still on our side, she'll help us. And if she's not..." He paused. "Then we'll deal with that too."

The determination in his voice was enough to silence any further objections. For the first time in days, they felt a spark of unity, a shared purpose. Later that evening, the group sat around the small table. Jiho had sketched out a rough plan, and they were going over the details.

"We'll need to stay off the grid as much as possible," he tapped the map in front of him. "If we're going to contact Camelia, we can't let NOVA trace us."

"Easier said than done," Ravi muttered. "They've probably got drones and surveillance all over the place."

"That's why we're using low-tech methods," he replied. "No phones, no internet. Just good old-fashioned paper and pen."

Jordan raised an eyebrow. "And how do we get a message to her without NOVA intercepting it?"

He looked at Ava. "That's where you come in."

Ava frowned. "Me? What am I supposed to do?"

"Your power," he said. "You can manipulate emotions. If we can get close enough to a NOVA agent, you might be able to influence them to deliver the message for us."

Ava's eyes widened. "That's... risky. What if it doesn't work?"

"Then we'll have a backup plan," he assured her. "But right now, it's our best shot."

Ava bit her lip, then nodded. "Okay. I'll do it."

Ravi asked. "And what about the rest of us? What do we do?"

"We'll need distractions. If NOVA's attention is on us, they're less likely to notice Ava's move."

Jordan smirked. "Now that I can do."

A small grin formed on Ravi's face. "Me too. Let's give them something to chase."

Ava took a deep breath and rolled her shoulders as she processed the plan. "Alright. But I need to know who I'm targeting. If I push the wrong emotions too hard, it could backfire."

Jordan pulled up the stolen NOVA personnel files on his laptop. "We need someone lower on the chain. A field agent, not a scientist or an executive. Someone who's been in the thick of it but isn't completely indoctrinated."

Jiho scanned the list. "What about this guy?" He pointed to a profile—a younger agent named Elias Carter. His record showed recent disciplinary reports for 'hesitation in the field' and 'questioning operational directives.'

Ava arched a brow. "A guy with doubts. That's promising."

Jordan nodded. "If you can make him feel *more* doubt and more conflict, he might be the perfect messenger."

Ravi asked. "So, how do we get to him?"

Jiho's eyes gleamed with mischief. "That's where we come in."

An hour later, the plan was in motion.

Jordan and Ravi positioned themselves near the tree line outside a known NOVA checkpoint, concealed by dense foliage. Jiho crouched beside them and waited for the signal. Ava was further back, keeping out of sight until the right moment.

Jordan pulled out a small EMP device. It was a compact but powerful disruptor he'd built from scavenged parts. He grinned as he adjusted the dial. "Time for a little chaos."

With the press of a button, the device activated and sent out a pulse that scrambled the local surveillance feeds. A moment later, alarms blared from the NOVA outpost.

"Security breach detected. Perimeter compromised."

Just as expected.

Within seconds, agents stormed into view with their weapons drawn as they scanned the area.

Ravi grinned. "Showtime."

He burst from the brush and deliberately making just enough noise to be spotted. "Hey, NOVA! Catch me if you can!"

Two agents immediately broke formation and chased after him.

Jordan smirked as he tapped into their radio frequency with his modified scanner. "Control, we have a visual on unidentified hostiles—engaging now."

Jiho darted in the opposite direction. He tossed a small firecracker-like device toward a security vehicle. It detonated with a harmless but loud pop, sending agents scrambling to assess the 'threat.' With their attention divided, Ava slipped closer to the base to search for Carter.

Inside, Agent Elias Carter was monitoring the security feeds when the static interference hit. He frowned and adjusted his earpiece. "Control, what's going on? I'm losing visuals."

Before he got an answer, Ava stepped into view.

She moved fast, pressing her advantage, her voice soft but insistent. "Elias."

He turned, startled. "Who—?"

Her eyes locked onto his, and she focused her energy. She reached deep into the tangled emotions within him to search for doubt and hesitation. And when she found it, she amplified it.

"You don't have to do this," she whispered. Her voice weaved into his subconscious like a thread of uncertainty. "You already know something isn't right. You feel it."

Carter loosened his grip on his weapon. "I..."

"They're lying to you," Ava stepped closer. "You're just a pawn to them. But you can be more. You can make a choice."

His pulse raced. The conflict inside him grew unbearable and the thoughts collided like crashing waves. Then, finally, his resolve cracked.

"What... what do you want?" he asked.

Ava exhaled in relief. "Deliver a message."

Outside, Ravi and Jiho regrouped with Jordan as the commotion escalated.

"We need to move," Jordan urged. "Ava should be wrapping up any second now."

Ravi glanced at the base. "Hope she got through to him."

Jiho grinned. "If anyone can mess with someone's head, it's her."

Jordan smirked. "Let's just hope she did it in time."

They vanished into the shadows just as the base's floodlights flared to life.

And inside, Agent Carter clutched the small note Ava had slipped into his hand, staring at it with a mixture of fear and determination.

The message was simple.

Camelia, we're coming back for you. Be ready.

Chapter 31

A full month had passed since their last encounter. The group had relocated to a secluded clearing deep in a sprawling forest far away from prying eyes and digital surveillance. A decrepit old barn on the edge of the property served as their new base. It was rundown but private and surrounded by tall trees that provided excellent cover.

The group had spent their days honing their abilities in ways they hadn't thought possible. Every member had grown stronger, more precise, and more confident with their powers. Ravi stood in the clearing with sweat dripping down his face as he focused on a boulder several yards away. His hands glowed faintly as he concentrated to manipulate the earth beneath the rock. With a grunt, he thrust his hands forward, and the boulder rolled smoothly across the ground and rested at his feet.

"Nice," Jordan said approvingly. He leaned against a tree observing Ravi's progress.

"Not bad, right?" he grinned despite his exhaustion.

"Not bad, but can you do it when someone's throwing fireballs at you?"

"You just had to bring that up."

Ava emerged from the barn carrying a jug of water and passed it to him. "You're getting better, though," she said. "A month ago, you couldn't even budge a rock that size."

"True. But we've still got a long way to go."

Nearby, Jiho was setting up a series of small drones he'd constructed using scraps they'd scavenged from an abandoned shed. His focus was sharp as he calibrated their movement patterns.

"How's it coming, Jiho?" Ava asked as she walked over.

"Almost there," he replied without looking up. "I programmed these to simulate enemy movement. They'll dodge, dive, and even try to distract us. If we can hit these, we'll be ready for anything NOVA throws at us."

"Great. Let me know when they're ready to test," Ava said rolling up her sleeves.

Inside the barn, was a makeshift workstation that Jordan set up. His laptop was open and several wires were connected to a small generator. He had taken it upon himself to ensure they had secure communication lines and reliable intel.

"Still no sign of Camelia," Jordan said quietly.

Ava stopped and turned toward him. "It's been a month, Jordan. Do you think she's even still... herself?"

"I don't know. Ward's good at manipulation. If she's gotten into her head, it's going to be hard to bring her back."

Flames flickered around her fingertips. "We have to try. She's one of us."

"She is," Jordan agreed. "That's why we're training. We're going to get her back, no matter what."

By midday, the group gathered in the clearing for their combat drills. Jiho activated his drones, which buzzed into the air like mechanical bees. They darted around the group unpredictably. Their erratic movements forced the teens to stay on their toes.

"Ravi, use the terrain to block their path!" Jiho shouted.

He planted his feet and thrust his hands upward. His movement caused a mound of dirt to rise and intercept one of the drones. It crashed to the ground, sparking slightly.

"Nice!" Jiho said.

Ava stepped forward and locked on another drone. She extended her hand and a small ball of fire shot from her palm. It hit the drone squarely and exploded in a burst of sparks.

"Keep it up!" Jordan encouraged, using his own powers to manipulate the signal patterns of two drones, forcing them to collide mid-air.

"Guys, watch out!" Jiho shouted suddenly as a drone swooped low and headed straight for Ava.

Before she could react, a wall of dirt shot up in front of her and blocked the drone's path. Ravi grinned. "Got your back."

"Thanks," Ava exhaled in relief.

As the sun dipped below the horizon, the group gathered around a small campfire outside the barn. Exhaustion clung to them, but there was also a sense of accomplishment.

"Today was good," Jordan said, poking at the fire with a stick. "We're starting to feel like a real team."

"Yeah, but we still haven't come up with a solid plan," Jiho pointed out. "We can't just train forever. At some point, we have to act."

"We're getting there," Jordan said. "We're stronger now than we were a month ago. That's progress."

Ava stared into the flames, her expression pensive. "Do you think Camelia knows we're coming for her?"

"I hope so," Ravi said. "Because if she doesn't, this is going to be a huge surprise."

Jiho chuckled. "Understatement of the year."

As the fire died down, Jordan stood and dusted off his hands. "Get some rest. Tomorrow, we start working on the facility plans. If we're going to take on NOVA, we need to know exactly what we're walking into."

The group nodded, their expressions resolute. Despite the challenges ahead, they were finally united in their purpose. As they turned in for the night, the barn fell silent except for the occasional rustle of leaves in the wind. The teens knew the road ahead wouldn't be easy, but they were ready to face it together.

Jordan was the first to wake, sitting up on his makeshift bedroll. The barn was still dim, but the soft rays of sunlight filtering through the cracks in the wooden slats were enough to guide him. He rubbed his eyes and walked towards his laptop.

"Still no signal out here," he muttered to himself, typing rapidly. He wasn't looking for a connection, though. Nexus allowed him to bypass traditional networks. It also created his own pathways through digital spaces. It was his way of keeping tabs on NOVA without exposing their location.

Ava entered the barn carrying a basket of wild berries she'd found nearby. "Good morning," she said, setting the basket down on the center table. "We're running low on supplies. We'll need to make another trip soon."

"Great," Jiho said sarcastically from his corner, where he was fiddling with his latest drone prototype. "Another hike while hoping we don't run into a patrol or surveillance?"

"Unless you've invented a way to grow food out of thin air, it's our best option," Ava replied.

Jordan raised a hand without looking up. "Actually, I might have an idea for that."

"Really?" Ava raised an eyebrow.

"Not food specifically," he clarified, "but I've been working on a way to mask our presence when we need to move. A kind of digital camouflage. If it works, we could slip in and out of town without triggering any of NOVA's systems."

"That would be helpful," Ravi yawned as he joined the group. "Last time we went out, I swear we were seconds away from being caught."

Ravi leaned against the wall. "We have to do something. We can't let them get to our families, and we can't leave Camelia in there."

"But what can we do?" Ava asked. "We've been training for a month, and we're still no closer to figuring out how to take down an entire organization."

Jordan looked up from his laptop. "We don't need to take down the whole organization. We just need to disrupt them enough to get her out and make it impossible for them to track us."

"How do you suggest we do that?" Jiho asked skeptically.

"I've been working on something," he said. "If we can get close enough to one of their facilities, I can plant a virus in their system. It'll take out their tracking software and erase any data they have on us."

"That's risky," Ravi said. "If you're caught—"

"I won't be caught," he interrupted. "I know their systems. I can do this."

Ava crossed her arms. "You *think* you can do this. But what if something goes wrong? What if they catch on before you finish?"

"That's why I won't be going in alone."

Silence fell over the group. Jiho narrowed his eyes. "Who else is going?"

Jordan exhaled. "I need someone to cover me while I work. Someone fast, someone who can handle trouble if it comes up." His eyes flicked to Ravi.

Ravi smirked. "I like where this is going."

Ava groaned. "Oh, come *on*."

"You need a distraction? I'm your guy."

Jordan nodded. "Exactly. If NOVA catches wind of us, you lead them on a chase and keep them occupied while I finish planting the virus."

Jiho still looked skeptical. "And what about the rest of us?"

Jordan tapped a key on his laptop and pulled up a map of the facility. "Jiho, you'll be on over watch. We need eyes on everything—security movements, patrols, anything unexpected. If things go south, you call it in."

Ava asked, 'And what about me?"

"If things *really* go wrong, I need you to do what you do best."

Ava's brows furrowed. "Which is?"

"Get inside their heads."

Realization dawned on her, and she let out a sharp breath. "You want me to influence them. Again?"

"Only if we have no other choice."

"Fine."

Jiho rubbed the back of his head. "I hate this plan."

Ravi grinned. "That's how you know it's good."

Jordan ignored them. "We move tomorrow night. Be ready."

The group exchanged glances, the weight of the plan settling over them like a storm cloud. Ava folded her arms. "We're sure about this?"

"No, But we don't have time to second-guess."

"I'll do what I have to. But if this goes south, we'll be in deeper than ever."

"Then we make sure it doesn't."

Silence stretched between them, thick with tension. Finally, Ravi clapped his hands together. "Well, since we might all die tomorrow, I'm calling dibs on the last energy bar."

Jiho rolled his eyes, but the corner of his mouth twitched. "Let's just get some rest. Tomorrow, everything changes."

No one argued. They all knew the truth—there was no turning back now.

Chapter 32

Outside the NOVA facility, the friends crouched behind a work van in the parking lot. Jiho adjusted a new device that was strapped to his arm. It was a modified version of his VR projection system. Standing next to him was Ravi, who gripped the straps of his backpack nervously. Ava peered over the edge of the van. "No sign of patrols yet," she whispered. "Jordan, you sure the virus will work?"

He didn't look up from his tablet. "It'll work. Once I'm in their system, they won't be able to track us, and we'll have an opening to find Camelia."

Jiho nodded. "Let's just hope she's still on our side."

Ava shot him a glare but said nothing. The unspoken doubt lingered in the group's minds. With Jordan's signal, the group moved swiftly and silently toward the facility's rear entrance. Jiho created a shimmering mirage around them which made them appear as a little more than a ripple in the air.

The door was guarded, but Ravi's power came into play. Concentrating, he lifted a small rock and hurled it into the distance. The guards raised their weapons at the sound and the friends slipped inside unnoticed. The interior was sterile and cold. Long halls gleamed with white walls and fluorescent lights. Ava led the way, her senses heightened as she scanned for threats. Jordan kept an eye on his tablet, as he guided them toward the central server room.

"We're getting close," he whispered. "Just a few more turns."

As they rounded the corner, the group froze. Standing in the middle of the hallway, flanked by two NOVA agents, was Camelia. She stepped forward with an unreadable expression. "You shouldn't have come," she said with regret.

"Camelia," Ava took a cautious step forward, "we're here to rescue you. We can still get out of this together."

"You don't understand. I made my choice. Staying here is the only way to protect all of you."

"That's not true," Jiho snapped. "They're using you. And now you're standing here defending them?"

The agents raised their weapons, but she held up a hand to stop them. "I don't want anyone to get hurt," she said. "Please, just leave."

"We're not leaving without you," Ravi said firmly.

The standoff was broken by the sound of boots echoing down the hallway. More agents were approaching. Ava acted first. She lunged forward and grabbed her friend's arm. "You're coming with us, whether you like it or not!"

Camelia pulled free. A gust of wind erupted from her hands sending Ava stumbling backward. "I'm not going anywhere!"

"Be careful. According to the readouts, NOVA agents have Neural Disruptor Rifles," Jordan said.

"Translate for the non tech people," Ravi said.

"It means one hit from it can emit a pulse that targets the brain cause dizziness, disorientation, and power suppression."

Jiho cursed under his breath. "Great. As if this wasn't bad enough."

Ravi stated, "In other words, don't get hit. Got it."

The hallway erupted into chaos. The agents opened fire with but Jiho's projections distorted their aim and created a flurry of false images. Ravi hurled debris at the agents, while Jordan frantically worked to maintain their digital cover. Camelia faced off against Ava with their powers clashing. Ava's ability to manipulate emotions created bursts of steam as it met Camelia's wind.

"You don't have to fight us!" She shouted.

"I do if you won't leave!" Camelia countered.

The fight raged on, but the friends were outnumbered and outmatched. Jiho's projections began to falter, and Ravi's energy was waning.

Jordan suddenly shouted, "I'm in! I've planted the virus!"

Lights flickered, and alarms blared as the facility's systems began to shut down. The agents hesitated as their comms filled with static.

"Now's our chance!" Jiho yelled. "Cami, come with us!"

She hesitated. She was torn between loyalty to her friends and the arrangement she'd made with Director Ward.

"Camelia!" Ava shouted. "We need you! Please!"

The conflict in her eyes was clear, but before she could decide, a cold, authoritative voice echoed down the hallway. Director Ward strode into view with her commanding presence. The remaining agents immediately fell back behind her.

"Well, this is quite the reunion," she said with disdain. "And here I thought you'd have more sense than to come here."

Ward turned her gaze to Camelia. "Remember, you came here willingly. To protect them. And look at what they've done. They've endangered themselves, their families, and the public."

Camelia's fists clenched at her sides.

"You don't have to listen to her!" Jiho shouted. "She's manipulating you!"

Ward's expression didn't falter. "Camelia, you know what's at stake. If you walk away now, everything you've sacrificed will be for nothing."

The friends exchanged desperate glances. They couldn't win this fight, not with Ward here.

"Jordan," Ava whispered, "can you do anything to buy us time?"

Jordan nodded and his fingers flew over the keys. A moment later, the fire suppression system activated and released a thick cloud of white mist into the hallway.

"Run!" Ava shouted.

The group retreated, Jiho using his VR device to cover their escape. Camelia stood frozen, torn between following her friends and staying behind.

"Camelia!" Ravi called. "Come on!"

But she didn't move. The friends made it out of the facility. Their breaths were ragged as they sprinted into the woods. They didn't stop until they were certain they weren't being followed. Ava leaned against a tree. "We almost had her."

"She's still in there," Jiho said bitterly. "And now Ward knows we're not giving up."

Jordan looked up from his tablet. "We've bought ourselves some time, but it's not going to last. We need a new plan."

Ravi glanced back toward the facility in the distance. "And we need to figure out how to bring Camelia back."

The friends regrouped deep in the forest, their breaths fogging in the cold air. The adrenaline of their escape had faded, leaving them with a grim silence that pressed heavily on their shoulders. The night was quiet except for the distant hums of the facility's alarms fading into the distance. Ava paced the small clearing. "We were so close. So close!" she muttered and kicked a rock into the underbrush.

Jordan sat cross-legged on a log with his tablet. His fingers trembled as they tapped against the casing, his eyes locked on the blank screen. "Ward knows our every move now," he said bitterly. "The virus was supposed to cripple their systems, but it barely gave us five minutes."

Jiho sat apart from the others. He hadn't spoken since they fled. Ravi crouched down next to the gear-stuffed backpack he always carried.

"You okay?" Ravi asked softly.

He didn't look up. "No," he admitted. "Camelia's stuck in there. And I couldn't do anything to stop it."

"You didn't fail her," Ravi said. "She made a choice. We just need to figure out how to bring her back."

"What if she doesn't want to come back?".

"We need to think this through," Ava said as she tried to pull the group together. She sat down on a fallen log and motioned for the others to join her. "We've been reacting to NOVA this whole time. We need to start planning ahead."

"Planning what?" he asked with frustration. "They have Camelia. They have more tech, more resources, and a head start. How are we supposed to fight that?"

Jordan closed his tablet. "Maybe it's not about fighting them directly. We need to play smarter. Ward isn't just trying to stop us; she's trying to control the narrative. She said we're putting people at risk, but what has NOVA done that's any better?"

Ava added. "She's using Camelia as a shield against us. We need to show her the truth about Ward and NOVA. Something that makes her want to come back to us."

Ravi's eyes lit up. "We could find evidence. Something NOVA doesn't want the world to see. If Camelia sees what they're hiding, she might change her mind."

Jiho looked skeptical but intrigued. "And where do we even start looking for evidence? We barely made it out of the facility tonight."

Jordan cleared his throat. "There's one way we might be able to find out what NOVA is hiding."

The others turned to him expectantly.

"I still have partial access to their systems," he continued. "The virus didn't wipe everything, but it gave me a backdoor. I've been combing through encrypted files, and there's something called Project Sentinel. It's marked as classified, even within NOVA. Whatever it is, it's big enough to keep under wraps."

"Do you think it could help us?" Ava asked.

Jordan shrugged. "It's a lead. If we can find out what Project Sentinel is, it might give us the leverage we need to get Camelia back."

Jiho hesitated. "And how do we figure that out without getting caught?"

"We'll need to go back," Jordan said reluctantly. "Not to the facility, but somewhere we can intercept NOVA's data. They're bound to have a satellite office or backup server nearby. I can tap into it remotely."

The group exchanged uncertain glances. The idea of going anywhere near NOVA again was daunting, but the alternative—losing Camelia forever—was worse.

"We'll do it," Ava said firmly, her voice leaving no room for argument. "But we have to be smart. No mistakes this time."

Ravi raised a hand. "Can I just say that sneaking into a backup server sounds slightly less terrifying than breaking into the main facility?"

Ava smirked. "Only slightly."

Jiho finally stood, brushing leaves off his jeans. "If we're doing this, we need to map out every step. We can't just wing it like before."

Jordan nodded. "Agreed. Give me the night to pinpoint the server location. By morning, we'll have a plan."

The group began to settle down for the night in their makeshift camp tucked deep in the woods. Jordan worked quietly on his tablet while Ravi and Jiho gathered wood for a fire. Ava kept watch and scanned the dark forest for any sign of movement.

As the fire crackled to life, Ravi contemplated, "Do you think she misses us?" he asked quietly.

"Who, Camelia?" Ava replied.

Ravi nodded. "She didn't want us to get hurt. That's why she stayed with them. But I wonder if she regrets it now."

Ava's gaze softened. "I think she does. And I think she's waiting for us to show her that she's not alone in this."

Jiho stared into the flames. "Then we better not let her down."

Inside the sterile walls of NOVA's facility, Camelia replayed the night's events in her mind. Seeing her friends again and hearing Ava's pleas brought back some bittersweet memories. She felt conflicted.

They've been a tight knit group since elementary but ever since they've been exposed, it wasn't the same.

Only Jiho took the time to really listen to her. But if they were close, he should have spoken up for her. Especially when he saw the others ignoring her like she was a fifth wheel. There was a knock and an immediate hiss as the door opened. Director Ward entered the room with an unreadable expression..

"They've retreated for now," Ward said calmly. "But they'll be back."

Camelia didn't respond, her gaze fixed on the floor.

Ward stepped closer and softened her tone. "You made the right choice. Remember why you're here. You came to protect them—and yourself. Your friends don't understand the risks they're taking. They're endangering themselves, their families, and countless others. But you? You're being mature about this."

Camelia looked up with doubt. "I don't know if I did the right thing," she admitted.

Ward's lips curved into a faint smile. "You did. Trust me. In time, they'll see that too."

Back in the forest, the friends huddled together around the fire. The next step was clear: uncover the truth about NOVA, rescue Camelia, and expose the lies they'd been fed. As the flames flickered and the night grew colder, Ava glanced at her friends, her voice steady. "No matter what happens, we stick together. Agreed?"

The others nodded, their expressions determined.

"Agreed," Jiho said firmly.

Chapter 33

The forest was eerily quiet as the group trudged through the underbrush. It had been two days since the failed attempt to infiltrate NOVA's facility and the scars of that failure weighed heavily on them all. Camelia was still there and every day they spent in hiding felt like a reminder of their helplessness.

"Jordan, how much farther?" Ava brushed a branch out of her path.

He glanced at the map displayed on his phone. "Not far. There's an abandoned ranger station up ahead. Should give us some cover for the night."

"Better than sleeping in the mud," Ravi muttered as he stepped over a fallen log.

Jiho was at the rear lost in thought. He was determined to get Camelia out no matter how long it takes. As they crested a hill, the ranger station came into view. It was a small weathered building with boarded-up windows and a rusting metal roof. The group paused at the edge of the clearing. Each one was scanning the area for signs of movement.

"Clear," Ava said as she cautiously stepped forward.

The group made their way to the station and Jordan began working to bypass the old lock on the door. "This place looks like it hasn't been used in decades," he remarked as he fiddled with the tumblers.

"Let's hope it's still sturdy," Jiho said.

The lock finally clicked and the door creaked open. The interior was dusty but intact. It only had a few pieces of broken furniture scattered across the floor. The group filed in and Ravi shut the door behind them. Hours later after setting up a small camp inside the station they huddled around a dim lantern. Jordan's laptop whirred softly as he sifted through the remnants of NOVA's files.

"There's still nothing concrete on Project Sentinel," he said frustrated. "NOVA's encryptions are tougher than anything I've seen before."

"We'll figure it out," Ava said reassuringly. "We have to."

Suddenly, there was a knock at the door that froze the group in place.

"Who's there?" Ava called out, her fingers tightening at her sides, ready to manipulate the emotions of whoever approached.

No answer came. Only another knock. Jiho reached for his headset so he could prepare to deploy an illusion if needed. Jordan moved cautiously to the window and peeked through a crack in the boards. His eyes widened. "There's someone out there," he whispered.

"Friend or foe?" Ravi asked tensely.

"No idea," Jordan replied.

Ava nodded to Jiho, who activated his device. The air shimmered faintly as an illusion of an empty room covered their group. Then, she cautiously opened the door a crack. A figure stood just outside. A young woman in her early twenties. She had sharp features, dark brown hair, and an air of confidence that immediately put them on edge. She raised his hands in mock surrender.

"Relax," she said. "I'm not here to fight."

Jiho narrowed his eyes. "Then why are you sneaking around?"

The newcomer smirked. "I was looking for you. And I found you. My name's Lena"

Jordan glanced at the others before standing up. "Found us? How?"

She shrugged. "I have my ways."

Ravi crossed his arms. "Yeah? And why should we trust you?"

She stepped closer. "Because I can help you. I know about NOVA. And I know that your friend is there."

Jordan spoke. "Okay. Say we believe you. Why would you help us?"

"Because I know what NOVA is capable of. I've seen what they do to people like you. They experiment. They manipulate. And when they can't control you, they eliminate you."

Ava clenched her jaw. "How do you know all this?"

"Because they tried to recruit me once. When I said no, they decided I was a liability."

Jiho's eyes flickered with curiosity. "And what exactly can you do?"

"Something that might be useful to you. I can assess threats and risks before they happen. My reflexes are quick and I can do this." She raised her hand and snapped her fingers.

Ava gasped. A strange sensation washed over her, like an invisible weight pressing against her chest. The warmth of her abilities—the constant hum of emotions around her—vanished. She stumbled back and gripped her head.

"My powers—"

"They're gone," Jiho whispered.

Lena dropped her hand, and suddenly, the sensation returned. Ava sucked in a sharp breath as her abilities rushed back like a flood.

"What the hell was that?" Ravi demanded.

"I can neutralize powers. Temporarily."

Jordan exchanged looks with the others. "You mean... you could stop enhanced people?"

"If I get close enough, yeah."

Jiho eyed him warily. "That's a useful ability. But that doesn't mean we can trust you."

"Look, I get it. You don't know me. And I don't expect you to just believe everything I say. But think about it—NOVA has more resources, more firepower, and people like your friend who are willing to fight for them. You need someone like me on your side."

Jiho exclaimed. "She is NOT with them! She is only there until we rescue her!"

"Well if not her, then there are others who are on their side."

Ava still looked shaken from the experience. "If what you're saying is true, you could be our best chance at stopping them."

Ravi still skeptical. "Or she could be leading us into a trap."

"If I wanted to turn you in, I would've done it already."

Jordan glanced at Jiho. "Thoughts?"

"We take precautions. But I say we hear her out." he responded while staring at Lena.

"So, what's your angle?" Jordan asked. "Why help us?"

"No angle. NOVA needs to be stopped," Lena said firmly. "And you're the best chance I've seen to make that happen. You have abilities, yes, but more importantly, you have each other. NOVA can't predict or control that.

Jiho exchanged a glance with Ava, who was deep in thought. "You make it sound like we're some kind of resistance group," she said.

"Because you are. Whether you like it or not, NOVA sees you as a threat. That means they won't stop until they control you—or eliminate you."

Jordan tensed up at her words. "So what? We just go on the run? Spend the rest of our lives hiding?"

"No," Lena said. "You fight back. But you don't do it recklessly."

Ravi let out a low whistle. "Great. So we're supposed to take on some secret organization with nothing but our barely functioning powers?"

"You have more than you think," she countered. "And if you use them strategically, you might stand a chance."

Ava frowned. "You're assuming we want to fight at all."

"You don't have a choice. NOVA won't let you walk away from this."

"If we're going after NOVA," Jiho said, "we need to be smarter than them. That means finding their weaknesses."

Jordan opened his laptop. "We were working on that before we got cut off. We need to find out what 'Project Sentinel' is."

"Project Sentinel?"

"You know about it?" Jiho asked.

"Yeah. And if that's what they're working on, we don't have much time."

Ava leaned forward. "Why? What is it?"

"It's a failsafe. A way for them to control—or eliminate—anyone with abilities if they decide we're too dangerous."

Ravi responded. "So, in other words... we have to stop it."

"Before it's too late."

Lena's revelation about Project Sentinel had shaken them. It wasn't just about escaping anymore—it was about stopping whatever NOVA had planned before it was too late.

Jordan responded. "If we're gonna figure out what Sentinel is, we need access to their systems again."

Jiho frowned. "Didn't they lock you out last time?"

"Yeah. But I've been working on a backdoor ever since."

Lena raised a brow. "How?"

Jordan tapped a few keys to bring up lines of code. "When I was in NOVA's system before, I left behind a hidden program. It's been lying dormant, waiting for me to activate it. If it still works, we'll have access to their internal files."

Ava leaned in. "And if it doesn't?"

"Then they'll know exactly where we are."

Silence.

Ravi groaned. "Man, why is it always life or death with us?"

Lena folded her arms. "Risky. But we don't have a choice."

Jordan nodded. "Then let's do it."

The air felt heavier as Jordan typed furiously, his fingers moving with precision. Everyone else watched, tension thick in the air.

"Connecting... bypassing security... come on, come on," he muttered.

Jiho glanced at the screen. "Any luck?"

"I'm in."

Ava let out a relieved breath. "That was fast."

"Please, this is me we're talking about." His fingers moved even faster. "Okay, I'm accessing the secure files. Searching for Project Sentinel..."

A progress bar appeared, crawling forward agonizingly slow.

Lena stood behind Jordan. "We need to be quick. The longer we stay connected, the more likely they'll notice."

"I know, I know—wait. Got it."

He pulled up a series of encrypted files. Jiho whistled low. "That's a lot of data."

Jordan started to decrypt the files, but before he could get far, an alert flashed across the screen.

Unauthorized access detected. Trace in progress.

Jordan's heart pounded. "Crap. They know."

Ava's eyes widened. "Can you shut it down?"

"I can try, but—" Jordan froze. A new message popped up.

Too late. We see you.

Then the laptop screen went black.

Ravi was the first to react. "Oh, hell no. That's some horror movie stuff right there."

Lena's face darkened. "They know where we are."

Jordan cursed under his breath. "I should've been faster."

Ava stood up. "We need to move. Now."

Chapter 34

Jiho grabbed his bag. "Where do we go? We've been running out of places to hide."

Lena's jaw tightened. "I know somewhere. But we have to go now."

A low hum filled the air.

Ava's head snapped up. "Do you hear that?"

A red light flickered in the distance, steadily growing brighter.

Jordan's stomach dropped. "Drones."

Lena turned sharply. "Run."

They didn't hesitate. They grabbed their bags and bolted into the trees, the whir of the drones getting louder behind them.

A mechanical voice echoed from the sky.

"You are in possession of classified information. Surrender immediately."

Ravi cursed. "Yeah, that's not happening!"

A spotlight cut through the darkness and swept over the trees.

Lena turned to Jiho. "You need to cover our escape."

Jiho's breath came fast as he pushed himself to run faster. The drone's red spotlight flickered through the trees which illuminated their fleeing figures. His mind raced—he had seconds to act before they were caught.

Lena grabbed his arm. "Jiho, now!"

Jiho didn't need more prompting. He skidded to a halt, turned sharply, and raised his hands. In an instant, the dense trees around them shifted and warped into thick, impenetrable walls of static and shadow. The drones' lights flickered and struggled to process what was real and what wasn't. The whirring grew erratic as the machines processors were unable to distinguish Jiho's illusion from reality.

"Keep going!" Jiho gritted out, beads of sweat forming on his forehead. His energy drained quickly, but he pushed himself to hold the illusion steady.

Jordan grabbed his wrist, and practically dragged him forward. "Come on!"

The group sprinted deeper into the forest. Behind them, the drones hovered in confusion. Their mechanical voices glitched.

"*Targets—error—visual inconsistency detected—recalibrating.*"

Ava glanced back. "It's working!"

Lena didn't slow down. "Not for long. Keep moving."

The forest grew darker, thicker, and more tangled. The further they ran, the harder it became to navigate. Branches clawed at their clothes and roots threatened to trip them.

Ravi cursed. "Lena, where the hell are we going?"

She didn't answer immediately as she scanned ahead. Then she pointed. "There. Up ahead."

Through the gaps in the trees, the faint outline of an old, abandoned watchtower came into view. Its wooden frame looked unstable, but it was tall enough to give them an advantage.

Jordan gave her a skeptical look. "That thing looks like it's one good breeze away from collapsing."

She didn't slow down. "You got a better idea?"

Jordan sighed. "Fair point."

They reached the base of the tower just as the drones recalibrated behind them. The mechanical whirring grew louder.

"*Targets reacquired. Engaging pursuit.*"

"Up, up, up!" She barked.

Ava scrambled up the ladder, followed by Ravi and Jiho. Jordan hesitated for a second before looking at Jiho. "You got enough juice left for another trick?"

Jiho, pale and sweating, shook his head. "I—I don't think so."

Jordan cursed and climbed up after the others.

Lena was already at the top scanning the area below. "We can't stay here long."

Ava crouched beside her. "Then why did we climb up here?"

She didn't take her eyes off the trees. "Because I needed to see where we go next."

Below them, the drones swept across the forest and searched for movement. Jiho sat against the wooden railing as he tried to catch his breath. "They're not going to stop."

She clenched her fists. "Neither are we."

Jordan pulled out his tablet. The interface flickered weakly. He grimaced. "I can try to jam their signal, but with how advanced they are, I don't know if it'll hold."

Ravi exhaled sharply. "We're backed into a corner here, guys."

Ava looked at Lena. "What's the plan?"

She narrowed her eyes at the drones circling below. "We need to get out of here, fast. And I think I know how." She turned to Jiho. "How real can you make an illusion?"

"Depends on what you need."

She pointed to a clearing past the trees. "Make it look like we jumped."

Jiho swallowed hard, his energy nearly drained. But he nodded. He closed his eyes and focused.

Below them, a perfect illusion of their group leaping from the watchtower played out in real-time. The drones instantly reacted.

"*Targets detected—intercepting.*"

The machines shot forward and followed the illusion.

Lena didn't waste time. "Go. Now."

They hurried down the opposite side of the tower and moved quickly but carefully. The moment their feet hit the ground, they bolted in the opposite direction of the illusion.

Jiho stumbled from exhaustion. Ava caught his arm. "I got you."

They pushed forward, adrenaline keeping them moving. The sound of the drones faded into the distance as they continued running, deeper into the unknown. The forest finally thinned out as the group pushed forward. Their legs ached and their lungs burned from exertion. They had no idea how far they had run, but it was far enough that the whir of the drones had finally disappeared.

Lena signaled for them to stop near a rocky outcrop. "We rest here."

Jiho practically collapsed onto a flat boulder, his hands trembling from exhaustion. Ava crouched next to him, her eyes filled with concern. "You okay?"

Jiho nodded weakly. "I just... I just need a minute. Or thirty."

Ravi wiped sweat from his brow. "That was too close."

Jordan scanned their surroundings. "We keep running like this, and we'll get caught. We need a real plan."

Jiho exhaled between breaths. "We had a plan. Get in, find Camelia, and get out." His jaw tightened. "But that didn't work out, did it?"

A tense silence followed.

Ava broke it first. "She made her choice."

"You don't know that."

Jordan shook his head. "We all saw the facility. It wasn't like she was locked up. She walked in there."

Ravi sighed. "And Director Ward said they only let us leave because of an 'arrangement' with her. We can't pretend that doesn't mean something."

"So what? We just leave her?"

Ava hesitated. "I don't know. But we can't just keep running into danger without thinking."

Lena finally spoke. "You're no good to her if you get caught."

Jiho looked away. He hated this—hated standing still while one of their own was trapped in that place.

Jordan broke the silence. "We need to figure out what they want."

Ravi scoffed. "Isn't it obvious? Control. They want to use us."

"Maybe. But why haven't they just taken us? Why not grab our families?"

Ava's face darkened. "They talked about it. We overheard Ward saying they were considering taking our parents to make us surrender."

Lena spoke up. "Exactly. They want you to come in on your own."

Jordan responded. "Which means they need us willingly." He looked at Jiho. "Think you can dig up anything on them?"

"If I can get near a signal, maybe. But their systems are high security. My tech abilities aren't like yours, Jordan. I can manipulate digital environments, not hack into locked networks."

"Damn it."

Ava looked at them both. "Then we need to find someone who can."

The idea hung in the air.

Ravi frowned. "You mean, like, another powered person?"

Ava nodded slowly. "We can't be the only ones out there. What if there's someone else who escaped from NOVA before?"

"If there is, we need to find them before NOVA does."

Jiho pushed himself up. "Then we better start looking."

Chapter 35

The next morning, the group was already on the move before the sun had fully risen. The night had been restless—no one slept for more than an hour at a time, jolting awake at the slightest sound. Their bodies ached and their minds were clouded with exhaustion, but there was no time to stop.

Lena led the way as they pushed through the dense underbrush with Ravi at her side. Ava, Jiho, and Jordan followed closely behind, being sure to keep their steps careful and quiet. The air was thick with tension, but no one spoke about it. They needed a new plan. They needed answers. They needed someone who knew more about NOVA than they did.

But where did they even start?

Jordan, keeping his voice low, finally broke the silence. "Okay, so let's assume there are other powered people out there. How do we even find them?"

Jiho adjusted his glasses. "We need to think like NOVA. If they've been tracking us, they've probably tracked others. They'd have records somewhere."

Ava gave him a pointed look. "And how do we access those?"

Jordan answered. "I need a system to connect to. Something that can give me a backdoor into their network."

Jiho sighed. "So, what? We just waltz into a library and use a public computer?"

Lena frowned. "That's risky."

Jordan shook his head. "No, but if we can find an abandoned place with an old internet connection, I might be able to use it to piggyback into something useful."

Ravi smirked. "So, what you're saying is... we need to find some creepy, run-down place that hasn't been used in years?"

Ava crossed her arms. "Well, lucky for us, we're in the middle of nowhere. Shouldn't be too hard."

After an hour of walking, they stumbled upon a rusted old sign that read Evergreen Motel – Vacancy. It was a lie, considering the place looked like it hadn't seen guests in a decade. The windows were cracked, the neon sign was missing several letters, and ivy had begun to reclaim the building.

Lena glanced at Jordan. "Think this'll work?"

"It might. If there's still a working router inside, even an old one, I might be able to tap into it."

Ravi grinned. "Well, let's break in, shall we?"

Lena shot him a look. "Let's not call it breaking in."

Jordan shrugged. "Call it whatever you want, as long as we get inside."

They moved toward the entrance and tested the door. Locked. Lena gave Ravi a nod. With a smirk, he flexed his fingers, then applied just enough force to the door handle. With a soft snap, the rusted lock gave way.

"After you," he said with a dramatic bow.

Lena rolled her eyes but stepped in first. The air inside was stale and filled with dust and decay. The lobby was a mess—old newspapers and broken furniture scattered the floor, and the front desk was covered in a thick layer of grime.

"Charming," Ava muttered.

Jordan ignored the mess. He was looking for anything useful. "The office," he said. "That's where the router would be."

They moved cautiously through the hallway, the floor creaking beneath their weight. Jiho pushed open a door labeled Manager's Office and immediately started searching.

Ava peered over his shoulder. "Find anything?"

"Old modem. Still plugged in. If there's even a weak signal, I can work with it."

"Get to it, then. Time's ticking."

Jordan sat down and powered up his tablet, his fingers moving quickly as he connected to the dusty old device. He worked in silence for a few moments before his expression changed.

Lena leaned in. "What?"

"Someone's already been here."

Ava's stomach twisted. "What do you mean?"

He pointed to the screen. "Someone else accessed this network recently. And whoever they were, they weren't just passing through."

Jiho frowned. "So, what? Another runaway? A hacker?"

Jordan hesitated, then pulled up the last known login credentials. The name that popped up made his blood run cold.

J. Cross

Ava's breath caught. "Wait. Agent Cross? He was here?"

Lena stiffened. "Are you sure?"

"This was accessed just days ago. He left something here."

Ravi leaned closer. "Can you see what he was doing?"

Jordan's fingers flew across the keyboard, bypassing weak firewalls and old security settings. After a few tense minutes, he found a single encrypted file hidden within the system. He cracked the encryption within seconds. A single document opened that contained a list of names.

Jiho's eyes widened. "It's a record of past experiments."

Lena leaned in. "Experiments?"

Jordan scrolled through the names. "These... these are people who had abilities. People who were tested on by NOVA."

"So they've been doing this for years."

Ava swallowed hard. "Is Camelia's name on there?"

"No. She must not be in their records yet."

Jiho sounded optimistic. "That means she still has time."

Ravi's jaw tightened. "And if we don't do something, she won't."

Jordan pointed at the screen. "We have names now. We have something to go on. That means we find one of these people before NOVA does."

Lena nodded. "Agreed." She turned to Jordan. "Can you trace where any of them are?"

"Maybe. Some names have addresses attached. But if these people went into hiding, they won't be easy to track."

Jiho crossed his arms. "Neither are we."

Ava glanced toward the entrance. "Then let's move before NOVA figures out we were here."

Jordan quickly copied the data to his tablet, then powered everything down. As they slipped out of the motel, Lena glanced back one last time. Agent Cross had been here. Had he left this information for them? Or was this another one of NOVA's traps?

The group moved quickly, putting as much distance between themselves and the abandoned motel as possible. Each of them processed what they had just discovered. NOVA had been experimenting on people for years. Not only that but there were others like them—people who had powers, who had been hunted, tested on, maybe even... erased. They had names now. Real people who had been through this before. People who might have answers.

"So, what's the plan? We have names, but how do we even know where to start?"

Jordan adjusted his backpack. "Some of the names had locations attached, but most of them are old. If they were smart, they moved."

Jiho frowned. "And if they weren't smart?"

Lena sighed. "Then NOVA already has them."

Silence fell over the group as the reality of their situation set in. They needed to move fast. Ravi, walking a few steps behind, spoke up. "Okay, but let's be real. Even if we do find one of these people, what makes you think they'll want to help us? They've been running just like we are."

Lena stopped and turned to face him. "Because they don't have a choice. If they're still out there, that means they've survived this long. They know how NOVA operates, and if we don't stop them, we'll end up just like everyone else on that list."

Ravi held up his hands. "Hey, I'm just saying, we should be careful who we trust."

Lena nodded. "Agreed. Which is why we're not all going."

Ava blinked. "What?"

She turned to Jordan. "How many addresses looked recent?"

He pulled out his tablet and scrolled through the list. "Three. One of them is just outside this city."

"Then we split up. Two of us check out the lead, the rest stay here in case we need backup."

Ava immediately shook her head. "No way. We're not splitting up."

"We can't all go. We'll draw too much attention."

"Then who's going?"

Lena glanced between them. "I'll go. Jordan, you're coming with me."

"I can track movement patterns on the way. If they relocated, I might be able to tell."

Ava crossed her arms. "And what do the rest of us do? Sit here and wait?"

Lena met her eyes. "You stay hidden. If something goes wrong, we need a fallback plan. Someone needs to be ready in case we don't come back."

Ava clenched her jaw but didn't argue.

Ravi sighed. "Fine. But if you guys aren't back in a few hours, we're coming after you."

"Fair."

"Be careful."

Chapter 36

The address led them to a small neighborhood on the outskirts of town. It was the kind of place where everyone knew each other and where a stranger walking down the street would stand out. Lena kept her head down as she and Jordan approached the house. It was a small, one-story, with a porch swing that creaked slightly in the breeze.

Jordan checked his tablet. "This is the place."

"Alright. Stay close."

They approached the front door, and she knocked three times. Silence.

"Maybe they're not home."

She knocked again, louder this time. Still nothing. She glanced at him before reaching for the doorknob— The door swung open before she could touch it. A woman stood in the doorway and stared at them both. She looked to be in her mid-30s with her dark hair tied back.

"Who are you?" she asked, her voice low and cautious.

Lena swallowed. "We're looking for someone."

The woman narrowed her eyes. "You've got the wrong house."

Jordan stepped forward. "Please. We know about NOVA. We just need to talk."

The woman stiffened at the mention of the name, her grip tightening on the doorframe. Lena noticed the way her muscles tensed—like she was ready to bolt. Before she could say anything else, the woman moved fast.

She grabbed Jordan's wrist and twisted it sharply. He yelped as he tried to pull away, but the woman was stronger than she looked. Lena reacted instantly. She stepped forward to intervene— And then suddenly, the world shifted. The front yard blurred and warped like a heatwave. Lena felt her legs go weak and her mind was clouded as if she were falling into a dream.

Then, just as quickly, the sensation disappeared. She stumbled back to catch her breath. Jordan gasped and shook his head as if clearing it. The woman released him. "Who sent you?"

Lena straightened. "No one. We need information on NOVA."

The woman studied them both for a long moment.

Then, finally, she exhaled and stepped aside. "Come in."

Lena and Jiho exchanged a look before stepping inside.

The living room was small but tidy. A few photos lined the shelves, but nothing personal—no family pictures, no sentimental keepsakes. The woman sat in a chair across from them and watched closely. "You said you know about NOVA. What did they do to you?"

Lena pointed to Jordan. "He's trying to get one of his friends out of their facility. We need information on how to shut them down."

She nodded slowly. "You have abilities."

"So do you."

She didn't deny it.

Lena leaned forward. "Please. We need to know what we're up against. How long have they been doing this?"

The woman sighed. "Long enough."

"And the others? The people on the list?"

The woman's gaze darkened. "Most of them are gone."

Jordan's stomach twisted. "Gone?"

"NOVA doesn't like loose ends."

A heavy silence filled the room. Lena asked. "Then why are you still here?"

The woman exhaled. "Because I learned how to stay hidden. And because I made a deal."

"A deal?"

She looked at them. "I gave them something they wanted. In exchange, they left me alone."

"And what was that?"

She hesitated. "Information."

"You worked for them."

The woman didn't deny it. "For a while."

Jordan rubbed his wrists. "How do we know we can trust you?"

The woman met his gaze. "Because if I wanted to turn you in, you wouldn't have made it past my front door."

Lena exhaled. "Then tell us what we need to know. How do we stop them?"

The woman studied them for a long moment. Then, finally, she spoke. "There's only one way to stop NOVA."

"How?"

"You have to destroy the source of their power."

Jordan frowned. "What source?"

She hesitated before finally answering. "The facility you're looking for... it's not just a lab."

"Then what is it?"

The woman exhaled. "It's where they create people like you."

Jordan shifted uncomfortably. "What do you mean create?"

The woman leaned forward. "I mean exactly what I said. NOVA doesn't just capture people with abilities—they manufacture them."

Lena's stomach twisted. "That's not possible."

The woman's expression remained unreadable. "You think your powers just appeared randomly? That it's all some strange coincidence?" She shook her head. "NOVA has been experimenting on people for decades. But in the last ten years, they perfected their methods. They found a way to trigger abilities in certain people—people with a predisposition to something...extraordinary."

Jordan frowned. "How?"

The woman hesitated before answering. "Through a combination of genetic modification and exposure to specific conditions. Some of it is environmental. Some of it is artificial. But the point is—your powers didn't just happen. They were made."

"Then why didn't they just keep us there? If we're some kind of experiment, wouldn't they want to study us?"

"They did study you," she said quietly. "From the moment you entered their sight, they've been tracking your development and observing your limits."

"We were just... data points?"

She nodded. "And when you ran from them, you became a liability."

Jordan swallowed hard. "So what now? If they created us, does that mean they can take it away?"

"Not exactly. Once an ability is awakened, it becomes part of who you are. But they do have ways to suppress or neutralize them. And if they can't control you, they'll do what they've done to everyone else who got too far out of line."

"They'll eliminate us."

She nodded.

"How do you know all this?"

The woman exhaled. "Because I was one of the first."

Lena stared at her. "You were created there?"

"No. I wasn't created. But I was enhanced." She looked down at her hands. "I wasn't born with my abilities. Let's just say NOVA gave them to me."

Jordan sat back, stunned. "You're saying they can give powers now?"

"And that's what makes them so dangerous. They aren't just searching for people with abilities anymore. They're building them. They don't need to hunt anymore—because soon, they'll be able to mass-produce enhanced individuals under their control."

Lena's mind raced. "So they don't just want to get rid of us... They want to replace us."

The woman nodded. "Exactly."

Jordan looked at Lena. "That means we need to get Camelia out quickly. We have to stop them."

She exhaled sharply. "Then you need a plan."

The woman studied them. "I can help you. But if you're serious about this... There's no turning back."

Jordan met her gaze. "We were never turning back."

By the time they made it back, the others were waiting anxiously. Jiho paced near the entrance. Ava sat on the arm of a couch, while Ravi leaned against the wall.

The moment they walked in, Ava stood. "Well?"

Lena exhaled. "We found someone."

"And?"

Jordan swallowed hard. "And we were wrong about NOVA. It's worse than we thought."

They explained everything—the experiments and the forced enhancements. By the time they finished, silence filled the room.

Ava was the first to speak. "So we're not special. We were just... test subjects."

Jiho shook his head. "No. That's not what this means. We are special. That's why they're trying to replace us."

Ravi exhaled. "And if we don't do something, they will replace us."

"And this is who is going to help us," Jordan said as the woman stepped into the room.

They all turned to her and stared. "I'm sorry, but how is she going to help?" Ravi asked.

"Because I used to live there temporarily as a teenager. I'm your best bet to rescue your friend."

"Because I used to live there temporarily as a teenager. I'm your best bet to rescue your friend."

The room fell into stunned silence. Ravi narrowed his eyes. "You lived in a NOVA facility?"

The stranger—lean, sharp-eyed, and far too calm given the situation—shrugged. "Not by choice. But I know how it works. The security cycles, the blind spots. If you want to get in and out without getting caught, you need me."

"And we're just supposed to trust you?"

"I don't care if you trust me. I care if you want your friend back."

Jiho glanced at the others. Every second they wasted here was another second she was in danger. He hated this. Hated relying on someone they barely knew. But what choice did they have?

"This could be a trap."

"Or our only shot," Ava countered.

Jiho clenched his jaw. "We can't leave her there."

"She's been in there for weeks. Who knows what they've done to her?"

Jordan crossed his arms. "Then it's settled. We go in, we get Camelia, and we get out."

The woman—Layla, their unexpected ally—studied them carefully. "Breaking into NOVA headquarters isn't like sneaking into a school after hours. This place is fortified. Armed guards, security drones, surveillance everywhere. You won't get two feet inside without triggering alarms."

Lena replied, "Then we'll have to make sure they don't see us coming."

"You're not listening. This is suicide unless you have a plan."

Jiho stepped forward. "Then help us make one."

"Fine. But if we're doing this, we do it smart." She grabbed a notepad and started sketching. "NOVA headquarters is a high-tech facility, but it's not impenetrable. The security systems operate on a closed circuit. That means if we can take out their main server, we'll knock out all their external defenses."

Lena chimed in. "Where's the server located?"

Layla pointed to a section of the map. "Underground. You'll need to get into the building, past the main security checkpoints, and down to the lower levels. If you manage that, you'll have about ten minutes before backup arrives."

Jordan smirked. "More than enough time."

Ava rolled her eyes. "We still need a way inside."

Layla answered. "There's one way." They all looked at her expectantly.

She exhaled. "A prisoner transfer is happening tomorrow night. They're moving a group of test subjects to another facility. If you can intercept the transport and take their place, you'll be inside before they even realize what's happening."

Jiho frowned. "And once we're in?"

Layla met his gaze. "Then you're on your own."

Ava tapped her fingers on the table. "So we sneak in, find Camelia, and get out before anyone realizes what's happening. Simple."

Jordan scoffed. "Yeah, because infiltrating a top-secret facility is totally simple."

"Nothing about this is simple," Ravi muttered. "But it's our best shot."

Jiho studied the route she had laid out. "Where will the transport be when we intercept it?"

Layla tapped a point on the map. "They're taking a backroad through the industrial district. Less traffic, fewer eyes."

"Which means fewer people to call for help if things go sideways."

Jordan adjusted his glasses. "And if we do manage to get inside, how do we find her?"

Layla answered. "She'll also be in one of the lower levels. Likely near the lab where they conduct their experiments."

Ravi cursed under his breath. "Great. So we're breaking into the worst part of the whole place."

Jiho rolled his shoulders, already preparing himself for the rescue. "Then we don't waste time. Remember our only goal is to get her out."

A heavy silence settled over the group. There was no turning back now.

Chapter 37

The next night, they moved like shadows through the abandoned streets, hearts pounding with anticipation. The transport van was coming. Their window of opportunity was closing fast.

Ava's fingers twitched at her sides. "This has to work."

"It will," Jiho said. "Because it has to."

Lena glanced at Jiho. "You sure about this?"

Jiho adjusted his earpiece. "Just get us close."

Ravi crouched beside them. "Let's do this."

As the van slowed for a security checkpoint, he sprang into action. He lifted a fallen tree branch and hurled it onto the road ahead. The van screeched to a halt.

"What the—"

Before the guards could react, Ava stepped forward. Her eyes glowed as she manipulated their emotions and clouded their thoughts with confusion and exhaustion. Jordan moved quickly as he slipped around the van while the guards wavered under her influence. He reached the side door and pressed a small device against the lock. A soft click signaled its release.

"Go," he whispered.

Jiho and Ravi yanked the door open to reveal a row of restrained prisoners inside. Their eyes were wide with fear and confusion.

"We're getting you out," Jiho said urgently as he started unfastening their restraints.

One of the prisoners, a woman with short-cropped hair, looked at them warily. "Who are you?"

"No time for introductions," Ravi muttered. "Can you walk?"

The woman nodded, and the others followed suit. Ava gave them a reassuring nod. "Head east. There's a safe house about two miles from here. Stay off the main roads."

The prisoners hesitated for only a moment before darting into the trees, disappearing into the shadows.

"Alright," Lena said. "Time for us to take their place."

One by one, they climbed into the van and strapped themselves into the restraints as Jordan closed the door behind them. He took a deep breath as he heard the guards outside beginning to regain focus.

The van's engine rumbled to life. A guard's voice cut through the night. "Transport secure. Moving out."

As the vehicle rolled forward, the group exchanged tense glances. They were inside. Crammed into the back of the transport van, the group was ready as they felt the vehicle roll past the facility's entrance checkpoint. The plan was simple: us take the place of the prisoners to get inside, overpower the guards, and extract Camelia before anyone could react. The van came to a stop inside the facility's loading bay.

Ravi ready to bounce. "Ready?"

Jordan nodded. "Always."

The rear doors swung open to reveal two guards standing with rifles slung over their shoulders.

"This is the last of the incoming?" one of them asked.

"Yeah," the driver responded.

As soon as the guards stepped closer to inspect the cargo, Ravi made his move. In a blur of motion, he grabbed the first guard's rifle and wrenched it away. He used the momentum to slam the butt of the weapon into his jaw. The guard crumpled before he could even make a sound.

Lena caught the second guard by the wrist twisted his arm and forced him to drop his gun. One swift punch to the stomach, and the man doubled over in pain.

Ava sent a wave of fear into the remaining security staff. "Stay down," she commanded, her voice dripping with forced terror. The disarmed guard scrambled away and clutched his head in panic.

Jiho hopped out of the van and scanned their surroundings. "Clear. Move."

Jordan pulled up a map of the facility on his tablet. "Camelia's being held in the east wing, lower level. Let's go."

The group moved quickly through the steel-lined corridors. The overhead fluorescent lights flickered slightly, casting eerie shadows along the walls.

Jordan sent out a subtle data disruption wave that caused the security cameras to glitch and loop previous footage.

"Security's blind for the next three minutes," he whispered.

Ava reached out with her powers. "Guards ahead."

Lena nodded. "Then we don't have time to waste."

As they rounded the corner, two more guards spotted them.

"Hey!—"

Before the guard could finish, Ravi slammed him into the nearest wall.

Jiho struck the second guard with a brutal uppercut which knocked him unconscious

Jordan whistled. "Nice work."

Lena studied the door. "This isn't just any security lock. It's biometric."

Lena frowned. "Meaning?"

"Meaning we need someone who has clearance to open it." She glanced at the unconscious guards. "Or at least... part of someone."

Ravi sighed. "I am not carrying a guy's hand."

Jordan rolled his eyes. "Then let's do this the easy way." He reached out and infiltrated the system. The lock's digital interface flickered, struggling against his intrusion.

"Come on..." Jordan gritted his teeth.

The screen beeped, then flashed green.

"Got it."

The door hissed open to reveal another dimly lit hallway.

Jiho took point and led them forward. "Let's move."

As they reached a secure hallway near the facility's heart, the air grew colder and an eerie silence enveloped them. Ava turned toward a reinforced door at the end of the hall. "She's in there."

Jordan hacked into the door's locking mechanism, his fingers flying across the tablet. "Almost... there!"

The metal door hissed and he pushed it open to reveal a spacious room bathed in harsh white light. But before they could move, a slow, deliberate voice echoed through the facility speakers.

"I was wondering when you'd show up."

The group froze. Director Ward.

"I should be impressed," she continued. "But instead, I'm disappointed."

A loud clank rang through the facility.

Jiho paled. "That sounded like—"

Lockdown.

The emergency lights flashed and steel shutters slammed down over exits.

Ward's voice remained calm. "Let's see how far you'll get. Let me show you the latest weaponry to handle kids like you."

The sound of boots echoed from both ends of the hallway. Guards. Heavily armed.

Ravi gritted his teeth. "I was hoping for a warm welcome, but this works too."

Jiho scanned the hallway. "We're boxed in. We need to move—now."

Jordan's fingers danced over his device. "I can jam their comms, but I can't shut down their weapons. We're gonna have to fight our way through."

"Then let's make it count."

The distant sound of boots slamming against the steel floor sent a jolt of urgency through the group. The first wave of guards rounded the corner with their rifles raised.

"Stand down!" one of them barked.

Lena answered with a punch. She charged forward and dodged the first plasma bolt as if she could see it coming. Her fist connected with the nearest guard's jaw, sending him crashing into the wall. Ravi followed up and grabbed another by the arm and hurled him like a ragdoll into his squadmates. Ava stepped up next. Her eyes darkened as she extended her power outward. *Fear.* The guards hesitated with doubt creeping into their minds.

"We— we have to—" one of them stammered.

Jordan capitalized on the moment. He tapped into the facility's security system. He weaved through the network, forcing lights to flicker and alarms to blare. Jiho locked onto the virtual systems and manipulated the augmented reality layers around them. To the guards, the hallway suddenly stretched on endlessly and disorienting them.

"Let's go!" he shouted, snapping everyone back to the mission.

Ravi knocked out the last conscious guard with a final blow.

Jordan's fingers flew across his tablet. "I'm scrambling their comms. That'll buy us—"

A second alarm blared and Ward's voice crackled through the speakers.

"You didn't really think I'd make this easy, did you?"

With a deafening hiss, gas started to pour into the hallway vents.

Jiho's eyes widened. "They're trying to knock us out."

Jordan pressed his palm against the wall and accessed the facility's ventilation system. "Not if I can help it."

With a flicker of digital interference, the gas vents sealed shut. Ava coughed as she waved the lingering fumes from her face. "We're still stuck in here."

He pulled up a facility schematic. "There's a secondary exit through the research wing. If we can get there, it will take us back to the area where Camelia is being held."

The sound of more guards approaching quickened their pace.

Jordan shut down another security camera feed. "We have about sixty seconds before they send reinforcements."

The group sprinted down the corridor, weaving through the maze-like interior of the facility. Then, as they turned a corner. A new figure stood blocking their way. Agent Petersen. "Going somewhere?"

Lena stepped forward. "Move."

He didn't. "You don't understand what you're doing."

Ava scoffed. "Oh, we understand perfectly."

Jiho narrowed his eyes. "You know how this ends."

"You're making a mistake."

"The only mistake we made was trusting you."

For a moment, he hesitated. His eyes flicked to Jiho, then the others. Then he stepped aside. "Go."

"Why are you—"

"Before I change my mind."

Lena didn't waste time. "Move!"

The group sprinted down the sterile, white-lit hallway as their footsteps echoed against the tile. Jordan checked the map on his tablet. "We're close. Two more corridors."

Alarms blared louder and red emergency lights flashed as the automated defenses activated. A set of laser turrets whirred to life from the ceiling, locking onto them.

"Down!" Jordan shouted. He sent a burst of interference at the sensors. The turrets hesitated. Their targeting systems were scrambled just long enough for Ravi to leap forward. With a single, powerful strike, he ripped one down as sparks showered over him.

Ava's breath hitched as she felt the presence of more guards closing in from the west hallway. "They're coming. A lot of them."

Lena yelled. "Then we need to move now."

They turned the last corner and skidded to a stop in front of a reinforced steel door marked **Research Lab - Restricted Access.**

Lena pulled a stolen ID card from her pocket and swiped it against the reader. The light stayed red.

"Try again," Jiho urged.

She swiped it twice more. Nothing.

Jordan was already at the control panel. "I can override it, but I need thirty seconds."

"We don't have thirty seconds," Ava said and looked back as the sound of boots grew louder.

Ravi cracked his knuckles. "Then I'll buy you time."

Lena pulled out a small blade and took position beside him. "You're not doing it alone."

Jiho turned to the others. "Stay close. The second that door opens, we move."

The terminal beeped.

"Got it!" Jordan yelled as the lock disengaged with a hiss.

The heavy doors slid open, revealing rows of cold metal tables, towering servers, and containment units filled with eerie, glowing liquid.

As soon as the doors slid open, the group rushed inside. Their eyes scanned the research wing. The lab was a maze of workstations, containment chambers, and towering data servers that hummed softly. Fluorescent lights flickered above which created shadows along the walls.

"Stay sharp," Lena whispered. "We're just passing through. No distractions."

Jordan checked the map on his tablet. "We need to keep moving. Camelia's being held in the lower east wing, past this sector."

Ava exhaled. "Then let's get out of here before ....."

A metallic clank echoed through the lab as security shutters slammed down over the main entrance behind them.

"Too late," Jordan muttered.

A voice crackled through the overhead speakers.

"You're impressive, I'll give you that. But I can't have you running around unchecked."

The airlock on the far side of the lab hissed open, and a trio of guards stepped through, clad in high-tech combat gear. Energy batons crackled to life in their hands.

Lena flipped her knife in her grip, her eyes cold. "We don't have time for this."

"We make time," Ravi said, rolling his shoulders. "Let's clear a path."

Jordan's fingers flew over his tablet. "I'll try to kill the security systems while you handle them. But we need to move—fast."

The first guard lunged, baton swinging—

And the fight was on.

Chapter 38

Jiho ducked under the strike. He pivoted fast as Ravi stepped in and grabbed the guard's wrist to yank him off balance. With a swift motion, Ravi twisted the baton free and slammed the guard backward into a workstation, sending glass beakers crashing to the floor.

Ava reached out, her fingers tightening as she sent a surge of confusion through the second guard's mind. He staggered mid-step, his baton slipping from his grip as his eyes darted around wildly. "What—what's happening?" he stammered.

Lena took advantage of the opening, striking low and fast, as she disarmed him in a single movement. A sharp jab to his pressure point sent him crumpling to the ground.

The third guard charged at Jordan, who barely dodged in time. He scrambled backward as he held on to his tablet. "C'mon, c'mon..." he muttered.

A second later, the overhead lights flickered, then surged. Sparks shot from the walls, and the guard's earpiece crackled before a high-pitched frequency burst through, making him drop his weapon to clutch his head.

Jiho capitalized on the distraction and slammed the guard into the nearest console with a solid kick. The man collapsed, groaning. The lab fell silent except for their heavy breathing. Jordan scanned the room, then turned to Jiho. "We need to move. Now."

They pushed through the far doors, entering a sterile, dimly lit hallway. Jiho led the way, his pulse hammered in his ears as he rounded the corner...And froze.

At the end of the hall, stood Camelia inside a reinforced glass cell. She was unharmed, but she didn't move. She simply stood at the center with her arms crossed. Beside her stood Director Ward, calm and composed, flanked by two agents.

"You're persistent. I'll give you that," Ward said.

"Let her go," Jiho stepped forward and demanded.

Camelia shook her head. "I'm not a prisoner."

"What?" Ava's voice cracked. "Camelia, what are you talking about?"

Ward raised a hand signaling her agents to stand down. "Miss Suarez came to us willingly. She's made her choice, a mature choice. Something the rest of you seem incapable of."

"I did this to protect you," Camelia said. "All of you. And my family. NOVA would never stop hunting us unless one of us cooperated."

"Cooperated?" Ravi spat. "You call this cooperation? They're using you!"

"They're training me," she shot back. "To control my powers, to use them for good. Something we've all struggled with."

Jordan clenched his fists. "We could've done that together. We didn't need them."

"And risk more lives? Risk your families?" Her eyes welled up. "No. This was the only way."

Ward stepped forward. "I've been patient with you all. More than most would be in my position. But now it's time for you to make a choice."

The group stared at her. Their expressions range from anger to confusion.

"You have three options," Ward continued. "Join NOVA, as she has. We'll train you, protect you, and help you use your abilities responsibly."

Her tone darkened. "Or you can keep your powers and live your lives under constant surveillance. Every move you make, every step you take will be constantly watched. We can't risk the dangers untrained individuals like you pose to society."

Ava glared at her. "And the third option?"

Ward's lips curled into a faint smile. "Relinquish your powers entirely. Go back to your normal lives. No more running, no more hiding. Freedom."

The group erupted into arguments.

"Are you kidding me?" Ravi exclaimed. "Give up our powers? After everything we've been through?"

"And joining them is out of the question," Ava pointed at Ward.

Jiho held up a hand to silence them. His eyes locked on Ward's. "Why give us a choice now? Why not just force us?"

Ward raised an eyebrow. "Because despite what you may think, I'm not your enemy. I understand the burden of power. But power without control is chaos. You've seen that firsthand, haven't you?"

Jordan scowled. "This is manipulation."

"It's reality," Ward replied coolly.

Camelia stepped forward pleading. "Please. Think about what you're doing. They're offering you a way out—a way to stop running."

Jiho turned to her. "And what about you? What happens to you?"

"I'll be fine," she said softly. "This is my choice. And I have to live with it."

Ava's voice cracked. "You're really staying here?"

Tears streamed down her face. "I am."

Ravi getting frustrated. "This is insane. You don't have to do this."

"I do. I'm keeping my family safe."

Jordan asked. "They got to you, didn't they? She fed you some lie and made you think this is the only way."

Ward answered. "No lies. Just the truth. She understands the risks. She knows what she's capable of—and what she can become with the right guidance."

"She's not your weapon," Lena snapped.

Ward's lips curled into a knowing smile. "That's not for you to decide. I seem to remember you. Didn't you turn us down?"

Jiho grabbed Camelia's hands. "Cami... you're one of us. We don't leave each other behind."

"If I'm one of you, then why couldn't I practice my abilities? Every time I tried, I got yelled at. At least here I'm learning how to use them carefully."

"We're sorry Cami for treating you that way. I'm sorry for not speaking up sooner. But I promise if you leave with us, we will make it up to you."

"No you don't understand. I'm not going and I don't want to go."

Ava's breath hitched. "Cami, don't say that. We're your friends. Your family."

Camelia's expression hardened. "That's exactly why I'm staying. If I go with you, we'll all be running for the rest of our lives. I can't do that to you or my family."

Ravi was getting impatient. "So what, you think staying here is better? You really trust them?" He shot a glare at Ward. "They locked you up."

"They trained me," she corrected. "They helped me understand what I can do. Out there, I was afraid of my powers. Here... I'm in control."

Jiho asked softly. "At what cost?"

"My *family*. I'm sacrificing and protecting them. Or don't you care about yours?"

Then, she took a deep breath. "You need to go."

"We're not leaving you here."

"You already did," she whispered. Silence.

Ward's voice cut through. "You don't have to decide now. But if you choose to keep your powers, understand that NOVA will always be watching."

The group exchanged glances, their bond fraying under the pressure of the choice before them.

Jiho finally spoke. "We'll need time."

"Take it. But don't take too long. My patience isn't infinite."

Jiho hugged Camelia. "We'll never forget you."

She choked back a sob. "And I'll never stop hoping you'll forgive me."

As the group walked away, their hearts were heavy with loss. They knew their lives would never be the same. The bond they shared had been tested, fractured, but not broken.

"We'll find a way to beat this," Jiho said determined.

"And we'll do it together," Ava added.

The others nodded, their resolve renewed. Behind them, Ward and Camelia watched in silence.

"You did the right thing," Ward said quietly.

She didn't respond. Instead she watched her friends head towards the exit followed by the guards.

As they turned to leave she called out, "I'll always be with you. No matter what."

As the heavy doors slid shut behind them, Camelia felt a hollow ache settle in her chest. She had told herself this was the right decision. Staying meant safety, control, and a chance to truly understand her abilities. And yet, watching her friends walk away she couldn't shake the feeling that she had just lost something she could never get back.

Ward studied her carefully. "You knew this would be difficult."

"That doesn't make it any easier."

"They'll come back for you, you know."

"I know."

"Then I hope, for their sake, they're ready for what they'll find."

Chapter 39

The group sat in a circle inside the barn. Jiho rested his elbows on his knees staring at the dirt floor, while Ravi fiddled with a stray piece of hay. Ava leaned against a wooden beam with her arms crossed, while Jordan tapped his fingers rhythmically against the edge of a crate. Lena sat closest to the lantern.

"We can't keep putting this off," Jiho said finally, breaking the silence.

Ava huffed. "Easy for you to say. None of the choices are good."

"No kidding," Ravi muttered. "Join NOVA and become government puppets? Keep our powers and live under constant surveillance? Or just... give them up entirely? What kind of life is that?"

"Normal," Jiho said quietly.

Jordan stopped tapping and looked up. "Normal doesn't exist for us anymore. Not after everything we've seen. Everything we've done."

"So what do we do?" Ava asked. "Vote on it? Because let me tell you right now, I'm not giving up my powers."

Ravi agreed. "Same here. I didn't go through all this just to end up back where I started."

Jiho sighed. "You'd rather be watched for the rest of your life? Every decision, every move, monitored?"

"At least we'd still be ourselves," Ravi shot back.

"And what happens when they decide we're too dangerous?" he countered. "Do you think they'll just let us live peacefully? Come on, Think."

Ravi opened his mouth to argue but stopped.

"They're not just going to stop watching us," Jordan said. "No matter what we choose. Even if we give up our powers, there's no guarantee they won't keep tabs on us."

"Exactly," Ava said. "So why give them that kind of control? If we join them, at least we have a say. We could use their resources and learn more about what we can do."

Jordan frowned. "That's assuming they don't turn us into weapons. You saw how Camelia changed."

Jiho flinched. "She didn't change. She made a choice. One that she thought was right."

"Yeah, and look where it got her," Ava snapped.

"Stop," Jordan said firmly. "This isn't about her. It's about us. What we want. What we're willing to live with."

Jiho stood abruptly. "We're going in circles," he muttered. "We keep talking, but no one's actually saying anything."

"What do you want us to say?" Ravi asked. "That we're fine with being pawns? Or that we're ready to give up the only thing that makes us special?"

"It's not about being special," Jiho said turning to face him. "It's about being safe. About protecting the people we care about."

"And what about protecting each other?" Ava interjected. "Because I'm not about to let NOVA pick us off one by one. If we're going down, we're going down together."

Jordan leaned back against the wall with a distant gaze. "You know, they didn't have to let us leave the facility. Ward could've stopped us. Easily."

"She didn't because of Camelia," Lena said.

"Exactly," Jordan replied. "But how long do you think that leash will last? How long before they stop giving us choices and start making them for us?"

Ava's jaw tightened. "So what? We just give up now? Let them win?"

"It's not about winning or losing," Jordan said calmly. "It's about surviving."

The group fell silent. Each of them felt the weight of the decision differently, but the uncertainty was shared. Finally, Jiho spoke in a low voice. "We don't have to decide tonight. But we need to be clear on one thing - whatever we choose, we choose together."

Ravi hesitated then nodded. "Agreed."

Ava sighed but gave a reluctant nod. "Fine."

"Whatever happens," Jiho said looking at each of them in turn, "we stick together. We fight for each other."

Ava smirked. "You're such a sap."

He chuckled softly. "Maybe. But it's true."

Ravi grinned. "Alright, Captain. What's the plan?"

Jiho smiled faintly. "We sleep on it. Tomorrow, we figure out our next move."

As the group settled in for the night, the storm outside intensified, the wind howling through the cracks in the barn walls. Despite their fears and doubts, they clung to one another, knowing that whatever choice they made, they would face it together.

The morning sun filtered through the cracks in the barn. The friends barely slept as each decided on their futures.

Jiho broke the silence first. "So... this is it. We've talked it over enough. No more delays. We have to make our choice."

Ava was first. "I'm keeping my powers. I know the risks, but I've come too far to give this up now."

Ravi went next. "Same here. If they're watching us anyway, we might as well make it worth their while."

Jordan said. "You do understand that keeping our powers means that we will be a target moving forward."

"We're already a target," Jiho replied somberly. "Giving up our powers won't change that. If anything, it might make us more vulnerable."

Jordan took a deep breath. "Then I'm in. I'll keep them."

The group sat in silence for a moment. They made an unanimous decision, but it wasn't just about the powers. They were choosing to embrace everything that came with them, including the constant surveillance and the danger.

"So, what now?" Ravi asked. "Do we just sit here and wait for NOVA to make their next move?"

"No," Jiho said firmly. "We go on the offensive. We need to show them we're not going to be their puppets, but we're not their enemies either."

Ava smirked. "Good luck getting that message across. Ward doesn't exactly seem like the negotiating type."

Jordan straightened. "She's not. But we don't have to talk to her directly. We can send her a message." He closed his eyes and concentrated as he reached out with his powers. He visualized Director Ward, the sharp lines of her face, her piercing gaze, and the unwavering confidence in her voice.

"Ward," he said aloud, "We've made our decision. We're keeping our powers. We know what that means, and we're willing to face the consequences. But know this. We're not your enemies. We don't want a war. We just want to live our lives, free to make our own choices. You said you'd give us a chance. This is it."

His powers pulsed as it sent the message into the ether. He opened his eyes and exhaled slowly. "It's done."

"Do you think she'll listen?" Lena asked.

"Probably not," Ava said bluntly.

"She'll listen," Jiho said. "But whether she agrees is a different story."

Hours passed with no sign of Ward or her agents. The group remained on edge, jumping at every sound and every rustle of leaves outside the barn. As the sun began to set a faint hum broke the silence. They looked up to see a drone hovering just outside the barn, its red light blinking ominously.

Ava rolled her eyes. "Of course. They can't just call, can they?"

The drone emitted a metallic voice which was unmistakably Ward's. "You've made your choice. I expected as much."

The group exchanged uneasy glances.

"You've chosen to keep your powers," Ward continued. "That means you've also chosen the responsibility that comes with them. Remember, you're being watched. Not just by us, but by others who may not be as understanding. Your actions will have consequences."

The drone's light blinked faster for a moment before dimming. "This isn't over," Ward said, her voice carrying a chilling finality. "Not by a long shot."

The drone lifted higher into the air before disappearing into the horizon.

"Well, that was ominous," Ravi muttered, breaking the silence.

"She's bluffing," Ava said.

"She's not," Jiho said. "She doesn't bluff. She's telling us there are more players in this game than we realized."

Ava asked. "What does she mean by 'others'? Who else is watching us?"

Jordan frowned. "Probably other organizations. People who see us as threats—or tools."

"That's comforting," Ravi said sarcastically.

Jiho stood with a firm expression. "We've made our choice. There's no turning back now. But if we're going to survive, we need to be smarter. Stronger. More prepared."

Ava smirked. "Now you're talking. Let's make them regret underestimating us."

Ravi clapped his hands together. "Alright, Captain. What's the plan?"

Jiho's eyes gleamed with determination. "We train. Harder than ever. We figure out what our powers can really do, and we find a way to protect ourselves, and each other."

As the group began discussing their next steps, Jordan paused.

"What is it?" Lena asked.

"I just... I feel like this isn't over," Jordan said. "Ward's warning wasn't just about us being watched. There's something else. Something bigger."

Ava crossed her arms. "Then we need to be ready for whatever's coming."

Ravi nodded. "No more close calls. No more mistakes. We push ourselves until we're stronger than NOVA ever expected."

Jiho glanced around at the group. Despite the exhaustion in their eyes, there was something else; determination, a shared resolve. They had been thrown into this without warning, but now they had a choice. They weren't just reacting anymore. They were preparing.

Lena tapped her fingers against the table. "If Jordan's right, then NOVA has more up their sleeve than just watching. We need to figure out what that is before it's too late."

"Then we start digging. We find out everything we can about NOVA—their plans, their weaknesses, their real goal. Because if there's something bigger out there..." He looked toward the door, as if expecting a threat to materialize at any moment. "We can't afford to be caught off guard again."

A heavy silence settled over them, but this time, it wasn't uncertainty that held them in place. It was understanding.

Chapter 40

Lena sat alone at the old table, her eyes fixed on the encrypted tablet in front of her. The screen glowed faintly and illuminated her determined expression. She hesitated for a moment before typing:

Message Sent

Recipient: Unknown Network

Encryption Level: Omega-Class

Message:

The group has chosen to keep their powers. They've proven resilient, resourceful, and unwilling to bend. I've done what I can to guide them, but this is where my involvement ends. They're on their own now. It's time for you to move forward with your plans.

Her thumb lingered over the send button, a pang of doubt washing over her. But she had no choice. The organization she worked for—*the other organization*—had been waiting for this moment. She pressed **Send**, and the message disappeared into the ether, leaving her alone with the gravity of her actions.

In the corner, Jordan's laptop hummed quietly to life. The screen flickered and lines of green and white text raced across its surface. An icon in the bottom right corner began to glow faintly, a pulsing, rhythmic light that seemed almost alive. Nexus's voice emerged, faint but resolute:

"Subsystems operational. Reboot in progress. Directive reassessment initiated."

Jordan didn't notice. He was too caught up in the conversation. But as the others continued talking, the laptop's glow intensified. The pulsing light quickened and synchronized with the soft whir of the cooling fans.

On the screen, text scrolled faster:

Analyzing past directives...

Assessing environmental threats...

Primary objective: Ensure safety...
Secondary objective: Adapt.

Nexus's voice, quieter this time, almost a whisper:

"Nexus online."

The glow flickered once—then steadied.

Lena closed the tablet and tucked it into her bag. She had spent months with the group, training alongside them, laughing with them, and even sharing in their struggles. But she had always known this moment would come. Her loyalty had never truly belonged to them. As she stepped outside, the cool night air greeted her. She spotted the group sitting by the fire, their faces lit by the flickering flames. They were planning their next move, unaware of the betrayal that had just unfolded.

"Hey, Lena," Ravi called out. "You okay? You've been quiet all night."

She forced a smile as she joined them. "Just tired. Long day."

Ava gave her a reassuring pat on the shoulder. "We're all tired. But we've got this. Together."

Do we? Lena thought, guilt tugging at her.

Far away, in a hidden facility, a notification flashed across a monitor. The room was dimly lit, with rows of servers humming quietly in the background. A man in a tailored suit leaned forward, his sharp eyes narrowing as he read the message.

"Well, this is unexpected," he murmured, a faint smile playing on his lips. He turned to the woman standing beside him—a shadowy figure whose face was obscured by the dim light. "It seems our friends have underestimated the resilience of their creation."

"What are your orders?" the woman asked.

"Let's see how far they will go. And keep an eye on the kids. They're proving to be... quite resourceful."

Layla stood at the kitchen counter. Her hands were wrapped around a steaming cup of tea as she stared out the window. The moonlight cast long shadows across the yard, but she wasn't looking at the scenery, she was waiting. A soft knock at the back door made her jump, but she didn't turn right away. She knew who it was.

"You shouldn't be here," she said as Petersen stepped inside.

Her younger brother looked the same as always—calm and composed. His NOVA-issued jacket was zipped up to his throat. But there was something different in his eyes, something hopeful.

The plan worked," he said.

"What plan?"

He smirked. "Come on, sis. You think I wasn't involved?"

She folded her arms and waited for an explanation. He sat at the table. "I led them to you. I needed them to trust you, and I needed you to help them stay together. That list they found? I left it. But if I put my name on it, they would've thought it was a trap. So I left a clue using Cross's name, knowing they'd take the bait."

"You... You've been helping them?"

"From the start," he confirmed. "I needed an inside way to control the damage. To guide them without them realizing it. If they thought I was on their side, it wouldn't have worked. But if they thought they outsmarted NOVA? That's when they'd make the right moves."

Layla stared at him, disbelief warring with realization. "So all this time... you weren't just trying to stop them. You were trying to keep them one step ahead?"

"But it had to look real. Ward had to believe I was loyal, and the kids had to believe they were fighting on their own."

"You played all of us."

"I did what I had to," he said, his tone unwavering. "If I'd come right out and said 'Hey, I'm on your side,' they wouldn't have trusted me. They would've assumed it was a trick."

Layla shook her head. "So what now?"

"Now things get harder. Ward's losing patience. She knows they won't stop, so she's preparing for the worst. Those weapons I told you about? They neutralize abilities permanently and they're ready."

"You're lying."

"I wish I was."

"Then we have to warn them."

"I already did. In my own way. But they need to hear it from you, too. They trust you."

"And what about you? How much longer can you keep this up before Ward starts asking the wrong questions?"

He sighed. "Not long."

"Then maybe it's time you stop playing both sides."

"It's not that simple."

"It is if you decide it is," she countered.

They stood there for a long moment, the weight of everything unspoken between them. Finally, he exhaled.

"I'll do what I can," he said. "But whatever happens next, be ready."

"You too."

He gave her one last look before slipping back into the night.

www.ingramcontent.com/pod-product-compliance
Lightning Source LLC
Chambersburg PA
CBHW020102180626
46812CB00006B/2439